VIETNAM

And The Summer Of Love

By

Bailley Adams

Hofmeister
Publishing

Minneapolis, Minnesota

Hofmeister Publishing

hofmeisterpublishing@outlook.com

ISBN-13 Paperback: 979-8-9869626-8-9

ISBN-13   digital: 979-8-9869626-5-8

LCC

First Edition

Printed in the United States of America

CHAPTER 1

SAIGON

Why was life so dry; so brittle—like a cracker? I was in the depths and sinking lower. I needed a savior, a demigod from Korea, a boy or a young girl? At any rate, I needed my life back. I just needed my youth. What ever happened to the Calypso music? I arrived in Saigon to make a fresh start. I thought it was the pearl of the East and that it would be my phoenix and my rebirth! I was here to save mankind and hopefully myself. I had just removed body and soul from another failing relationship and I needed a rest. My hopes and grand illusions had been cracked. I was a wreck. Where was my life going? Whatever happened to the music?

Like a babe lying on the tundra snows, I have always considered myself helpless. I thought the exotic East could give me what I was looking for. Would it? Could I bend and mold it into my own shape? I thought I could. I thought I could draw from it everything I needed and walk away a free man. What a fool I was! If you think I am a cynic, well good! This has been a cynic's War and I have been a cynic's fool. Yes, I had thought the air of Saigon would be sweeter for my presence. But contrary to opinion, when I arrived in the early hours of the morn, the sun was rising in the East not the West.

I could see Vietnam from the window of my airplane as the first rays of the dawn lightened the sky. The twinkling South China Sea had finally brought me to the edge of this emerald landmass. But the closer I came, the more it would change. At first from my airplane window high

1

above the clouds, it looked like an enchanted isle. As we got closer, I saw it as a lush paradise dotted with people and small villages. But when the airplane landed, I was caught in a transition that I was totally unprepared for. The lush landscape had been rudely scarred, and in its place was the largest Military arsenal in the world. In every direction you looked there was Military weaponry being unloaded and stored. The scene was incredible! There were hundreds of jeeps, hundreds of tanks, hundreds of airplanes, hundreds of helicopters, hundreds of caterpillars, hundreds of barrels of oil all lined up endlessly waiting to be used; and I wondered who in God's name would ever pay for all of this?

I wasn't ready for the sterileness and the steel of Army life. I liked color, flashing eyes, panel-lined reception rooms, intrigue, and Grand Marnier. What the hell was I doing in this rat hole? Men in helmets and dust; some bloody War! I guess I just wasn't ready. I hadn't properly prepared myself. I collected my belongings from the airplane, stood up, and I had the definite feeling I was about to enter another world.

I can still remember the sensation I had when I first got off the plane and immediately became engulfed in the hot, muggy air. It was like the tight grip of an enormous octopus; and as long as I was in Saigon, I would never escape it.

I was excited as I came down the steps of the airplane. I had arrived! I expected an embassy official to be here to meet me, but it looked as if I was on my own. Good, that was even better! I was like a child in a toy store, and I wanted to savor every moment of it. I watched a human chain of Vietnamese coolies unload my luggage. Then I caught an Army transport into town and sat back as the speeding jeep introduced me to the countryside.

The coastal land near the airport was filled with shallow water that was crystal and glowing in the morning sunshine. Overhead the sky was filled with bellowing white clouds. I was struck by the stillness and the serenity of the land. In the middle of the wetlands a lone boy was sitting on the back of a water buffalo with the golden dawn behind him. A bird flew across the horizon. Somehow the scene seemed captured in time as an enduring symbol of peace and tranquility.

One thing for sure, the American at the wheel knew how to drive! No chicken, pig, child, or pedestrian was spared. Our jeep shot through villages leaving people and livestock scrambling for safety.

Once the land between the airport and Saigon had been countryside; now it was covered with cheap housing complexes built by the French and later added to by the Americans. As we passed the shantytowns and approached the sprawling outskirts of Saigon, the traffic became ten times worse. Hundreds of Japanese Hondas, American Military trucks and jeeps, antique Citroens, motor scooters, and old Peugeots without mufflers battled their way into the old City. But my driver refused to slow our progress. I became convinced he was either a madman or he had a hot date waiting. In no time at all we had crossed the main plaza and were in front of the Continental Hotel. I lifted my suitcase out of the jeep.

"I'll meet you next year in Monaco for the Grand Prix races." I said, and I swaggered off.

Jesus, that man had nerves! Maybe all things were possible in Saigon. I thought to myself as I walked into the Hotel.

The Continental Hotel was a colossal monument to the Republic of France! Here I was in the middle of Saigon with the grandeur of France before me. The Hotel was a classic period piece! Any moment I thought I would see two French plantation owners in white suits stroll

3

down the steps and beckon for their rickshaws. Bigots or not, the French knew how to live! I climbed up the enormous steps and went through the elegant French doors.

The lobby was a sanctuary of space and light. The heightened ceilings gave the room a cool and almost petrified look. Huge fans churned silently away on the ceiling while drooping ferns guided my way to the front desk. It was a long trek in getting there, and I wondered what the Vietnamese thought of this miniature polo field. Napoleon Bonaparte would have been at home.

I was signed in by a short, mealy mouthed Frenchman named Louie. In the beginning I had thought Louie was one crack concierge. But underneath his professional French veneer, he was one of the most lewd and sinister persons I have ever met. After the French defeat in Vietnam, any Frenchman with brains would have left the Country; the hacks stayed on. Later I would come to know of his many vices.

Louie handed me the key to my accommodations, gave me a rather mysterious smile, and guided me up to my room. I thanked him with as much grace as I could muster, asked him about the ventilation system, and got rid of him with an American dollar bill. When they are not tripping over their egos, the French are such sluts.

I put my suitcase on the bed and started to unpack. An ancient ceiling fan gently brushed the air across my body creating an almost erotic sensation. I liked it! This room fit my mood. The dramatic French windows and the tropical slat doors made me think I was in the Caribbean. I wanted to put on my swimsuit, rush down to the warm water and slip my body in; but the traffic horns down below reminded me that this was no tropical island.

The French provincial bed in the corner made me think of my Mother, a neurotic who had always loved her bed. She had married five times and through it, I acquired an instinct for survival. Discreetly I had an air of aloofness, sported a red tie now and then, and never cried in public. She was the one who was always in tears. I would never come to understand her eternal search. She would traipse after men, win them, and traipse on. What was it all for?

I thought I would wash up and see if the American Embassy was still standing. The Hotel's bathroom facilities were a bit antiquated, but then I didn't expect to be staying at the Ritz. The French did have strange ways. Why did they always insist on two toilets in every bathroom? That was one of the universal truths I would someday find out. Saigon would come to teach me many things.

I left the Hotel with Louie noting my departure and walked out into the bright mid-morning sun. The Continental Hotel was near the French Catholic Church that sat on a high hill overlooking the City. I thought the Cathedral was a little over-bearing considering most Vietnamese were Buddhists, but then the French never did trifle with details. Tu Do Street or Rue Catinat as it was called in the old days started at the Cathedral and worked its way down to the Saigon River. I decided not to fight gravitational force, but flow with the Street down to the waterfront then catch a cab over to the Embassy.

I was ready to explore! I wanted to find the timeless East with its dragons, lotus flowers, birds, and pagodas. This was my chance to experience the sweep of the oriental roofs and search out the old marketplaces and cafes. I was excited! I wanted to reach out and kiss even the dry, old hags who came toiling up the Street in their black formless dresses. Yes, I was alive! I was caught in a sea of conical hats and ringing rickshaw bells and I loved it! I liked too the distinction of being White; it made me feel important. Maybe that is why the French stayed here and fought for 12 years—alas the suffering French ego!

As I walked down the Avenue lined with wrought iron balconies and tall, delicate trees, the flower markets were just receiving their morning deliveries. Everywhere I looked there were fragrant flowers. I loved the flowers, the binding, flowing, sensuous heat, and these oriental women! Like china dolls in porcelain boxes, they were exotic and enticing. I liked to watch them as they passed by. Many of them wore a long-sleeved dress with a long flowing skirt in panels. Their black hair was piled high above their heads or hung long and straight down their backs. They were so fragile and elegant. They seemed to emulate the mysterious East. Every once in a while, I would straighten my tie. It was a nervous habit I had that came from those guilty pangs that attack us when our minds wander seductively.

It seemed hard to believe that this was a City at War. The streets were filled with people, the grocery stores were stocked with food, jewelry shops were selling gold, and the markets were filled with fresh fruits and vegetables. I passed Chinese druggists, tailor shops, beauty parlors, teashops, chop suey booths, tire pumping stations, and dress shops. Each enterprise had an oriental magic and charm to it, and all were doing a thriving business. But it was the action on the Street that I liked the best.

Saigon was the home of the entrepreneur! No merchant stayed in his shop. Street vendors were an important part of shopping, and there were dozens of them peddling their wares. Some sold sweets and soft drinks. Others promoted their goods while some offered services like shoe shines or car washes. It was pure red-blooded capitalism, a delicate system that has never been cultured, caring, or polite; and somehow without price tags and credit cards, it made me a little nervous. But we believed in it, and sometimes we went to War over it.

The day was getting hotter. I had reached the waterfront and it was time to head over to the Embassy. As I looked for a taxi, a local street urchin approached me carrying a basket filled with coke cola, beer, coconuts and a few bananas. He looked undernourished for a ten-year old, but inwardly behind those enormous dark eyes, he was probably a true philistine shark. I decided to watch my step.

"Hey you, you American; you buy coke. Beaucoup coke. Very good price." He had a winning smile on his face and it was true salesmanship, but I wasn't taking.

"Hey you, you American; you number one, you buy coke." He implored.

I tried to wave him off and kept looking for a taxi.

"You number one, American; you number one. Beaucoup coke, beaucoup beer. You buy!"

There was a certain urgency in his voice. I looked at his tattered clothes and his dirty face and I thought of Oliver Twist; but no, if I gave him a dime, he would want a dollar. Besides my dignity was offended by this unruly child who dared approach me. After all who did he think I was?

"Hey American." His eyes narrowed as his voice dropped. "You want girl. You want boom-boom? Beaucoup lay."

I looked down. A ten-year old hustler on the streets of Saigon. I could not believe it! Whatever happened to decency? With a little bit of seething rage, I told him to get lost. Somehow that got to him.

"You bad, American; you very bad!"

The words were not tossed out lightly. They came through clenched teeth, and as he turned to go, I felt an enormous power inside of him; a power that had been waiting for decades to surface.

I caught a cab and I was relieved to be inside sheltered from what seemed to be a harsh and unruly world. Rubbing elbows with the peons has never interested me. I enjoyed cultural contacts and exchanges, but I am always one who never likes to get too close. In the taxi I felt safe. The Vietnamese at the wheel drove like a maniac, but then who didn't in Saigon? I decided it was a primitive form of self-defense.

We had taken some back alleys where the street narrowed, and we were moving along at a terrifyingly fast clip when our pace came to a screeching halt. I went flying forward into the driver's seat. I popped my head up. Outside it looked like a Manhattan traffic jam. Across from where we were stopped, the houses were so close you could see right in. All the windows and doors were open and you could smell fermented fish sauce cooking and see laundry drying. I crawled back onto the seat and pondered my fate. I wasn't excited about staying in the taxi with the sun beating down so I got out of the taxicab to see what the problem was.

As I started forward, I saw that the whole street was backed up. No one was moving. At the head of the line two US Army vehicles had collided causing all traffic to stop. A fight was in progress. Two American soldiers were pounding the hell out of each other. The men were enormous brutes, and you could feel the tension in the air. I had seen fights in school and in bars. I remember men tearing at each other, ugly with hate; their fists high ready to swing hard and violently. In the end each would be torn and bleeding.

The Vietnamese were crowded around. There was a festive gleam in the air and you could tell they were enjoying the fight. Money began to appear as fast bets were being made. I looked at the smiling crowd and the two American giants destroying each other, and I wondered if maybe our efforts in Vietnam weren't being misdirected.

Two American MPs arrived breaking things up. The money quickly disappeared as the police waved back the crowd. The soldiers were resisting the police. It looked like an enlarged brawl. I drifted back to the taxi and waited for the street to clear. Soon we were again on our way!

We came up to the American Embassy. It looked like an enormous white whale washed up on the shifting sands of the Saigon seashore. I was not proud of the two bayonet soldiers stationed outside of the Embassy's main gate. If this was the image of America, I did not like it. I paid off my driver, approached the chalk white building, and I went inside.

The room was freezing. There was a Vietnamese woman at the front desk who looked suspiciously half French. She was very helpful despite the 12 sweaters she had on her back. When we came to Vietnam, we brought our own weapons, soldiers, culture, and even our own glorified air! I wondered if she liked the air conditioning and whether or not she would ever become accustom to it. She was very pleasant and kind and gave me explicit directions to my new office. I thanked her and departed. On the way down the hall, I passed a man with a patch over his eye. On the next floor I passed a man with only one leg. A little War weary, I dropped into a chair outside the office of the man I was going to be working for.

"Well, where are they?" A loud voice demanded.

In the next room I could hear a string of apologies.

"I want those God damn papers here before lunch! Is that clear?"

The words came floating out through the open door almost smacking me in the face.

A lamb! I'll be working for a lamb! I thought quietly to myself. But before I had time to rejoice, my associate came storming out of the room leaving a trail of cigar smoke and a few dazed molecules in his wake.

Jesus Christ! I thought. It's 100 degrees out on the Saigon streets and in here I've got a Mexican hot tamale on my hands. Well, things could be worse. Right now, I needed a drink. Every hard-working diplomat needs a drink before noon. I turned around and retraced my steps. I was ready to go back to the Hotel and bury my head in the sand. With a few rounds of Martinis, I knew I would be back to normal or would I?

CHAPTER 2

It was wonderful to be back at the Hotel. There was something of a womb like security in being there. I trotted down the long lobby and made a sharp left into the Bar. The lobby was a pale white with oriental rugs and bric-brac here and there; but the walls of the Bar were covered with a dark teak wood and gave one the immense feeling of well-being.

There was a long corridor of teak wood that you traveled along and then it opened into an enormous room; a dark, masculine room. I could feel the protective warmth enclose over me as I slid into the Peacock Bar. The rich teak color of the walls told of many wily tales and drained Sherrys. I could see the old Frenchmen sitting at their tables slyly ruling their own worlds. The eternal electric fan hummed overhead like a clock ticking, waiting, and ticking.

There were no windows in the Bar only French doors that led out to an enclosed courtyard. The Bar was a mammoth structure built to last for centuries. I manfully walked up to it and ordered a drink.

"Whiskey and water." I demanded of a somewhat paunchy bartender. He looked like the village butcher with his fat hands and rolled up sleeves. "Do you know Huey Lake?" I asked.

"Oui, Monsieur."

"Does he come here often?"

"Oui."

I was content to let it lie at that. There was a sulking American sitting at the end of the Bar. I thought I would go over and cheer him up.

11

"Not many women around here." I said looking around.

"The fewer the better." He replied.

"You a civilian?"

"I am a businessman." He said with clarity. "I'm in Vietnam to make a fortune."

"On what?" It seemed like a logical question at the time.

"On the War. There are 250,000 troops scheduled for Vietnam and I'm here to outfit them. Beer, barstools, condoms, stainless steel sinks, ping-pong tables, stereos, refrigerators, air conditioning—whatever you need. I've got it."

"But are these things really necessary to fight a War?" I asked.

"Who cares? If the Government is buying, I'm selling."

It sounded a little cynical, but it was probably the hard nose of reality speaking. Just then my eye caught a ghost of a vision shutter and struggle across the room. It was a man, or half a man, haunted by something vicious and evil. His body was gaunt and he had a worried look in his eyes. Was he sane or half sane? His eyes shifted constantly; he seemed driven.

"Who is that?" I asked the bartender.

"An old warrior."

"French?"

"No, American."

"Does he come here often?"

"No, hardly ever."

I watched him and kept watching him. He was like a ghoulish demon or a drying carcass on a tortured desert. But then no one seemed to care, or worry, or be concerned. The Bar was beginning to fill up. Tough men with pistols on their hips were strolling in. They came up to the Bar bigger than life. You could see the scars on their faces and the wrinkles deep in their dark flesh. I found myself shaking hands.

"Henderson, 2nd Battalion."

"Belmont Dexter, Diplomatic Corp."

"Cornelius, 2nd Battalion."

There seemed to be little interest in conversation only a preoccupation for some serious drinking. Well, they had just met the right person.

"Where are you from, Henderson?" I asked.

"Fort Bragg."

Oh good! A total Military man. He probably joined up at 16, ate steel nuggets for breakfast, and guarded the Fort on Holidays.

Another whiskey and water was placed in my hands. "When are you guys going to win this War?" I asked.

"It ain't ever going to be won. We're putting in our time, getting our promotions, and moving on. There'd be no place to go without this War. So why end it?"

Well, he had a point. Where is the glory of being a soldier if you did not have a War to die in? There would be no need of someone crying and sobbing over your departure, no reason to write poorly misspelled letters home, or devastate the economies of other countries.

"Hey! Bell—ding ding!" I turned around and there was Huey Lake.

"Huey, Jesus!" I said shaking his hand. "How the hell are you! I knew I would find the right watering hole sooner or later!"

Huey and I had gone to Harvard together. He was short, had ruddy cheeks, and a perpetual glow about him. No matter where he went, it was party time! Women loved him; he was adorable. He was America's homegrown boy—polished and fresh. Huey Lake— spinach clean, Huey Lake! We had spent a lot of good times together.

"I'm fine." He said. "I got your letter and I've been watching for you. How do you like this shit hole?"

"I think it is great! I am up for this War! There is nothing like a War to make you feel manly! Let me buy you a drink." My friend, the bartender, poured me a drink and I handed it to Huey.

"Thanks, Ding Dong. Here's to you." He said and he drained his glass. "Christ, it's good to see you! How long have you been here?"

I looked at my watch. "Eight hours."

"You've got a lot to learn, baby." There was an unsettling pause.

"What's happening States side? How's Maureen?" He asked.

"Maureen and I are no longer together."

"What! Why?" He asked in alarm.

I shrugged. "It just didn't work out."

"I'm sorry, Dex." He said genuinely.

"Everything seems fine in the States." My mind trailed off. "There is some vague resentment over the War, but nothing overwhelming. We checked out just in time. It's no longer the same good old Harvard Square."

"Do you remember the Harvard/Yale football game in our Senior year when we went to the Owl Club to pick up mayonnaise jars filled with milk and laced very generously with brandy?"

"Oh yes, I think at the end of the game we did more swaying than cheering."

"I remember your date tried to go into the Club with us, and we had to tell her that she was persona non grata because she was a girl. Boy, was she pissed! Where was she from; some hick town—Minneapolis?"

"Yes, I think she was. Those were the great days! No cares, no responsibilities. Life was one long party."

"I miss the Club. Have you been back lately?"

14

"No, I don't get back often. But Huey, how are things with you?"

"I am here defending Democracy and making the world safe for mankind."

"Do you like what you are doing?"

Huey shrugged. "I like flying."

A striking woman walked into the Bar. All eyes turned toward her. She was accompanied by an Army heavy weight, and it seemed the entire room was standing and saluting.

"Jesus, who is that?" I said almost falling off my chair.

"That is Christine Blakely. She is an Army nurse at the Hospital."

"An Army nurse! She looks more like a cross between Joan of Arc and Cleopatra. When do I meet her?"

"Right now she is with a Major General and I think she is tied up."

Out of the corner of my eye I saw the strange, haunted man grope his way across the room and leave.

"Bell."

I looked at Huey.

"I've got to fly up the coast tonight, but I will be back tomorrow. Why don't we meet here at 6:00 o'clock tomorrow and we can have dinner together?"

"That sounds great! I've been up for 24 hours, and I think I have some recharging to do." I said. We shook hands. Jesus, it was good to see Huey again!

Finding myself surrounded three layers deep by the Military, I was feeling more secure about being in Saigon, and I was becoming more determined to meet Miss Blakely with every drink.

"Who is Christine Blakely?" I asked the men standing near me.

"She's a God damn bitch."

15

"She's as hard as nails." His sidekick added.

Their buddy, somewhat of a philosopher, continued. "She's everything you ever wanted, needed, or desired. Only she doesn't walk, talk, or breathe. And if she smiles, you can be sure it is not for you."

Well, this woman had quite a reputation! These men were fresh from the field, and they still had their flak jackets on.

"She'd sooner step on you than look at you." One of the soldiers continued.

"Ya." The shorter soldier growled. "When the sun set, it forgot to warm her."

"She'll put you in your coffin before you know what's happened to you." Our philosopher continued, and then he downed his drink.

Well, that was a solid round! I wondered if they were all on target. I turned and watched her and my determination began to waiver. I have been given many things in my life, but good looks were not one of them. I was the guy the girls never wanted to dance with and through it all, I gained a certain fortitude. But as brash as I am, there are times I have cold feet. I can be brave; men are always brave, aren't they? But sometimes I lose my courage. Well, it was now or never. Someone had just summoned the General, and Christine was sitting alone. I began my 100-mile march.

"Miss Blakely?" I said.

"Yes." She looked up startled.

"May I sit down?" I didn't give her time to answer, but sat down quickly in the General's chair. "My name is Belmont Dexter. I am with the Diplomatic Corp." I said shaking her hand.

She had that troubled female look, that don't touch me look, and that time to pack up look.

"I noticed you from over there and I wanted to meet you."

She kept looking at me.

"Is there a chance I could see you?" I seemed to be talking very fast. I looked up. There was a long shadow over me. The General was back!

"General, Sir." I said rising from his chair. "Excuse me, Sir! It was nice to meet you, Miss Blakely." I tried to leave gracefully. What an ass! I wanted to kick myself for being such a raging, royal asshole!

After my flattering episode in the Bar, I decided I needed rest. I stumbled up to my room and hit the sack. I awoke in the morning sort of a flaming ball of fire. I looked down at the baking sidewalks below, and I decided to wander down to breakfast. Surprisingly enough, I managed to secure a 'New York Times' in the lobby.

The restaurant was located opposite the Bar on the Easterly side of the building. It was a warm, sunny room well planned for late morning breakfasts. The ceiling was high like the ceiling in the lobby giving the room a very dignified look. All the tables were covered with white tablecloths and a bouquet of flowers graced each table. The Hotel's silverware was impeccable! The French were so civilized! Even the bone china was in the best of taste. I sat down elated. I have always appreciated good living!

A lumbering French waiter approached my table.

"My name is Pierre. I am here to serve you." He said in a defeated voice. Pierre definitely had a resigned outlook towards life. He had a long, scrupulous nose and the saddest eyes I have ever seen. Though he was quite tall, everything about him drooped. His shoulders drooped, his eyes drooped, and his mustache drooped. If you threw a glass of wine in his face, he would probably say thank you. He was married to a small Chinese woman. I had met them one day in the marketplace. She was giving holy hell to some hag selling fruit. I thought they were

17

going to attack each other. But she came away with her purchase all smiles. When Pierre introduced his wife, I knew she was one crafty woman. They were the oddest couple I have ever met.

"I'd like coffee with cream, cereal, and some orange juice."

"Oui, Monsieur." Pierre said and he lumbered off.

I began to read my newspaper. Across the way was a gentleman with a long, narrow face and a hawk like nose. He wore a gray, well tailored suit, and he was sipping tea from a delicate teacup. He had that distinctive British look about him. He was very neat and proper. In fact, he appeared to be the image of respectability, but there was something about him that fascinated me. He looked so perfect, so self-contained, so immensely secure. Yet when I exchanged glances with his piercing eyes, it was as if I could hear him snarling inside, and I knew then that there was something black, terrifyingly black in the deep recesses of his formidable character. I wondered who he was and what he was doing here. As I glanced down at my newspaper, I had the definite feeling I would be seeing him again.

CHAPTER 3

It was another exciting day at the Embassy. I walked into my office and found my associate's door closed. So I sat in a chair next to a young man by the name of Rip Snyder. He was a journalist from UPI.

"You waiting for that guy?" I pointed my finger at the closed door.

"Yep."

He had a nice Southern drawl and a deadpan face.

"Do you work at the Embassy?"

"Nope."

That's what I like, a man of many words. He was probably a flaming torch from the CIA.

"What do you do?" I asked inquisitively.

"Journalist, UPI."

Well, we had finally gotten somewhere. "I thought you guys were supposed to be out in the field covering the War."

"This is a special assignment."

"Ah." I said nodding my head. "What is it on?"

"South Vietnamese corruption."

"You mean the South Vietnamese are corrupt?"

He studied my face for a moment. "Filthy corrupt."

"Why are you here at the Embassy then?"

"Because the Embassy supports it."

"Supports it!" I burst out.

"What do mean supports it?"

"US policy is to cooperate with the Vietnamese in every way and that means condoning the graft, theft, and blackmail of the South Vietnamese elite who run this City."

"How do you know the Embassy knows about the corruption?"

"They know; but if they want to fight in this Country, they've got to support the Government, and if the Government is corrupt, then they will look the other way."

"That doesn't make a lot of sense. It is the people of Vietnam we are trying to help."

"The people are the last to be helped. They are the ones who bear the brunt of this War. Saigon is run like a Mafia stronghold—the whole system works on kickbacks, and all the money goes into the pockets of the South Vietnamese officials. The rich get richer and the poor get poorer. It is pure exploitation at its finest hour, and we condone it. In fact, we make it all possible."

The door to the office flew open.

"Ok Synder, get your ass in here." My associate snapped and a stream of smoke came belching out of his cigar.

The door slammed shut again. Ten minutes later it re-opened.

"We're just guests here. Remember that, Synder, we're just guests." He said walking Synder to the door. "What the South Vietnamese do here is their own business."

Well, so much for social justice. I thought to myself. It looked like my turn was next. I stood up.

"Mr. Griffin? My name is Belmont Dexter. I am to be your new Assistant." I said extending my hand.

"Oh yes, Belmont, we've been expecting you." He said giving my hand a hearty shake. "Those God damn reporters. They're at me like a pack of wolves." His hand went to his forehead. "I wish they would go hang themselves on the highest UPI pole! We all hate reporters here. They're always sticking their nose into things they have no business being in." He stopped for a moment as if meditating.

"Well, I'm glad you made it. How do you like this damn cesspool?"

"I like the Continental Hotel! It's a great old place."

I was looking at his short, stubby hands. He was a gruff old character that's for sure. He gave me a hard look.

"I want to be back in the States with my wife, Dexter. We have a small bungalow outside of Miami that we've had for years. I want to sleep with my wife in the night and during the day, I want to fish. That's all I want."

Was he pleading with me or apologizing? Whatever it was, I was beginning to feel like a God damn priest. I politely looked away.

"Ok Dexter, let me show you your office."

We toured the office and then went into the Map Room.

"I want to explain to you pacification. See this map, Dexter? Every one of those red pinpoints indicates one of our secured hamlets. But see how spread out they are. We don't have the troops to guard all those hamlets. So what happens is that we fortify an area and spend a great deal of aid money in developing it. Once we're done, we leave and go on to the next hamlet. The Viet Cong come in and re-take the village. Then we have to come back and fight the Viet Cong. In the process the village is reduced to rubble, and we're right back where we started from. It's a no win situation."

"Can't the village defend itself?" I asked.

"Many times the villagers are the Viet Cong."

21

"What about the South Vietnamese Army?"

"They don't like to fight." He said tightly. "Our job here is to coordinate the Military and the pacification effort. Believe me Dexter, it's a thankless, God damn frustrating job. People are screaming at us all the time." He said with his cigar clamped between his teeth. "If it's not the Military, it is the aid people. But the ones to watch out for are the political elite who run this City! We're fighting here with one arm tied behind our backs! Tomorrow I'll go over all the details with you. Right now I have to go. It is best to start work around 6:00 am. Nice to have you aboard, Belmont." He said shaking my hand.

"Yes, Sir. It's nice to be here."

I met the rest of the people in the department then I went on up to see the Ambassador.

"Is the Ambassador in?" I asked the receptionist.

"Who is calling, please?"

"My name is Belmont Dexter."

"Are you Belmont Dexter!" She seemed to almost fall over with awe.

"Yes."

"Oh! Your Mother has called a dozen times. Is everything all right at the Continental?"

"Yes fine."

"I'll tell the Ambassador that you are here!"

The Ambassador came out immediately. "Belmont, how are you?" He said magnificently. "And how is your charming Mother?"

"She is good."

"Come into my office. When did you get in?"

"Yesterday morning."

"Isn't Saigon superb?"

"Well, to tell you the truth, I'm not sure I like it yet."

"Oh you will, Belmont. You will! Wait until you meet some of these oriental women. They are wonderful! How is everything at the Continental Hotel?"

"Everything is fine."

"Good, the Continental Hotel is really the best place in town. Say Belmont, the Mrs. and I are having a black-tie reception at our villa on Friday night. Why don't you come?"

"I'd like to, Sir."

"Good! Plan around 7:00 o'clock."

"Thank you, Sir." I said extending my hand. "I look forward to Friday."

"Thank you for stopping by, Belmont. If you need anything, please let me know."

"Thank you, Sir. I will." We shook hands and I departed.

Leaving the Embassy was like running into a brick wall. Once out of the air conditioning, my body shivered and shook until it finally adjusted itself to the incredible heat outside. I decided to walk back to the Hotel. It was about four in the afternoon, and I had a couple of hours before I was to meet Huey at the Peacock Bar. Letting my mind drift, I began to stroll down the boulevard.

The three cultures had a curious way of mixing. Unlike the Americans, there was something soft and gentle about the Vietnamese and French presence in the City. I liked the trees that dotted the boulevards. They were so delicate and protective as they guarded the City from the intense heat of the day. But when the Americans arrived in Saigon, they cut down all of the trees to facilitate the flow of traffic through the streets and we installed air conditioning in all US offices.

American bars were everywhere. They were called 'Denver High' or 'California Dreaming'. Outside pictures of shapely Vietnamese girls were lit up in neon flashing lights of red, white and blue. Hard thumping rock music wailed from inside. It seemed like a total insult to the serenity of the Vietnamese culture.

It was strange to be in Vietnam. I didn't feel like a guest. I felt like an intruder. In English, gaudy billboards advertised American products everywhere in the City. The target market? The American soldier stationed in Saigon. The Vietnamese were not even considered a part of the market. In their own society, they were almost totally ignored. That would become part of their mentality; their cross—to succeed, to be recognized! Life began just over the mountain top and it didn't matter how you got there; the goal was to arrive!

I was just coming up to the Caravelle Hotel. It was regal and stately and not too far from the Continental Hotel. Out in front was a wonderful terrace with wicker armchairs and straw canopies to protect you from the sun. I felt I was back in Nice watching the women with the deep blue sea rolling in. Then I saw her sitting alone at one of the tables and everything stopped. Should I approach her, just go and order something to eat and casually say hello, or go on by? I hesitated for a moment. Then I decided to press my luck.

"Miss Blakely? Belmont Dexter."

She looked up. "Oh, hello." Her face did not seem quite so chilly.

"May I sit down?"

"Yes." She said tentatively.

"I would like to apologize for last night. I did not mean to intrude."

She smiled. "You were very funny."

Funny? A quick panic swept over me. "Oh yes, I always

try to amuse my Superiors. It is a little game I play."

"Why are you so nervous?"

"Nervous? Me?" I stuttered. "Well, to tell you the truth, I am afraid I am bothering you and if you would like me to leave, I will …." I began to rise.

"No, please stay."

I looked down at her. She sounded actually nice. I sat back down.

"How long have you been here?" She asked.

"I just arrived 2 days ago."

"Then you hardly know the Country. Vietnam is a fascinating place."

"Yes, I like the culture very much. Why are you here?" I could not help asking.

Why was she here? She thought to herself. "I wanted a warm climate and a cause."

"So here you are!"

"Yes."

"Are you a humanitarian?"

"No, I am just a solitary person who is doing what I can."

"I hope if I get wounded, you will be there to save me." I was looking into her beautiful blue eyes.

She smiled. "I must go now."

"Miss Blakely, may I call you Christine?"

"Yes." She said.

"There is an Embassy party this Friday night and I was …well, I was wondering if you would go with me?"

She thought for a moment. "Yes, I would be happy to go with you."

"Oh, thank you." I breathed. "I could pick you up at 6:45. Where do you live?"

"I live at the nurse's compound near the Hospital on Cong-Lu Street."

I stood up as she rose.

"I will see you on Friday! It is a black-tie reception."

"Good. I will be ready."

She had a beautiful smile. She held out her hand and I shook it. I watched her walk all the way down the long, narrow terrace.

CHAPTER 4

I had just scored and I was walking on air! Secretly I wished
I had a bullet hole in my chest so Miss Blakely could dress my wound
and nurse me back to good health. She would be grave and concerned
and of course she would cry. As I walked, I could feel her hand on my
forehead, and I thought of her coming to me late at night. It was a
euphoric dream all the way to the Continental Hotel.

Right now, I loved Saigon! I loved the yellow and pink stucco
buildings with their colonial shutters, the beautiful tropical gardens and
the vegetation. I loved the flower markets, the Chinese and Vietnamese
pagodas, the lush botanical gardens, and this gentle, serene culture.

I loved the mystery, the intrigue, and the back streets of Saigon!
There was a gaiety to the City. In a way it all looked normal. Lovers
strolled down the streets holding hands, children walked happily by.
There were even women in mini-skirts with 1960s big bouffant hairdos.
Everywhere you looked, there was activity. The City was growing and
bursting with high energy!

The sensuous, warm air surrounded me, caressed me, and made
me whole again. Fie to the New England ice and cold! This is where
I belonged. I wanted to open up the Vietnamese hearts and minds to
my way of life! Like the Missionaries of old, I wanted to convert them
to my ideology! Because we Americans were adamant about imposing
our beliefs on to others as if it was our divine right. Conquer the old
West or conquer the East, we knew no bounds; and with our long
tentacles we would try to grasp and hold and finally dimmish any

competing world views by mass extinction or polite coercion because our way was the *only* right way!

I cut through the central market with its maze of stalls and shops. Tarps were strung from all angles shading the rows of colorful fruits, vegetables, and tubs of fish glistening in the sunlight. There was ivory, silk scarfs, cotton, cinnamon, and spices, rare woods and aromatics all displayed out in the open air. I was hailed by many vendors, but I continued on my way back to the Hotel.

Once there, I went upstairs to change and went back down to the Bar. There was a band playing in the dimly lit Peacock Lounge. The Bar was packed. Everything was dark and warm and masculine. The music dripped with sensuality. From across the room a tall woman walked onto the stage with thunderous applause. I could not take my eyes off of her. She looked like someone you wanted to keep on a silver divan for when you came home late at night.

Nicole DuBois sang at the Peacock Lounge regularly and when she did, the Bar was jammed. She wore a tight sequenced dress that showed a faint outline of her breast and had a split up the side that flashed long, sexy legs. Her voice was low and husky. From a distance she was every sexual feeling I had ever known. Every time she swayed her hips, I thought I would melt. If this was Tuesday, how was I ever going to make it to Friday?

Enthralled, I kept edging closer. Unfortunately, I got too close. On stage she reeked with passion, sending our hormones to out of control places, but up close you could see the caked eyelashes and the sagging cheeks. She had been a vision, a phantom of my imagination. She was like all women with their electric rollers and tombstone smiles. She was glossy and beautiful until you looked beneath the surface and saw all the cracks; and once you found them, it would never be the same. I thought

Vietnam would take me from all of that. I thought I would be strictly in the company of men, and I would not have to deal with these sad, troubling emotions. Yes! Vietnam was an illusion and it would come to teach me many things.

I turned away and began to look for Huey. I found him in a corner at the back of the room talking with another man.

"The first sign of an attack, Huey, is when the South Vietnamese Army cuts and runs." The Army man said.

Huey grinned.

"I'll tell you something else, Huey. The Vietnamese are becoming so stinking rich from this War, they are beginning to keep French servants. It's disgusting! I want out. This is a filthy swamp and I want out!" He said again.

Huey saw me. "Hi Dex! I'd like you to meet Captain Barry Winthrop. Barry's with the 1st Cavalry."

"Captain." I said extending my hand. We shook hands.

"Remember what I said, Huey."

Like a sage, the Captain nodded to me and left.

"Who was that?" I asked.

"One of America's fighting best."

"He sure was skittish."

"We all become skittish after a while. Let's have a drink." Huey said draining his glass.

I noticed his face was already flushed. Huey found our friend the bartender and produced two drinks.

"Cheers!" We clanked glasses and drank heavily.

"How was your trip?" I asked.

"Good. Did you get into any trouble?"

"None at all." I lied.

Huey was silent for a moment. "Dex, what's the most important thing in life?"

"That's a hard one. I guess I'd have to say love and security."

"Wrong, Dex. It's money—that saintly bird with peacock wings. It's the only thing worth fighting for."

"Huey, you've got to slow down. You're a couple of drinks ahead of me and that's not fair."

"Oh yes, it is fair. Damn fair! The only thing about this world is that it is fair. Those who are bad get theirs in the end."

A youngish looking boy with wire-rimmed glasses approached Huey.

"Hi Randy. Meet Belmont. Randy's a writer for the *Sun*."

Randy nodded to me then turned to Huey.

"I wonder if you have any money I could borrow?" Randy asked.

"Well sure, Randy. How much do you need?"

"$30 bucks."`

"Here, kid."

"Thanks, Huey. I'll get it back to you!" He said and left.

"Are you the official Bank?" I asked.

"They know I'm a soft touch. It's easy to be caught short in Saigon! In this City money rolls off your fingertips."

"Isn't there something about professional integrity in Journalism?" I asked.

"No one has integrity in Saigon. This is the end of the world."

The band began to tune up and Nicole DuBois swept onto the stage amidst much clapping. The band played blues and swing. There was a bass, a sax, a clarinet, and a few horns. The sound was pure and the hours seemed immortal. It was as if we were on a slow-moving ship; strangers on a endless voyage. Nicole Dubois was singing in the brackish light. Cigarette smoke curled up to the ceiling. The room was filled with sensuality. Enchanted, we listened to her sing and became buried in our own distant thoughts.

It was after nine before Huey and I staggered out of the Bar. The light was almost gone now. Huey insisted that we take a cab to a restaurant called My Khans which was down by the riverfront. But I decided the walk would do us good. Huey relented and we started down the boulevard.

"This climate is fiercely hot, Bell. Fiercely hot!"

I was wondering just how plowed Huey was.

"Keep walking, Huey."

He brought his left hand up to his head and saluted me good-naturally. We kept walking.

"The back streets are the best, Bell! We'll explore some later tonight."

"I'll follow you!" I said gamely. We were going at a good pace.

A Vietnamese prostitute came up to us.

"GI, you buy me. Me very good."

"Ya, and next day I'd wake up with a good case of clap. No thanks, doll-face." Huey said. We walked on.

One of the many delicacy vendors came up the street carrying a basket filled with rice husks. They worked the City squares, the waterfront, the markets, and the temples.

"Belmont, you've got to try one of these eggs! These eggs are the best damn eggs in the whole world!"

"The WHOLE world?"

"The WHOLE bloody world."

"What are they?"

"Duck eggs."

"Oh terrific."

31

"They are delicacies, Bell, delicacies!"

He hailed the vendor, a young girl with long black hair; and he asked her for 2 eggs. She reached deep down into her basket and smilingly brought up two warm eggs. Huey handed her money giving her a generous tip.

"I want to keep her out of the bars. She looks like a sweet young kid." He confided.

I knew what he meant. We continued on our way. A teenage boy approached us.

"Hey Joe, you give me 5 piasters."

"Get lost." Huey snarled.

The boy moved off.

"Street kids. The City is full of them. If you give them money, they'll go down to Le Lai Street and shoot up."

"Shoot up?" I looked at him.

He put his hand to his arm and pushed with his thumb. It's a bad culture, Dex. It's filthy and bad and we have created it all."

I looked up. There was a sagging Vietnamese flag.

We arrived at the restaurant just in time to catch the sun set. The sky was red and it made the water a glowing pink. The restaurant was located on a floating barge that was tied to a jetty. It was titillating to be down by the River. The barge was an open-aired restaurant with a thatched roof. Oriental lanterns hung from the beams, and on each table there was a flickering candle enclosed in glass. The sad plunking of music drifted across the water and the delicious aroma of food cooking was in the air. It was still pleasantly warm out, and I was feeling vastly hungry and content. From across the River, small lights danced on the water from excursion boats and traffic going up and down the River. The Port was a hotbed of activity, and I settled back to enjoy the bustle.

All the people in the restaurant were Caucasian except a few Vietnamese who were probably either wealthy or well placed. I ordered Huey a cup of coffee and he became a little more sober.

"Why are you here, Bell?"

We were seated on the River side of the restaurant inches from the water. The scene was tropical and full of romance.

"I want to be heroic!" I said. "I want to go behind enemy lines, break codes, forge documents, and blowup bridges. I'm in search of life!"

"What do you mean?"

"I'm 31 years old. The Autumn leaves are dropping down all around me!" I looked up. "I'm afraid I'm not tough, that I am weak and impotent and that there is no meaning to life. There is something here I have got to find."

"This isn't the place for you, Bell. It's rotten and it stinks. Go back to the States and work in a Ghetto, or help build housing in the inner city, but *do not* stay here."

The waiter came to our table. He was a very small, frail man. Huey didn't have to speak Vietnamese, the waiter accommodated him in fluent English. Huey ordered our dinner. The waiter quietly bowed and left.

"I'm scared." I said. "I've got to test myself. This is a test. This is a big test."

"Why a test?"

"I want to show outwardly that I am strong because inwardly I have doubts whether I am a man, whether I have self-worth, whether I can be productive anymore; and it scares the hell out of me."

"This isn't the place for you to prove yourself. You and I don't belong here. This isn't our War."

"Why isn't it our War? We are here to protect the freedom of the Vietnamese!"

"No." Huey said cynically. "What we are doing here is protecting US interests and the Saigon elite from their own people. This place is depressing. It is like an endless succession of Chinese boxes. The environment is bad here, Bell. Women carry grenades in their baskets, kids steal from you, spies are everywhere, and the Government is hopelessly corrupt. The only thing I want to do is to make some money and get the hell out of here!"

"There is more at stake than just money!"

"That's easy for you to say, you've always been surrounded by money; but I haven't, and that's what I want!"

"What about the Vietnamese, do you think they should be taken over by the North?"

"It is better than what they have now. The Government here is pathetic and the South Vietnamese Army is a joke. The Viet Cong are smart and they are tough and they have the people on their side. No matter what the US Government says, we are losing this War.

If you send an overwhelming force after the enemy, they disappear. If you send out a small force, the Viet Cong overwhelm us. The US Government tries to rebuild the villages we destroy, but the supplies usually end up in the hands of the South Vietnamese Army officers who turn around and sell the supplies on the Black Market or right back to the Viet Cong. Try finding a good razor blade at the PX. Shit! They are all being sold on the Black Market. The same is true for lumber, cement, fire extinguishers, forklifts, trucks, and jeeps. You name it. It's a million-dollar enterprise for them. But it's all official and accepted! What is worse, the US Army has become so hard up for their own trucks that they go and lease the same stolen trucks back from the South Vietnamese Officers. The South Vietnamese officials are in everything —gambling, prostitution, opium, extortion, and Black-Market money. This City's got a smog problem, a municipal garbage problem, a traffic problem, inflation, and juvenile delinquency problems. And we created it! We created it all!

We have destroyed the Vietnamese economy, we have destroyed the social fabric of their society, and we have uprooted an entire population all in the name of democracy. We are losing this War, Bell. It's like the fire in the ship's hole that continues to burn, and soon it will bring down the entire ship. Oh, but don't let the American people know. Christ, Bell! I hate the whole thing. I want out!"

Our meal came and Huey looked surprised. The waiter passively dished out the food. Then he slipped away. Huey was becoming much too serious. I decided to bait him. "I think this food is poisoned." I whispered to him under my breathe.

"No, no. They don't do it that way." Huey said. "They do it to you when you least expect it. They'll wait and thoughtfully pick the right time." Huey paused. "You know it's not their fault. We just happen to support the wrong Government."

Huey was certainly adamant! I decided to change the subject. "I like the weather here. It beats Vermont."

Huey seemed jarred for a moment. "Dexter, you're a damn frick'in diplomat, you know that? I don't know why I waste my time talking to you."

I sighed in relief. Huey was back to normal.

"There are some great spots off Tu Do Street that I want to be the first to introduce you to. Since we're in Saigon, we might as well enjoy it for what it is."

"Let's live it up, Huey! I'm ready for action!" I told him.

"Hey Bell, how is your Mother? Your very alluring Mother?"

"Josephine is fine. She certainly misses you though."

"Really? I'll have to pay her a call when I get back to the States." Huey's eyes twinkled. He and my Mother had always gotten along famously. "Ok Dex, I'll take you in tow. But the first thing you've got to learn is to be careful of the Vietnamese. I'm not going to be around to watch out for you. I am usually in flight over Laos or Cambodia."

"I think I can manage." I said smiling.

"The Vietnamese are cunning. They are amazing liars, and they will try to take advantage of you whenever they can."

Just then the waiter came to our table and Huey instantly shut his mouth. The waiter bowed and handed Huey a slip of paper. Huey opened it up and read it.

"Excuse me, Bell. I'll be back in a couple of minutes." He said casually leaving his chair ajar.

The breeze off the River made the candle on our table flicker. I could hear the water splashing against the barge as it moved on its way towards the Sea. I was feeling carefree from the rice wine we had been drinking and life seemed very full. Life, women, and opportunities had all fallen into place.

Watching the lights moving across the water made my thoughts drift to Christine. She was attractive. Probably too attractive for her own good. She had sensitive eyes. The kind of eyes that had fathomless depth; and there was something about her that made you want to take care of her. Maybe it was the tight way she held on to older men. Perhaps it was her midnight eyes or her cold stares that so desperately needed the sunlight.

Whatever it was, there was an attraction there, a powerful attraction. I liked to think of her wheat-colored hair and the graceful way she moved. But like a flower growing in a swamp, she seemed so out of place. Why was she here? Whatever possessed her to come to Vietnam?

I wondered how I would make love to her. Would I slowly take off her clothes and replace each garment with a torrent of kisses or would I just let myself go and move without knowing or stopping. I wasn't sure. A lot depended upon her. Some women are tender and so beautiful. But would the desire be there for her? That was the question.

I looked down at my watch. Huey had been gone for 25 minutes and I was becoming concerned. I looked out over the water. The air was warm and heavy. Everything seemed so tranquil. I decided to get up and stretch my legs. There was a commotion on the bank of the River, and I thought I would go over and see what it was. I walked across the gangplank and onto the riverbank.

A group of Vietnamese stood looking down at a body sprawled out on the bank of the River. They were talking excitedly. I thought some American had been knocked out or was drunk. I went down the embankment to get a better look. It wasn't a drunk American. It was Huey! He lay in the thick mud with his throat cut. The blood was oozing out and lay in a puddle beside his head.

His eyes were as wide as his mouth. He looked frantic and his face was screwed up in agony. I knelt down beside him and put my hand on his wrist. There was no pulse. He was dead. Very dead! Huey—of all people, Huey! He was so pure and likable. He was a wonderful American and he gave his life to die in this hole. Some homage! I closed my eyes. I could feel the wetness roll down my cheek. There was nothing more I could do. I just looked down at him.

A procession was passing by. I looked up at the road. Everyone wore white and carried torches. There was no chanting or whispers; only a gong, the darkness, and the movement of fire. I heard an ambulance in the distance and I saw lights flashing. But no one stopped or yielded or said anything. It was like a rising tide. They all had expressionless faces as they continued on their slow, silent march.

I was badly shaken. Saigon was not quite so sweet as when I first arrived. I watched them put Huey's body into the ambulance, and I asked them where they were taking him. Then I left. I was raging inside. I went back to the restaurant to try to find out who had given the note to Huey. Our waiter was standing by the railing watching the commotion on the riverbank. I spotted him and went over.

"Who gave you that note?" I shouted.

"I not know."

"You are lying! Who gave it to you?"

"I not know."

I let my left fist fly leaving him sprawled out on the gangplank. The gooks, the damn frick'n gooks! I walked away in disgust. I caught a cab over to the morgue to make sure Huey got the best of care. Then I went back to the Hotel. When I went in, the Bar was still packed. I went out to the courtyard in the middle of the building. It was quiet there and I needed to be alone. I sat there until the sun came up the next day.

CHAPTER 5

The first thing I did in the morning was to go to the Ambassador. I went up to his office, but they said he was out of the Country and would not be back until Friday. They suggested that I speak to his Deputy, Mark Townsend. So I did.

Mark was a pretty boy from Houston—a pansy and a snob. You would think with Vietnam being the upcoming issue in the world that the Embassy would have some top-notch people on its staff. As it was, Mark was a blank introvert unaccustomed to having his feathers ruffled. I told him what happened to Huey Lake. Mark said he was sorry but he could not help. Murder was a Vietnamese problem and out of the hands of US jurisdiction.

I was ready to throw daggers. I could have strangled him on the spot. I gnawed at him like a dog with a new bone. Finally, he suggested I talk to someone in the CIA. Mark withdrew not particularly graciously, and in came a man called DeAngelo. He was a short, dark Italian wop with very intense eyes.

"Are you a friend of Huey Lake?"

"Yes."

"I knew Huey Lake. He dealt with a fast crowd. Anyone of them could have picked him off."

"What do you mean?"

"Just what I said. If I were you, I would keep out of this." He gave me a long, intense look. That was all he said.

I spent the rest of the day trying to get Huey's body out of hock.

It seems the Vietnamese were not going to let him go home. I was asked to go over to the Ministry of Social Welfare to straighten out the paperwork so Huey's body could be released and sent back to the States. I did not like any of this. There seemed to be a deadly quiet surrounding Huey's past. The only thing I wanted was to get him home where he would be safe. And right now, that seemed like a gigantic task.

The Ministry of Social Welfare on Tu Do Street was a run-down building in need of repair. It was built around a courtyard with offices opening onto long, dark corridors. There was no glass in the windows only faded green shutters that were warped and stained by years of monsoon rains. Bats flew in and out of the windows and there were birds nesting in the corners of the ceiling. Plaster was chipping away from the interior, and you could see how rainwater had run down the walls. I kept stumbling over rubble on the floor that had accumulated from broken tiles. All the paint on the walls was faded.

This place was a dump! It had dust three inches thick and it reeked of colonial decay. Women sat at desks, but they didn't do anything except knit. It took me an hour before someone would talk to me, and then they asked me to come back in a week. No, I was going to straighten this out now!

The small Vietnamese man nodded and asked me to sit down. The room was filled with all kinds of people waiting for papers. I found a seat next to a plump English woman who was eating bonbon chocolates from Herrods in London.

"'ello Love, 'ave a chocolate."

"Thank you." I said popping the chocolate into my mouth absent-mindedly. My mind was on getting this thing over with as fast as possible.

"Are you an American?"

"Yes...I am sorry. Belmont Dexter." I said shaking her hand and rising slightly.

"ow are you?" Mrs. Carr said. "It is nice to meet you."

She was a merry sort. She continued to babble on about her native Britain. She had grown up in a London suburb and she loved the sea, but she liked it here too. Her husband had been an honest tradesman and after he died, she wanted to do something for charity. So she came to Vietnam to run an orphanage for Vietnamese children. She talked non-stop. Thank God, she spared me her political views!

A siren went off at the Post Office and everybody began to leave.

"What is that?" I asked.

"It is noon lunch, Love. The Vietnamese take a two-hour lunch during the day."

"A two-hour lunch! But what about all these people who are waiting?"

"Oh, they will come back."

"Come back! I don't have time to come back!"

"I'm afraid you will 'ave to, Mr. Dexter. This is Vietnam you know." She said with a plucky little smile. "See you at 3:00 o'clock."

I was not sure what Mrs. Carr meant when she said see you at 3:00 o'clock. What was I going to do for two hours? By the time I got back to the Embassy, it would be time to come back down to the Ministry. But I was back here at 2:00 o'clock on the dot! Only the Government staff did not show up until 2:45 and they refused to start work before 3:00 o'clock. My blood was boiling. I walked up to the counter and demanded that something be done! But I was told they could not find my papers. Somehow my papers had been misplaced.

"What the hell do you mean, misplaced? I am not leaving this building until I get those papers!" I shouted. I was upset! I looked down behind the counter, and I saw a stack of files lying on some broken down shelves and several piles of paper cast on the floor. The piles of paper looked ancient and had frayed ends where the mice had eaten away at them. It was apparent they did not have a filing system. Christ, maybe they didn't even know what a filing system was!

"I try. Please take seat." The Vietnamese man said.

I walked forlornly back to Mrs. Carr.

"Mrs Carr, I am at a loss. You have got to help me." I said sitting down.

"Why not grease his palm a little, ducky."

"You mean give him money?"

"Yes, dear."

"You think he wants money?"

"Why of course, dear. That is the only way anything gets done here. Without money your papers will be delayed for months."

So I went storming down to the Bank of Saigon to withdraw $100 in small bills. I was not going to give these bastards any more than I had to. I asked for a couple of envelopes too. I might as well be discreet about it. I went back to the Ministry of Social Welfare and stepped up to the counter.

"I really do need these papers." I said earnestly and handed him the envelope.

He went over to the wall and looked in it. Then he came back.

"We find papers." He said raising the papers in his hand triumphantly.

I looked at him steadily. I was not happy. I had just spent four hours playing Mickey Mouse.

"All Ok. No sweat. Go to Interior Office. Get signature."

"Thank you." I said humbly, and I walked over to Mrs. Carr.

All the steam in my valves had finally been released.

"Well, Mrs. Carr you really helped me. I hope I will see you again in Saigon."

"You will." She smiled broadly.

Released! I was so happy! This really had been a nightmare! I walked down the steps and across the plaza to the Ministry of Interior. The building was in the same state of disrepair. After much looking, I found the right office, explained my problem, handed over my little white envelope, and waited for another miracle to be performed.

"I sign." Said the Vietnamese. "Go back to Social Welfare, get signature."

"But I was just there. Why didn't he sign it then?"

"Before he sign, he make sure I sign." The Vietnamese said smiling.

I could be doing this all day. How many hoops did I have to go through? I was furious! I went marching back to the Ministry of Social Welfare. I threw the papers on the counter.

"Sign them!" I shouted.

"You come back next week."

"Sign the damn papers, you bastard."

"Come back next week."

"I am not going to come back next week. I want the papers signed now! I slipped him another white envelope. He again went over to the wall and looked inside.

He came back and signed quietly. That frick'n bastard! I thought to myself.

Mrs. Carr was smiling up at me. "Come visit me for tea, Love. I am with the Children's Refugee Orphanage on Rue Le Pasteur."

"Thank you, Mrs. Carr. I will try." I said furiously and I walked out. I have never felt so humiliated in all of my life!

CHAPTER 6

I got Huey's body squared away, and he left for the States the next day. It was not a pleasant experience calling his family to tell them the news. But the worst part was calling my Mother and breaking it to her. She was outraged and accused me of not taking care of him. There was not a lot I could say.

I decided to forget Huey and concentrate only on this evening and my date. I knew I had to look my best. Knowing Christine, she would probably be looking around for some safe port, and that meant an older man with graying hair whose cockles she could warm but probably not ignite. The old bird would have seen too much action for that.

It was hard to out dress the Military men with their chests all full of medals so I thought I would try for an extra smooth shave. The Ambassador had lent me a driver and a jeep for tonight, and I was very much in his debt. I was anxiously looking forward to the evening. At the appointed hour "Charles" called up to my room and I came down. My driver was a young kid just out of high school.

"Charles Watkins, Sir." He said saluting.

I saw the glow in his eyes. I was wearing a tux, and I must have cut a grand figure coming down the steps of the Continental Hotel. I wished I had had a little gray at my temples. But, oh Charlie looked young! His hat fell down over his ears and his hair was in his eyes. He seemed like a clumsy, conscience-stricken teenager dragged painfully from his too short-lived youth.

I thought back to the lazy Summer I spent on the Cape after I graduated from prep school. I had my college days ahead of me—

football games, Hasty Pudding, college mixers, nights at the library, milling around bookstores and coffee shops, and growing up in Harvard Yard. Whoever worried about working or paying bills? And God forbid, who ever thought about the Draft?

When I was eighteen, I had never felt freer. It was the Summer of 1963, and it was spent down by the sea with the warm sand and the ocean breezes. I had just started to experiment with sex and it was awesome! All I cared about was my girl, the sun, the sea, and my new Chevy with the big back seat. Not for the next four years did I ever have to worry about a thing; and certainly not War! War was not for starry-eyed youths; it was for old and cranky Generals.

Our jeep was an open-aired Military jeep. I climbed up in the front. "Onward Charles." I commanded.

We started out with two hesitant jerks. Charles was not known for his clutch driving. We were headed toward the airport where the US Army Hospital was located. It was the evening hour and the light had a filtered glow to it. I felt oddly bizarre in a tuxedo driving through the back street slums of Saigon. Somehow the open aired jeep made one feel too close to the wretched poverty I was traveling through. Beggars, stray dogs, piles of rubbish, evil smelling alleys, boys urinating on the walls; you wondered how life went on.

Charles hooked a sharp turn and we were in front of the nurse's compound. It was a white shinning building with a veranda in front. I trotted up the stairs and asked for Christine. Christine looked gorgeous as she came down the stairs. She had on a white silk blouse and a long flowing skirt made of oriental silk.

"Hello." Christine said and she smiled radiantly.

"Wow! You look great! Come on, we have a bit of a ride ahead of us." I escorted her out.

"Oh, you may want to bring a scarf with you. My car is a bit breezy."

"I've got one." She said with a wide smile and she pulled out a beautiful flashing pink scarf.

Smart girl; thinks ahead. I liked that. We walked out into the sultry air.

"Christine, meet Charles."

"Hello." She said gaily.

"Good evening, ma'am."

"We are in his hands." I said and helped Christine into the back of the jeep. I crawled up beside her. Charlie managed to move the jeep smoothly into the street and we were off. When we arrived in front of the Ambassador's elegant villa, every light was blazing! The oversized mansion was a lavish affair. It was of course French left over from the grand old days of French Colonial rule. It reminded me of the sad state of tarnished silver.

Outside there were high gates protecting the house and the inner gardens. As we went through the gates, we entered a whole new world which functioned at a different rate and on a different level. It was called royal opulence! The party was being held for several US Senators who came over to get a firsthand look at the War. I was surprised to see how many American wives were here. We could have been at any of the Embassies on Wisconsin or Connecticut Avenues. Maybe Wars were not so bad after all. I carefully helped Christine down.

As we went up to the door, the glowing light tumbled out. Inside people were smiling, glittering and golden. The room had an enormous chandelier made of finely cut-glass prisms. It was a giant sphere and it flooded the room with a sense of elegance and well-being. There was

47

ornate moldings on the walls and tall French doors. The Ambassador and his wife were standing there to greet us.

"Well, hello Belmont. I am so glad you could come!"

"Mr. Ambassador." I said shaking his hand readily. "I would like you to meet Christine Blakely. She is a nurse at the US Army Hospital."

"I am delighted to meet you! I would like you to meet my wife."

The women were engaged in a conversation and the Ambassador leaned toward me.

"I am sorry to learn of your friend's death. It is very unfortunate."

"I would like to find out who murdered him. Is there any way you could help me?"

The Ambassador's face winced. "I wish there was some way I could help, but I am afraid there is not."

He seemed very frigid on the subject, and I decided this was not a good time to pursue it. Christine turned to me and smiled.

"Do not let this girl get away, Belmont. She is much too pretty! Go on in and enjoy yourselves!"

The orchestra was playing! We fluttered in like a pair of doves looking for a home to nest in. Having just arrived in Saigon, I knew virtually no one. I decided the best strategy was the buffet table. But before we could get there, Mark Townsend intercepted us. Mark had not been very helpful at the Embassy. He seemed like a shady character. The kind that never tells the entire truth or had boundless insecurities locked up inside of him. I have an unwritten dictum which I have always followed. Never trust a man with a mustache. And men with beards are even more suspect! That is how I felt about Mark. His mustache and his arrogant ways kept me on my guard. Mark dressed to perfection. He seemed so smooth, you just wondered where all the wrinkles were. I decided he probably platonically conceived himself one afternoon with a septic little smile and has been true to himself ever since. I was about to two step him.

"Hello, Mr. Dexter. I see you are getting to know Saigon." He said peering at Christine. But Christine was my trophy, and I was not going to introduce her to him.

"Hi, Mark. This is Christine. Yes, I did get everything straightened out with Huey. He is home now. I don't want to cut you, Mark; but Christine and I are starving. Excuse us while we go and crash the buffet table." I said and guided Christine away.

"Who was that?" She whispered.

"Some creep over at the Embassy. I avoid him at all costs. You are hungry, aren't you?"

"Starved."

"Good! So am I!" We headed across the room.

The long buffet table was covered by a delicate, yellow tablecloth. In the middle was an enormous vase filled with tiny white flowers offset with pink roses. On the table amidst all of this softness was a dazzling display of glittering silver and endless chafing dishes holding stuffed artichokes, liver pates, smoked salmon, toasted nuts, anchovies, pickled oysters, exquisite little shrimp, smoked pheasant, oysters on the half shell, octopus, roast beef, smoked salmon rolls, French brie, and crab-meat all garnished with watercress and tropical fruits. I knew there had to be a few French chefs left in Saigon! Christine and I delighted in exchanging tastes.

As the orchestra was tuning up, we wandered over to an exhibit that was set off in one corner of the room. Articles of a captured Viet Cong soldier were being displayed as if they were relics from some distant War. We were both enchanted by the simple garb of the enemy—the black pajamas, the sandals, the hammock, the canteen, the knapsack.

Somehow it all seemed more thrilling enclosed behind glass. This was the spirit we were fighting. This was the force that would come to beat the most powerful Army on the face of the earth.

Christine kept running into people she knew. We chatted amicably with them. One man she introduced me to was a suave Frenchman by the name of Mr. Boissande. He was very continental, very collected, and he had years of experience in Vietnam. It seems in his youth he had stalked the countryside for '*Agence France Press*'. He knew the ropes and he loved to talk.

"The French were very smart when they came to Vietnam. Instead of wasting men conquering the nation, they simply dismantled the economy. Yes, we French built roads, bridges, canals and sanitation systems, but it was all financed by heavy taxes imposed on the farmers. We created monopolies and in effect controlled the markets. Then we used the markets to squeeze out the Vietnamese farmers. We imported rice so that the price of rice dropped substantially. When the Vietnamese rice farmers could no longer make ends meet, they were forced to sell out to the wealthy French who coveted the land and its riches. Having been a fiercely self-sufficient people, the Vietnamese were now totally dependent on the rich landlords and they were always at their mercy.

What is not understood are the injured racial feelings, the misery, and the desperation to gain what was lost. This is the reason they leave their homes and fight under overwhelming odds. They have left their wives, children, and their jobs to fight rather than acquiesce to the humiliation and the injustice. There is quite a force up in those hills. Do not under-estimate them!"

Christine spotted someone she knew and fluttered away like a butterfly while I helplessly watched her go.

"Now, what does the Vietnamese want?" He continued. "I will

tell you what they want! Lower rents and taxes, ownership of the land, fair prices for their products, respect, and a reasonably fair and honest government. Is that too much to ask?"

I was not listening to him. I was watching Christine, and I was very anxious for her return.

"Is that too much to ask?" He asked again.

"No, not at all."

"Well, you Americans are making the same mistakes we did. Why can't you see that? We helped make the Vietnamese dependent upon us, but so are you! You have destroyed the structure of their lives, and you have herded them into the cities like cattle where they cannot care for themselves. You have taken away their dignity, their homes, and their livelihoods. And you expect to win this War?"

Christine came back to us radiantly and Mr Boissande began holding up fingers.

"The United States has used 1) unprecedented reliance on destructive chemicals 2) the most massive aerial bombardment in history 3) and the deadliest anti-personnel weaponry ever designed to kill."

"Mr. Boissande," I said quietly. "I hate to interrupt you, but I did promise Christine the first dance. Will you excuse us?"

"Of course! I am sorry. You two have more to think about than War." He said winking at Christine. "Goodbye Ma cherie, I will see you later. Goodbye Belmont."

"Thank you, Sir." I said shaking his hand, and I took Christine's arm.

"Christ, who let him through the front door?"

"You were very rude."

"I do not care; I want only to be with you, and tonight I have been sharing you with everyone. How can you say that to me when I have

51

been suffering all evening? Please let's dance."

There was a 12-piece orchestra playing and the music was beautiful. I gathered Christine into my arms. She danced wonderfully.

"That guy talked like a madman. There is not a chance we are going to lose this War!"

"Let's not talk of War. I see too much of it every day." She pleaded.

"What do you do on your days off?" I asked.

"I have been working at an orphanage for Vietnamese children."

"Could it be the Children's Refugee Orphanage?"

"Why yes, how did you know?"

"I know the famous Mrs. Carr." I said.

"She is a charming women."

"Oh yes, charming! What else do you do besides taking care of the sick, the maimed, and the homeless?"

"I swim at the Cerde Sportif."

"What is that?"

"It is a Club in Saigon that has a wonderful swimming pool."

"And you like that?"

"I love to swim!"

"Do you like to dance?"

"Yes, I love to dance!"

"You dance very well." I said holding her closer to me.

We both listened to the music and we were both silent in our own worlds. Then came the dreaded tap on the shoulder. A Military man dripping with metals took her away from me. Christine was on top of the world. But how couldn't you be when you are young, beautiful, and desired? The world was at her beck and call and she knew it! I watched Christine on the dance floor. Every two minutes she would have a new partner. They would hold her tightly and move her gracefully around the floor like a leaf on the morning breeze. She was a very popular nurse in her white silk dress, white high heels, and long flowing hair. I saw my chance and I took it.

"Hello again!" I said gathering her close to me.

"Hi!"

There was a gorgeous August moon coming up over the garden, and we could hear the crickets and the bullfrogs keeping time to the music. I felt Christine's feverish hand on my shoulder and her soft cheek against mine. I could smell the gardenia scent she was wearing. The night was warm and steeped with intimacy. I maneuvered Christine out onto the terrace where it was very private. I brought her over to the corner of the wall and softly kissed her. She kissed me too, but she suddenly pulled away.

"I would like to go home." She said in a tense voice.

I could tell by her voice that she was upset. I nodded gravely and I escorted her out. We hurriedly said goodbye to the Ambassador and his wife. On the way home we did not say one word to each other. I walked her to the door.

"I am sorry. I hope I did not step out of line."

She looked at me. "Goodnight."

"Goodnight." I said, and I watched helplessly as she walked slowly down the hall.

CHAPTER 7

I did not sleep well that night. I lay tossing and turning. I did not want to think about Christine, but I did. There was no hope for me; only a long, lingering desire. I have always been attracted to the mothering kinds of women who dote on you. So why was I attracted to this Italian iceberg, this frozen Madonna? What power did she have over me to keep me tossing and turning in my bed? But I wanted to get closer, and I would!

The next day I called the Hospital to see which day Christine had off. Then I called Mrs. Carr and told her I would be delighted to come to tea. This was my lateral approach. It was a bit sneaky, but I decided to give it a try. We were going to have lunch together. The children would be taking their naps at twelve o'clock and Christine would be free to sit and chat. It had been Mrs. Carr's suggestion. She had a young nurse she wanted me to meet and wouldn't I stay and have lunch with them under the banyan trees? Of course I would. I would be delighted to!

Finally it was Wednesday. The Orphanage was located in the middle of the City on a side street. It was an old French compound and it looked condemned. The house was surrounded by walls with a wrought iron gate and a bell in front. When I arrived, I could see children in the courtyard playing in the morning sunshine. They were all barefoot and some hadn't any pants on. When I was admitted in, they ran to me as if I was the greatest excitement they had seen all week.

They laughed and giggled, and I picked one of them up and

carried her into the house while the other children followed us merrily. I had brought some bright colored jellybeans with me; and if I had been a hit before, I was now a full-fledged deity as I distributed the jellybeans to each child. Mrs. Carr greeted me in the hallway and invited me inside. A Vietnamese woman came out and took the children in for their naps. They passed by me smiling and waving. Breathless and open, each one was precious with their dark, straight hair and shinning eyes!

"Mr. Dexter, 'ow nice to see you! Come out in the back where it is cool. Christine should be 'ere shortly. She is just putting the children down for their naps."

I followed Mrs. Carr out to the back. There was a wooden table and chairs under a huge banyan tree. The front of the building protected us from the harsh glare of the noonday sun, and it was very cool under the enormous tree. I pulled out a chair for Mrs. Carr and helped her get seated.

"Thank you, dearie." She said settling in. I sat down beside her.

"Well Love, 'ow is everything with you?"

"Hopeless."

I could picture Mrs. Carr chatting away to Christine, and I wanted all the sympathy I could get. I threw her a long, dejected look.

"Well my, that does sound bad."

"I really feel lost here; lost and alone."

"Oh my." She seemed at a loss for words as Christine came out of the house to join us.

"Christine!" Mrs. Carr brightened. "I want you to meet Belmont Dexter!"

"Hello Mr. Dexter." Christine said coolly.

55

"Hello, Christine."

"Why, you two know each other."

"Yes."

Mrs Carr looked chagrin.

Over lunch Mrs. Carr and I had a two-way conversation. I teased and cajoled her and tried to amuse and flatter her. She loved it! Christine sat back listening to us carrying on. She finished her lunch.

"It was nice seeing you again, Mr. Dexter." Christine said and excused herself.

I gave Mrs. Carr a shattered look and followed Christine. I saw her turn into a room at the end of the hall. It was a room full of babies. Some were still asleep.

"Christine, why are you giving me the cold shoulder?"

There was a two-year old standing up in her crib with her arms outstretched to me, and I picked her up as I swooped down upon Christine. At least someone wanted me.

"I have work to do."

"Everyone has work to do. I have work to do!"

The little girl I was holding gave me a big hug and started to play with my hair.

"Then why aren't you working?"

I shifted the little girl to my other arm.

"Because I came here to see you."

"Belmont, I don't think we should see each other anymore."

"But why not? I'm wild about you!"

"I don't want to be pushed into a relationship."

"Look Christine, I do not know anyone here. I am lonely and I would like to get to know you. It is that simple. Is that so bad?"

Christine had finished changing the infant's diapers, and

she put him back into the crib. She took the child from me and gently replaced her with a wisp of a baby and a bottle.

"Oh Christine." Babies were foreigners to me; I could feel my legs sag. "I have never held a baby before. What if I drop him?"

"Her. You won't."

The baby was so tiny. I was afraid I would hurt it.

"What if she starts crying?"

"Give her a hug and she'll stop."

I was not too sure. Frankly, I was deadly afraid of children. But I managed. In fact, I was feeling rather paternal, and I watched eagerly as the baby sucked heartily on the bottle nipple. Christine finished changing the two-year old's pants and let her sit on the table. The child smiled up at me.

"She likes you." Christine said.

"I am glad somebody does."

"Am I that difficult?"

"Yes." I answered truthfully. "Sometimes you can be normal then all of a sudden you drift away into a shell."

"I don't mean to be distant."

"Look Christine, can't we just enjoy each other."

"Yes, as friends we can."

Friends were a start. I wasn't sure if I had won or not.

"Sunday is my day off, Christine. Why don't you come over and have Sunday breakfast with me? The Continental Hotel has a wonderful brunch, and then we could over to the Cerde Sportif for a swim. What do you think?"

Christine considered it for a moment. "I have a four o'clock shift, but I could go until then." She said tentatively.

"Good!" I said as if a milestone had been crossed. "You won't let me down, will you?"

"No."

"I will wait for you in the Continental Hotel lobby around 9:00 am on Sunday."

The baby I was feeding had gone to sleep in my arms. Christine gently took her back to her crib. Seeing that, the little girl on the table again stretched out her arms to me. I picked her up.

"What is her name?"

"It is Kimi. She is up for adoption."

"Adoption? Why?"

"She is AmerAsian. She belongs to neither side. No one wants her."

"No one wants her! She is very cute and so happy!"

We took Kimi back out to the courtyard to play.

"I will see you at nine on Sunday!" I was overjoyed.

Christine waved and went back inside. Elated, I went off to thank Mrs. Carr.

CHAPTER 8

It was past nine o'clock on Sunday morning, and I was pacing around the lobby of the Continental Hotel like a madman. Thank God I was not born a woman! Men were the thinkers and the doers. Women were the ones who waited. They waited for someone to ask them to marry them, they waited for their babies, they waited for their husbands to come home at night. Finally, Christine came through the entrance and all my fears were swept away. Now that she was here, I felt infinitely better.

"Hi!" I said elated.

"Hello." She smiled.

"Did you have any trouble getting here?"

"None."

"Are you hungry?"

"Starved!" She said flowing over like a flooding stream in May.

Christine ran hot and cold. It was difficult at times understanding her. Sometimes she seemed to be glowing with life, and other times she seemed so lost and reclusive.

"Good, follow me!" We started down the length of the lobby.

"You look very happy this morning." I said.

"I am!"

"Why?"

"I am usually happy."

Christine was carrying a tote bag, and I could smell the coconut oil from her suntan lotion. It was an exciting smell. It made me think of the sand and the sun and the morning beach with the birds diving into the water.

We walked into the dining room. The room was golden with sunlight and Pierre was there to seat us.

"Bonjour." He said bowing politely.

Christine smiled. "Bonjour."

"Hello, Pierre. We need a table."

"Oui, Monsieur Dexter."

He led us off to a table by the window. I seated Christine and sat down. Pierre brought us a pot of coffee and fresh orange juice in delicate glasses. There were flowers and fruit on the table. I poured Christine a cup of coffee and then I poured a cup for myself. I enjoyed breakfasts. I particularly liked eating them with women. There was some kind of unwritten intimacy there and I missed having it.

"Do you go to the Cerde Sportif often?" I asked.

"I usually go with a group of nurses from the Hospital at least once a week."

"Then you are a regular! You will have to introduce me to all of your beau's at the Club."

She smiled. "You must keep your girlfriends under lock and key."

"No, but I like to know what my competition is."

"Well, you needn't worry. There isn't any."

"None? That is hard to believe. You are far too pretty not to have any."

"Remember, Belmont. We are just friends." She whispered.

"Oh right. I forgot."

Pierre came over to take our orders and that comment floated off into the air. We both decided on omelets with sumptuous mushrooms and freshly baked croissant rolls.

"Where are you from?" Christine asked.

"I grew up in a little town called Bronxville just outside of New York City. I have lived though in California and Boston, and one year I went to school in India."

"Where do you like best?" She asked.

"I guess I like Washington DC the best. I have grown accustom to Georgetown. My friends are there. I own a house there. It is home."

"Do you come from a large family?" She asked.

"No, there was just me."

Our breakfast came. We ate and chatted and poured ourselves a last cup of coffee.

"Where are you from?" I inquired.

"Great Fish, Montana."

"Do you like it there?"

"It is very nice."

I wanted to ask her more about herself, but she didn't open up. She had some sort of invisible line and once you tripped over it, the curtain came down. We finished our breakfast.

"Are we ready to go?" I asked.

"Yes!"

Christine gathered up her beach bag. I went upstairs to get my things. I called a cab, and we were on our way to the Cerde Sportif for a morning swim.

Neatly trimmed hedges and high white walls surrounded the Cerde Sportif. From the outside all you could see was the Spanish tile roofs. Tightly sealed, this was the foreigner's playground. Built in the days of the French, it still maintained its elegant, exclusive nature. It reminded me a lot of the Indian Creek Club in

Florida. But unlike that venerable old Club, when you walked in through the front door you did not nod to yourself and say 'yes, I have arrived'. More you went to the Cerde Sportif to be with your own. It was an oasis opened only to those with white skin and round eyes. Its presence stood as if to say with a certain mocking: 'you do not belong here. It is only for us'.

Christine and I went gaily through the front door. With the relative coolness of the morning, we could feel the day begin. It was warm, but not blistering hot outside. The long chilly arcade was dim and refreshing. In the middle of the courtyard with the sun blazing down, I could see the swimming pool surrounded by tables shaded by indigo blue umbrellas with white fringe. Colorful orange deck chairs dotted the pool area.

Resting on the lounge chairs were many fit, good-looking bodies of high-ranking Military men tanned deeply by the tropical sun. I even noticed some French girls. Those sly, sexy French women can always be spotted on any beach anywhere in the world. There is something on their foreheads that says: 'I am French'. I followed Christine.

"The changing rooms are over here. I will meet you out at the pool." She said.

"Good."

The changing room had a classic age-old country club smell of mildew to it. This is probably the very room Oscar Wilde changed in with his bridge-playing buddies. I got quickly into my conservative swimsuit. No swim briefs for me! I came out first.

The scene was leisurely naked and sensual. A Vietnamese waiter dressed in a formal white jacket was serving drinks. I found two lounge chairs and sat down in wait of Christine. She appeared like a golden girl —long, tawny, glowing. Christine was American, totally American;

beautifully American! She had a strong, healthy body, radiant, clean features, smooth skin, a happy smile and a will of her own; an iron will. She was wearing a two-piece swimsuit, and I loved seeing the curvature of her hips.

"Hello." She came to me smiling.

"Hello!"

"I am glad you are with me. I never like to come here alone." She said sitting down.

I knew what she meant. She had just turned every head in the house. She was like some vast fertile pasture that you wanted to come and nibble on. She was like one of the stars in the universe that was beaming and glowing and magnificent. And you wanted her. You wanted the morning kiss, the soft touch, the gentle smile, the flaming nights; but how did you ever cut through her armor?

"Do you burn? I have some suntan lotion if you would like it." She offered.

"Will you put some on my back?" I asked tentatively.

"Yes." She said obligingly. "We better not stay too long. The sun here is very hot!"

She smoothed the oil all over my back. The suntan lotion felt wonderful, and I loved feeling Christine's touch.

"There!"

She smiled as she lay back in her chair. Christine loved to sit in the sun and let it warm her; let it melt away all the bad things and cleanse her. Sometimes when she had her eyes closed, she had the deep cosmic feeling of wanting to make love to the universe. She loved the sky and the water and the soft breezes that caressed her and held her.

"Don't you love the sun? I wish the sun would capture me and take me away!" She said.

"Really?" I looked at her with one eye shut. "What are your other fantasies?" I asked amused.

"My other fantasies? They are all normal."

The sun dipped behind some bellowing clouds then reappeared with all of its brilliance. It was as if Christine was running naked in the wet grass with the sun ravishing her and turning her golden.

"I suppose you want a white knight to take you away also."

"Yes. That would be nice." She said.

I lay back in my chair. Maybe this wasn't such a good idea after all. Just lying half naked next to Christine in the noonday sun, I could feel myself becoming aroused. "I think I will go in for a cool dip." I said.

"OK."

I got up and dove into the pool. It was not too long before someone wandered over to Christine. Christ! Why hadn't I defended my territory? I got back out of the water. He was even sitting in my chair!

"Belmont, this is Derrick Flynn. Derrick, this is Belmont Dexter." Christine said introducing us carefully.

I extended a dripping hand. This was the man I had noticed at breakfast the first day I had arrived in Saigon. In a swimsuit he had very long limbs, and it seemed to me a sunken personality that bordered on treachery. I have an odd intuition about people. A smiling face and a murderous heart that is the kind of feeling I had about Flynn as I shook his hand.

"Hello, Mr. Dexter." His eyes were very cold like two tight masks covering up a steel rimmed heart.

"Mr. Flynn." I returned with a curt nod.

"I knew your friend Huey Lake. It is a pity he is dead."

"You knew Huey? How?"

"He was an acquaintance of mine."

Mr. Flynn had a British accent, and I wondered how Christine had ever known him. He turned to Christine.

"If you would relay that message, I would appreciate it." He said standing up.

"Yes, I will." Christine promised.

"Good to meet you, Mr. Dexter."

I nodded.

"Good bye." He said in a muttering voice.

"Goodbye." Christine and I said in unison.

"Who was that?" I asked.

"He is an Englishman who lives in Saigon."

"How do you know him?"

"He knows several nurses at the Hospital."

"He seems very menacing, almost sinister." I said.

"I know. He doesn't seem like a lady's man, but he seems to know them well."

We enjoyed the sunshine and the pool. Around two-thirty we decided to change and head for home. It had been a wonderful day! I was not sure how sunburned I was going to be tomorrow, but it had been worth it! We found a taxicab, and I took Christine back to her quarters. It was a dusty trip back to the Hospital.

"It is cool on the veranda. Would you like to come in for a while?"

"Yes, I would!"

We got out of the taxi and I paid the taxi driver.

"I think I can find something cold for us to drink with maybe even some ice in it!"

"Great!"

On the second floor of the nurse's compound there was a large veranda that spread the length of the building. Christine took me upstairs. An odd allotment of wicker chairs and settees were scattered about. Christine asked me to sit down, and she went off to get the drinks. I put my swimsuit and my towel on the floor.

"Here, this should hold us." Christine said handing me the glass. "I hope you like ice tea."

"Yes, I do." I took a sip. It was cool and refreshing. "This is a nice veranda. I bet half of the US Army has been up here."

"I think more than half of the US Army has tried to get up here, but we have some very tough Military Police."

"You mean after curfew, you couldn't climb out of your window and run away with me in the night?"

"Probably not."

"Darn."

There was a pause.

"Who is Huey Lake?" Christine asked.

"Huey was a close friend of mine. He was murdered last week down by the River."

"Murdered! Why didn't you tell me?"

"I don't want you to worry about being in Saigon."

"I don't worry about being here. I know it is safe. Why was he murdered?"

"I don't know, but I plan to find out."

"I am sorry, Belmont."

It was close to four o'clock. "I had better be going." I said.

Christine walked me downstairs.

"Thank you for the breakfast. It was a wonderful day!" She said.

"It was fun! I feel better now. At least I know one person in Saigon!" I waved as I left.

The next day Christine called me at my office.

"Belmont, this is Christine."

"Hi!"

"You forgot your swimsuit and your towel yesterday."

"I knew I would forget something. Sorry." I said. Actually, I had left them there on purpose so I would have an excuse to call on Christine again.

"Are you free for lunch today?" She asked.

"Sure!"

"Could you meet me at the Caravelle Hotel at twelve o'clock noon?"

"Yes!"

"Good, I will see you soon."

The Caravelle Hotel had a rundown, tattered restaurant on the first floor with old world charm and delicious French cooking. Christine was right on time. She had just scored another point with me.

"Hello." She said smiling and looking radiant.

"Hi!"

She placed a freshly washed towel and swimsuit in my hands. I had left it a soggy mess on the floor of the veranda. Now it was being returned to me clean and fresh.

"Thank you! My you nurses can do wonders, can't you!"

"You forgot it."

"You distract me!"

She smiled as we walked inside and found a table in the back. The restaurant had an antiquated atmosphere to it, and I enjoyed sitting there with Christine as we waited for our lunch.

"They are sending me to Dak Tu up in the Highlands of Vietnam." Christine said quietly.

"Dak Tu! That is where all the heavy fighting is!" I burst out. She had caught me off guard.

"That is why they need us."

"But you can't go up there. You're a woman."

"It is safe, Belmont."

"Not with rockets flying in and out!"

"I didn't ask you here to upset you. I only wanted to tell you that I would be away for a couple of weeks."

"A couple of weeks! When do you leave?"

"Tomorrow morning."

"Tomorrow! Why so soon?"

"I don't know. I was just informed this morning."

"Well, I suppose it is safe. But will you call me when you get there?" I was really concerned. Dak Tu was no place for a woman! All in all, it was a pretty grim meal. After we finished, I found a taxi for Christine.

"The Cerde Sportif won't be the same without you." I said as I opened the door of the blue taxicab for her.

She smiled. "I'll be back!"

"You won't forget to call, will you?" I said resting my hand on the taxi door.

"No." she promised.

I wanted to kiss her, but I held out my hand instead. She gave me hers. Heavy rain clouds had moved in from the Sea and it began to drizzle.

"Be careful of the Marines up there. It is not the Viet Cong I am worried about. It is my own brothers!"

She laughed. "I will be careful." She said. She smiled radiantly with all of her glowing, youthful charm and climbed into the taxi.

I watched the taxicab go down the street. For me, all the lights had just gone out in Saigon.

CHAPTER 9

Christine's medical team arrived in Dak Tu by helicopter. From the cockpit windows of the American helicopter, they could see the twisted peaks and scraggy ravines that surrounded the old Fort. Of late there had been heavy fighting in the hills. Search and destroy missions were being sent out daily. For this reason, the US Army was moving its best medical personnel forward.

Like a figurehead raised brazenly above the Sea, the Fort at Dak Tu stood majestic and impregnable on a high knoll overlooking the Kakjram Valley. From the long vistas of the Fort, you could see a small river winding its way along the valley floor. Fierce winds blew constantly sending a ghostly white mist up through the mountainous terrain. The winds were always strong as if warning of some impending danger. The Fort was a relic from the past. It had been abandoned years ago by the French. Now it had new life breathed into it by the American occupation.

The Fort was surrounded by barbed wire and land mines, and it was backed up by big guns and fighting aviation. In the middle of the Fort there was room for a small airstrip. To each side of the runway there were stacks of supplies and many sandbagged bunkers. The Fort was barren of any vegetation. To the West there were rows of tents. You could see laundry drying and soldiers milling about. At each watchtower there were machine guns that stood careful guard over the lonely valley below.

Red dust kicked up as the helicopter came closer to the ground. Several men emerged and turned to help Christine.

"Can you make it?"

"Yes." She said over the loud noise of the helicopter.

"Here we go, one big leap."

All four of the medical team were on the ground, and they bent low and moved away from the wind and the whirling blades of the helicopter. Captain Morley took them directly into the Triage area of the Hospital that was located next to the airstrip.

"Gentlemen, this is Captain Stark, the Hospital Commander." Captain Morley said introducing them.

"Captain Stark, this is Doctors Hoffman, Hitchcock, Shapiro, and Christine Blakely."

The Captain shook hands with everyone.

"Welcome to Dak Tu." Captain Stark said. "We have a couple of doctors rotating back to the States so your presence here will be extremely helpful. I want to give you a quick tour of the compound and then take you over to your living quarters."

Captain Stark showed them the Hospital. It was built of wood and had a tin roof. There was a long, concrete walkway which connected the Hospital to the doctor's quarters. In the Hospital there were five operating rooms and a x-ray unit. Generally when the wounded came in, they were patched up and sent to Saigon or Japan for convalescence. Only the worst cases were operated on here.

The Hospital Commander showed them the graves, the mess hall, the latrines, the headquarters, and the Officer's Club. Then he brought them back to the Hospital and their new living quarters. Christine had a room down the hall with a screened porch in the back facing the mountains. The doctors were together in a large room up front. They began to unpack their gear.

"Hey, that nurse is frick'n gorgeous." Dr. Hitchcock said.

Bill Hitchcock was a young, viral intern from California. The other two doctors were family men; and they thought of Hitchcock as amusing —sometimes clever, sometimes crude, and always obnoxious.

"Yes, but she doesn't like you, Billy." Doctor Shapiro said.

Noah Shapiro had lived with Bill for the last five months and he loved to taunt him.

"Doesn't like me? Didn't you see her drooling behind me in the helicopter?"

"I think that was air-sickness, don't you, David?"

"Yes, she certainly looked pretty sick." Doctor Hoffman said.

"Ya well, sick or not, I'd like to stick it to her." Doctor Hitchcock said.

Down the hall Christine was unpacking her clothes. She had not brought much with her except her Army fatigues and her black Army boots. She hung up her shirts and took out her toilet articles. Then she went out to the porch to sit down. It was the twilight hour. She sat quietly watching the velvet dusk turn the mountains a deep purple. It was a spectacular Vietnamese sunset. The sky was full of brilliant colors and soft golden light. The stillness of the twilight sky was so beautiful in its final glory.

This was the most difficult time of the day for Christine. It was magnificently beautiful, but if it was not shared with someone, somehow it made her feel very much alone. She began to think of Belmont and the party they had been to. Why had she been so cold towards him? She had enjoyed the party, and it had been wonderful to be away from the Hospital with all of its suffering and sadness. Why then had she pulled away from him? Why was she always afraid to get too close?

She knew why. Kisses were like daggers coming to rip her apart. They were the hurt and the rage of long past when love, confidence, and

71

trust had all been shattered, and out of the pieces had come a very hardened and abandoned woman. Would she never risk herself again? Did she never think that the other person had feelings too. That perhaps a kiss was a show of affection. That it was tame and gentle and spoke of love.

And what about the other person? Did they not have needs equal to her own? Why must she always lash out? Why had she ruined the evening? She knew why, but she wasn't going to dwell on it. Tomorrow she would be back at work. It was better not to be involved. Work would take her away from these thoughts, and then she wouldn't have to dwell on them anymore. She could just lock them away.

Her mind drifted to the early morning helicopter ride from Saigon up to the Vietnamese Central Highlands. It was the time of day when the soft morning light had made everything golden. The countryside was green and lush and so still. There were birds flying high above; quiet and graceful. Lazy, slow-moving streams flowed across the serene land and glistened in the early morning sunshine. The streams originated high in the mountains, and they brought life-giving water down to the Sea.

From high above Christine had seen lazy water buffalo quietly grazing with friendly white birds sitting on their backs, and farmers dressed in black wearing conical hats working hard in their golden fields. It seemed like a peaceful, storybook land. It was in stark contrast to the cold metal of the American helicopters, the deadly machine-guns that were always aimed at the ground ready to shoot, and the earth-shattering noise that the helicopters made everywhere they went.

There was a knock on the door. She went over and opened it up.

"Hello, David."

"Are you ready for dinner?" Doctor Hoffman asked.

Doctor Hoffman was a keenly sensitive, thoughtful, and absolutely reliable man. He was the kind of Doctor you would want at your bedside if ever you were gravely ill. The Doctor was older than the rest of the surgeons in Vietnam and Christine enjoyed his company.

"Yes, I am." She said smiling.

They walked down the concrete walkway to the Doctor's quarters. Noah Shapiro was there to intercept them and invited her in.

"Well, what do you think, Christine?" Doctor Shapiro said showing her the room.

"I think it looks very ship-shape!" She replied approvingly.

Next to his bed Doctor Hoffman had placed a picture of his wife and his kids. He was from beginning to end a dedicated family man. This year in Vietnam had been hard on him. He wanted very much to be back in his small town in the Midwest with his wife and children.

"We can bring in another bed if you'd like to join us, Ms. Blakely." Doctor Hitchcock said coyly.

"No thank you. I like my own room." Christine said.

There was an uneasy tension in the air. The four went out and crossed over to the Mess Hall. The chow line was long. Christine felt somewhat out of place as men kept staring at her. The four medical personnel found a table and sat down. Doctor Hitchcock moved very close to Christine. Christine concentrated on her food. Doctor Hitchcock watched her steadily.

"Christine is a very Christian name." He said to her.

"I like it." She said coolly.

"How old are you?" He asked.

"27."

"Have you ever been married?" Dr. Hitchcock asked.

"No."

"Why not?" He demanded.

"I just haven't." She said tensely

"Do you have a boyfriend?"

"No."

"So would you like to screw around?" He asked.

Christine didn't say anything. She could feel the blood rising to her cheeks.

"Come on Bill, that isn't very nice talk." Doctor Hoffman broke in. "Why don't you let Christine eat her dinner?"

"Because I prefer that she eat me?"

There was a silence at the table. This was going to be a very difficult three weeks.

Christine stood up and left.

"Nice job, Hitchcock. Why didn't you just rape her on the table so we could all watch." Doctor Shapiro said angrily.

"Ah, she'll get over it." Doctor Hitchcock said smiling.

"I don't think you won any points there, buddy." Doctor Shapiro added cynically.

Later that evening Doctor Hoffman knocked on Christine's door.

"We are going over to the Officer's Club. Would you like to join us?" He asked.

"No, I think I'll stay here, David." Christine said.

"I'm sorry about Hitchcock. I am afraid we are not going to be able to do anything about him. He's a good doctor. I've seen him work. But unfortunately, he's a little socially retarded."

"I would like to stay out of his way." Christine said.

"We will see if we can't work some scheduling wonders."

"Thank you, David." She said gratefully.

They said good night and she closed the door.

CHAPTER 10

There were rugged mountains along the spine of Vietnam. They were amazingly beautiful and they were steep and very grand. Majestic mahogany and teak trees rose a hundred feet tall and loomed over the jagged ridges and deep ravines. They were the first canopy, and they protected the dense undergrowth of the jungle. Everywhere ridges and rock outcroppings showed themselves like stark masters; relentless and unforgiving. It was an unpopulated jungle wilderness; a place where one could easily go and hide. For that reason, the National Liberation Front (NLF), better known as the Viet Cong or just 'Charlie' by the US soldiers, built and maintained a vast network of paths and trails through the thick jungle; and they were moving an unprecedented amount of supplies from the North to the South of Vietnam. The outpost at Dak Tu stood as a reminder to the Viet Cong forces that the journey into the South would not be easy.

An American rifle platoon was just returning after three days in the bush.

"Why don't them damn VC come out and show themselves?" Brody said. "We pack in 60 pounds of gear, hump through the the jungle when it's 100 degrees, fry our brains out, and all we got to show for it is nothing! Shit, when I do see them gooks, I'm gonna blast their heads off." Brody was a young nineteen-year-old from Oklahoma.

"Ya, well you're gonna get your chance tomorrow." The radioman said.

"What! You mean we're gon'na have one day rest and go back out?"

"That's what six says."

"Shit, the Heavies are crazy. They're always crazy. Why don't they just for once do something that makes sense?"

"Frick'n Brass." Link Chesney said.

"Ya, they're gon'na get us all killed!" Swanson added.

Inside the American Fort, the soldiers passed a group of bare-chested men sitting on folding chairs behind a wooden structure in the 99-degree heat sipping beer as if they were sunning themselves on some LA beach. You could see the heat radiating off of the metal chairs.

"Hey, look at them bums sitting on lounge chairs with a beer in hand trying to catch the rays!" Link said as the squad passed by. "We're out at a firebase, and we need water and new socks and more ammunition; and the reason we don't get it is cause these slugs are out here catching the rays."

"S-h-i-t!"

"Ok, keep moving you guys. You've still got to get over to Station D and get your tents up." Sargent Rollins barked. He had a stoic face carved out of granite. Some called him a one-man army.

Once at Station D, the men began to put up their tents for the night.

"Man, I can't wait for that first beer." Swanson said.

"Ya, I hope we got mail." Brody said.

"You mean you haven't heard from your little piece of ass." Swanson shouted.

"Shut up!" Brody said.

"Ya, well Bobby's got her now. He's probably out at the drive-in doing it to her right now."

"Shut up!"

Swanson started to take off his shirt.

"Hey Swanson, put your shirt back on. You look indecent." Link Chesney shouted at him.

"In decent? Long and strong—that's in decent." Swanson said confidently. Everyone just shook their heads and grinned. Swanson had a very fertile mind.

"Ok Brody, go get us some beers. Tonight we gon'na get higher than a Georgia pine! Who's ready for a little stud?" Harlan Greentree was an expert poker player. The men had washed and were ready to relax.

"Man, you've got to be kidding. I'm so tired I couldn't lift a feather."

"That's cause you're a lightweight, Harrison." Harlan taunted him.

"Ya, well you've already cleaned me out once this week."

"Well, you write home to your rich 'ole daddy and tell'm you got'ta have some money cause after this here War, I'm going back to the streets of Watts, and you is going back to the country clubs around Pacific Palisades; and we ain't never gon'na get this rare opportunity to meet this way again."

"Oh really, what do I do in the meantime for money?"

"Don't worry about a thing, I'll carry you."

The Sargent came up. "Mail call!" The men crowded around him.

"Harrison, Chesney, Swanson, Greentree."

"Nothing for me, Sarge?" Brody asked.

"No, Brody, nothing for you."

"Ah, shit!"

"Don't worry, Brody, she'll write." Link Chesney told him. They were the best of friends.

"Ya, but why don't she write?"

"Maybe she did and it's on its way or maybe one of her letters got lost."

"Shit! I HATE this War!" Brody screamed totally out of control.

"Don't worry Brody, you only have 42 days left." Link Chesney told him.

"Ya, but 42 days may be too late." Brody said angrily.

"Come on Brody, you guys in this game or not?" Greentree yelled at them.

"Ya, we're in." They said as they sat down.

"We're going to start with a round of stud. Jokers to open. Games over at chow time."

"You better deal straight, Greentree; and none of this double talk." Chesney said.

Greentree dealt a hand and looked at his cards. "Man, I couldn't beat an egg!"

"Sure Greentree—sure. That's what you always say." Link Chesney said scornfully. He was into Greentree for $200.

"What you go'in to do Hairy-cins?" Greentree asked Harrison.

"Ok, I'm in. In for a dime, in for a dollar."

The men were working on downing as much beer as they could before supper. The game went on until chow time, but by then Harlan had gotten just about everyone's money. But no problem! There was always more where that came from.

The next day the men were up at four o'clock in the morning. It was dark. The camp looked like a graveyard. They put on their gear, and silently moved out of the Fort well before the sun came up. Each man carried a full pack, extra ammunition, mortars, and a M-16. They were glad for the early morning march because they knew that in a couple of hours, the jungle would turn into a raging furnace.

They were a tough, young group of men with a distrustful outlook on life. They lived an outdoor existence sleeping in tents, eating from mess kits in the rain or under the blistering sun, seldomly bathing and constantly swatting flies. It was a hard life. They had dirty boots, dirty fingernails, and sweat filled uniforms. They coped as best they could by just counting the days. How many days left? How many days?

Their eyes were seasoned and piercing. Their steps were alert and careful. The knowledge of death was a constant companion. They respected the jungle, and they approached it single file knowing that it was infested by the VC, and that at any minute they could be ambushed or hit by a sniper, step on a pungi stick, or be ripped apart by a bouncing betty or toe popper. Fear was always with them. It paid to be alert. It paid to watch for the slightest shadow or sound.

They left the security of the Fort and headed up the steep mountain terrain with its savagely red clay soil and dense jungle cover. The plan was to make contact with the enemy; and if possible, take a prisoner. Generally, the Viet Cong would fight only if it was to their advantage. Then they would break contact and move away. But up here in this blood-covered mountain top, the enemy was holding their ground, and the Military wanted to know why.

The jungle was damp as the squad picked its way through the twisted bamboo and thorny undergrowth. The early morning dew made the foliage slick so that the soldiers grabbed on to vines and branches as they went up the mountain. But sometimes the men would slip in the dark; curse, get up again and toil on. They continued to climb in single file and in silence. Each man was privy to his own thoughts. By now they were accustomed to the dank jungle smells of rotting debris. They continued to keep themselves apart and focused with every step.

The first Easterly pink of the morning sky was just beginning to break and the jungle was becoming alive with the sounds of wildlife.

Birds were twittering, monkeys were making threatening noises, and colonies of termites were painstakingly keeping the jungle floor clean. Pools of light were filtering down from the tall teak trees that the men were passing under. At certain points, the mountain would produce granite outcroppings so that the squad had a natural vantage point from which to view the valley below. But they were careful to skirt these openings because they did not want to be observed by the enemy.

The jungle had an appealing lushness to it. It was rich and green and full; and its changing features provided the only variety for the soldiers as they hiked through the dells and valleys, cliffs and broken rock formations dripping and covered by the jungle's fertile growth. But the jungle's beauty was deceptive. Well camouflaged behind any rock or broadleaf tree could be a Viet Cong with his AK-47 aimed at your head ready to shoot.

Because the trails were the life-blood of the Viet Cong, the American patrol stayed away from them. But as they went up the steep slope, they ran into a trail that ran East and West away from the drainage line. Link Chesney was at the head of the patrol. He halted it immediately and went down on one knee. Brody came up to him.

"What is it?" He whispered.

Chesney pointed to the black coil running down the trail.

"Holy shit!"

"Tell the Sarge to come here with Harlan." Chesney whispered.

"OK." Brody said and he moved quietly away.

The Sargent moved through the thicket with Harlan behind him and looked at the wire. He knew from experience that the NLF never laid communication line except to link up a battalion with its regimental headquarters.

Sargent Rollins looked down the length of the trail.

"Get Six on the line." He said to Harlan.

"Six on the hook, Sir."

"Six, this is Bravo. I've just spotted communication wire running up the trail."

There was a pause.

"Bravo, this is Six. Follow the wire, but be careful."

"Roger that."

The jungle was beginning to heat up as the rifle platoon followed the wire along the trail. Huge thunderclouds had rolled into the area and it began to rain. The path was slippery and caked with mud. In ten minutes, a deep ravine feeding off the Western edge of the trail opened onto an outcropping of granite and a fast-moving stream. Above the noise of the splashing water Sargent Rollins and Private Chesney could hear a singsong chatter. They exchanged glances. Sargent Rollins stopped the patrol again.

"You and Brody go check out the stream and be extra careful!" Rollins said.

The two men took off their packs and crawled through the wet foliage on their bellies. Sargent Rollins spread out his men along the trail and told them to ready themselves, and not to shoot until the enemy was halfway past the column. He planted Harrison at the end of the line to chase down any strays for interrogation.

The rain had stopped and there was a new sweetness in the air. Link Chesney and Brody Hawkins crawled back and reported seeing eleven VC by the edge of the stream.

"Did you see any rucksacks?"

"Ya, they were all wearing them."

Rollins was delighted. He smiled ear to ear.

"OK, they'll be coming our way."

The squad waited a long time. They looked at the leaves, the wet bark, their feet. Tiny teardrops of water splashed down upon their guns and on to their fatigues as they patiently waited. After a time, they began to see figures coming down the path. The VC wore black pajamas, sandals, and conical hats. You could hear them jabbering. Hearts began to pound and every M-16 was trained on them.

When they were clearly in the middle of the column and Sargent Rollins could see the white of their eyes, he yelled. "Kill them!"

Each soldier fired until their clips were empty. Within seconds Rollins yelled: "Ceasefire."

The eleven bodies were turned into a bloody pulp. The platoon waited under cover for ten minutes. Then they moved out.

"Sorry about that, Charlie." Swanson said as he skirted around the gory mess.

Sargent Rollins moved his squad on up the trail. One hundred meters further, they found a cluster of five buildings and a mess hall. Some of the buildings had been smashed by artillery. In one of the buildings there were two tons of rice and they knew then that they were in a NFL stronghold.

"How do we destroy all of that rice, Sarge?"

"Leave it. We'll call in some air tomorrow. Right now, I want to see where that communication wire is going." Rollins said.

It began to drizzle again. The squad took out their ponchos and pressed on up the trail. Tall trees rose 100 feet into the air. Then three layers of canopy filled in all the spaces below. Giant water drops fell from limb to limb, and finally crashed down upon the jungle floor. It was hard to believe that anyone would live in such a harsh part of the world with its scorpions, millipedes, ticks, and the empty vastness of forests quiet and still.

As the squad penetrated deeper into the region, the jungle became even more dense, darker and gloomier. It was past noon and the jungle was heating up into a hot sauna. The men toiled forward forgetting their discomfort and pain with thoughts only of what lay ahead. The trail brought them back to the riverbed and on up into a narrow draw where steep granite cliffs rose up on each side. It was cool in the draw and the men enjoyed the clammy moistness. All of a sudden enemy fire broke out from all sides.

"Take cover!" Sargent Rollins screamed.

Men dove into the foliage around them. Bullets were coming in hot and heavy. Shouts for medic were rising from all directions. Bullets screamed overhead, bark was splintering off of trees, and red dust was being kicked up off of the ground. Chesney, Brody, and Harrison were all hit. Those that were cut down in the first couple of seconds were still on the trail. The squad was pinned down by the automatic fire. The only thing they could do was to stay down and cling as tightly as they could to the life-giving earth.

Sargent Rollins crawled over to Harlan.

"Get Six on the line."

"Six, this is Bravo. We're in a ravine. We've hit some kind of a hornet's nest. We're taking heavy fire from all sides. I've got heavy casualties. Half my men are wounded. Seven look to be dead. I'm afraid they'll outflank me and close up my rear. If they do that, my Frick'n goose is cooked. What can you give me?"

"Bravo, this is Six. Third Platoon is on its way. Give me your coordinates and I'll send in artillery."

"Six, this is Bravo. Fighting could become hand to hand. If you keep your ships overhead, I'll try and back my men out of here." Rollins said.

"Bravo, this is Six. Roger that."

Twelve meters away, a VC skirmisher was crawling up on a group of soldiers. Swanson turned around and pumped several rounds of lead into him. The VC skirmisher stopped dead.

"Man, that's getting a little too personal." Swanson said to himself.

"Hey Jacobs, did you see that?" Swanson shouted. Swanson reached over and shook him. Jacobs rolled over and Swanson saw a bullet had penetrated Jacob's forehead.

"Jesus!"

The whole world was quivering and recoiling from the battering of explosives.

Rollins crawled over to Swanson.

"Jacobs dead, Sir."

"We're moving out. Pass it on to move 50 meters down the trail and then turn due West."

"Jacob's dead."

"Follow the sun. Find a bivouac for the night. Then at daylight follow the drainage line down to the valley. Keep yourself low. You got that?"

"Jacob's dead."

Sargent Rollins looked at Swanson oddly. "I can see he's dead. Your responsibility right now is to the living so button that up soldier. Pass what I said down the line or I'll can your God damn ass." Rollins growled and moved away. He went over to Harrison.

"I'm not going to make it, Sarge." Harrison had a gaping hole in his chest and he was in tremendous pain.

"Listen, Harrison, you are going to make it. Now we're pulling back I want you to crawl 50 meters down the trail and then head due West towards the sun. Rest up the night then follow the drainage line down the slope, and Harrison if you don't make it off this mountain; I'm coming back up here and kicking your ass all the way down the Frick'n mountainside. Now get your ass moving. Is that clear?"

Sargent Rollins could soon hear the gunships overhead taking some of the pressure off. He crawled over to Brody and Link Chesney.

"Brody's hurt bad, Sarge."

"Will he make it?"

"He don't say nothing."

"You follow Harrison down the slope. Make sure he keeps going. I'll take care of Brody." Sargent Rollins crawled back to Harlan. The light was fading from the sky.

"OK Harlan baby, it's just you and me and we're going to cover each other going out of here. We'll take Brody as far as we can."

"The radios gone, Sir."

"F....! Ok move out." He said in a cold, hard voice.

Night was beginning to fall. The platoon had been pretty well annihilated. There were just a few men left. Now the only fight was to make it back to the Fort at Dak Tu alive because there was no one else who was going to come out and save you.

CHAPTER 11

The next morning Christine woke up early. She was still hungry from the night before. She got out of bed and started to get dressed. The morning air was very cool, and it reminded her of her childhood home in the Rocky Mountains of Montana. She remembered her Father rising early in the mornings. He would brew the coffee, start the bacon frying, and build a roaring fire in the stone fireplace before the family emerged from their warm beds. The mountain air was cold at sunrise so getting out of your cozy, well blanketed bed was not always easy. You had to be coaxed out of bed by the smell of bacon sizzling in the frying pan or the smell of logs crackling in the fireplace because you were at the edge of dreams where astounding magic occurs, and keeps you racing from one door to the next.

You do not want to come back into the world. But there are wonderful smells in the kitchen. Your Father is making breakfast, and the sun is rising in the East. So half awake, you slowly open your eyes to the new dawn, but it is so hard because you have been watching time clocks flying through the air, and you see babies carrying horses. It is very hard to leave this wild and zany world where you are safe and warm; but you must. It is a new day on a continuum of endless days which is known as life. We all follow a path; and we think we have choices, but do we? There are always those little circumstances in life that are so difficult to explain.

As she rose, Christine could hear the wind thrashing about in the trees on the mountains above. She put on two pairs of socks and a sweater. Who would ever think you would need a sweater in Vietnam?

Christine found out that the nights were very cold and the days were very hot in the South Vietnam Highlands.

It was still dark as Christine walked over to the Mess Hall, but there was a crack of light that announced that the sun was about to rise. As she went inside of the Mess Hall, the empty space seemed strange after being so crowded with soldiers only hours before. Naked light bulbs hung from the ceiling sending out a harsh morning glare. Everything looked much too real. She found a few wrapped sandwiches sitting on a tray. She took a sandwich and a cup of coffee. Christine sat down and began to eat her food, but before she could finish, there was a loud siren letting the camp know that the helicopters were bringing in the wounded and all Hospital staff needed to be up and ready to assist.

Now the earth was gaining light. A sharp glow came from the East and daylight appeared. Thank God for daylight in this cold, thankless world where young men were sent out as pawns to be sacrificed so that the rest of us could be free. But free from what? That was the all important question. Just what did we gain from the War in Vietnam? What does mankind gain from any War?

Christine went out to the tarmac. She could see a helicopter hovering over the ground. Once it landed, wounded soldiers were being unloaded. She went over to help, but she was unprepared for what she saw. This was Christine's first introduction to War. She had always seen the wounded in a clean, white Hospital after they were clean, patched, and sedated. Now she was seeing all too clearly what War really was. Mass casualties were being carried off the battlefield just as they had fallen. Their broken and severed limbs were tucked in beside them. They were covered with mud and dirt. Filthy tourniquets were wrapped around their appalling wounds. It was as if Christine had descended into Hell or had been shipwrecked into a sea of filth and blood. The wounded did not scream, they did not moan, they just clutched their litters and looked up at her as if to ask: 'Why me?' She could see the pain on their faces. She could see how scared they were. 'Am I going to lose my arm? What about my leg, am I ever going to walk again?' They were brave and young and you had to ask yourself why God have we done this?

Christine helped to sort out the wounded. Right pelvis leg not present—gone, probably still lying on the battlefield. Multiple penetrating wounds of the left chest and flank. Multiple wounds of the scalp. Christine came over to Brody who was in a semi-state of shock.

"Karen, where are you? Karen?" He kept asking.

"You will be all right, Brody." Christine said to him softly as she checked his vital signs and lightly touched his arm. She did all she could for him. The next soldier had a through and through of the right upper arm with unstable fracture of the humerus. He was stabilized and sent to x-ray. Every case was gruesome. There were gapping chest wounds and stomach holes. Arms were missing; feet were gone. That was the way it was. The Doctors operated as best they could on the bodies and the mangled flesh.

Later in the afternoon, a Colonel came into the Triage area looking for one of his soldiers. He was tall, very pale, and had fine features. He walked over to Christine.

"I am looking for a soldier by the name of Private Brody Hawkins. Do you know where he is?"

"Yes, he is over here." Christine said and she brought the Colonel over to Brody.

"Brody, this is Colonel Wheeler. We can't locate your squad, Brody. We need some information from you. Can you tell me where you last saw your platoon?" Colonel Wheeler asked.

"They got us in the draw, Sir. Everybody got hit. All my buddies. All my buddies!"

"How far were you from where the rice was stored?"

"50 meters; maybe a little more."

"OK soldier, get some rest." Colonel Wheeler could not help but see the emotional pain this boy was in. "We are proud of you, son." The Colonel said.

"Yes, Sir."

Colonel Wheeler turned to Christine. "Thank you." He said.

Colonel Wheeler walked heavily back to headquarters. He was tired. He had been up all night hoping for information on his men. Brody was the first glimmer of hope that any of his platoon was still alive. He had been picked up in the early hours of the morn by a helicopter that was circling the area where the men had last been seen. Colonel Wheeler wanted to bring in the B-52s, but he knew he was in a checkmate position without knowing where his squad was located. The only alternative was to get another platoon up into that mountain ridge. But they were still an hour away and making slow progress.

On the other side of the mountain there was another Company that was being hard pressed. Why was the enemy standing and fighting? Colonel Wheeler kept wondering. Generally, the Viet Cong would make contact and then retreat. Something big must be up in those mountains. He thought.

The Commanders had discussed the situation, and many felt that the resistance would be over in a couple of weeks as the enemy moved through the area. With this difficult terrain, the Commanders did not want to get too heavily involved in a dogfight around Dak Tu. The word had been sent down to increase the intelligence and send out more feelers. But Colonel Wheeler had his doubts. He had never known the enemy to string combat wire for a one-night stand. And everywhere he placed his men, they were getting hit. Either the Viet Cong were looking for a fight or they had an unbelievably large force up in the mountains. Only time would tell.

A week had passed. What remained of the platoon made it back to camp. Only Harrison was unaccounted for. Those who were wounded were cleaned up and sent on to Saigon.

The fighting was still intense on the other side of the mountain. Christine and the other medical staff were being kept extremely busy. Nerves were becoming somewhat frayed. There was too much blood, too much pain, and too many fatalities. But life went on. You had to keep working. You had to keep going. You had to just concentrate on the present and forget about tomorrow.

After the day was over, total exhaustion brought needed sleep. When there was free time, you either went to the movies or wrote short letters home. There was a routine to it all: more choppers, more wounded, more dying; the night came, the day began: more choppers, more wounded, more dying. And for what?

The only thing that broke the constant routine was the mortar attacks. Usually, they came late at night or just before dawn. The Hospital compound was particularly vulnerable as it was located near the airstrip. There were times when Christine had been asleep and had been woken up by the warning sirens. She immediately would drop to the floor, crawl under her bed and prayed for her life. In time the mortar attacks became part of her day. They were harassment tactics, and they usually stopped after a few rounds. Someone out there didn't want you around. Someone wanted you gone or dead!

CHAPTER 12

After a major offensive in the mountains that month, Doctor Hoffman pulled Christine aside.

"Could I talk to you for a moment?" Doctor Hoffman asked.

"Yes." Christine looked up at him. She could see the strain on his face.

"We are taking enormous casualties up in the mountains every day, and we keep losing so many of our soldiers. Doctor Shapiro and I thought if we could move our Mobil Surgical Unit closer to the fighting, we could save a lot more of these kids. I talked to Colonel Wheeler to see if we could set up shop at his firebase camp higher up on the mountain. It has a strong perimeter and it is guarded by the Marines. They keep supplies there and helicopters are constantly flying in and out. It should be safe. Doctor Shapiro and I thought you would be a great help to us. Would you come?"

Christine trusted the Doctors completely. "Yes, of course."

"It will be pretty tough living conditions. The food will be bad, we will be in tents, and there is no place to shower regularly."

"I grew up in The Rocky Mountains, David. I should be fine."

"I do not think we will be there too long. Colonel Wheeler said he was going to pull back his men and reassess the situation. But for now, we are just losing too many of our boys. Could you be ready by this afternoon?"

"Yes, I have very little to pack."

"Thank you, Christine. You have been great!" Doctor Hoffman said.

"We are making a list of medical supplies that we will need. Think of what you want to bring, and I will touch base with you in an hour. You don't mind another helicopter ride do you?"

"Oh no, there is nothing like a good vibrating ride in a helicopter to keep all your bones in place!" She smiled at him.

Doctor Hoffman laughed. "Good! I will talk to you in an hour. Thank you, Christine!"

The helicopter ride was just a short 30-minute hop up to the base camp. From the helicopter, Christine could see how steep the mountain was and how inhospitable it seemed. She wondered how anyone could move in such thick undergrowth and how these young soldiers dealt with the jungle, the heat, the insects, the exhaustion, and their own fear.

The Marines had dynamited a plateau off of the top of the lower mountain to make a landing zone for the helicopters. They had cut down all of the trees and had removed all of the undergrowth. All that was left were blackened stumps on a bald, scarred mountain top. Landmines were placed around the camp and were duly noted. There was a way in and a way out. The camp looked small to Christine but very secure. She could see weaponry and medical supplies stacked neatly in rows and ready for use. There were tents pitched and the Doctor's Mobile Surgical Unit was up and running.

They had been at the camp for several days. They were extremely busy after a battle or they had no work at all for as soon as they operated on a wounded soldier, he was air-lifted out of the camp and sent back to Dak Tu or further on to Saigon. The helicopters worked all hours of the day evacuating the wounded on to and off of the base camp.

For the last week large, foreboding thunderclouds had rolled in from the Sea. The heat was stifling, but it did not rain. There was a tension in the air. Everyone just wished it would rain, but the brutal heat continued on. The Marines, fully armed, stood watch over the lonely outpost. They watched over the camp all hours of the day. They stood ready. They were always ready for action!

The Viet Cong had also been watching the camp. They had kept constant surveillance over the camp from higher ground ever since the camp had been built. The Viet Cong had high powered binoculars. They watched every move that was made in the camp from many different angles. The Viet Cong needed the weaponry and the medical supplies, and it was all sitting right there in the broad sunshine like a fresh crop of corn waiting to be harvested.

The Viet Cong knew where the landmines were. They knew how many sentries there were, they knew the timing of the helicopter drops. They had watched the base camp from the beginning. Now it was time to strike. The Viet Cong had rehearsed their attack for seven days. They had four Viet Cong soldiers assigned to each American soldier. Every Viet Cong was assigned a target. Each Viet Cong had a large knapsack and twelve minutes to get in and out. Their strategy was to attack and withdraw; rarely would they hold ground. They used the weather and the terrain to aid their attack and to take the advantage.

It had all happened so fast. The camp was overrun by swarms of Vietnamese men dressed in black. They waited until the last helicopter had left the valley. Then they stormed the camp from all sides. No one had a chance. It was the equivalent of a South Dakota massacre where all the buffalo and the Indians lay dead and rotting in the long prairie grasses. Nothing had survived, breathed or was moving. There were just a lot of bodies rotting in the noon day sun. It was an American slaughter at its finest hour only the roles had been reversed. After the attack came the silence. It was an eerie silence and you could see vultures circling high above. It was now quiet; very, very quiet.

As they came into the Triage unit, the Viet Cong shot both Doctors. Christine screamed as they attacked. "David!" She cried as she fell to her knees to help her fallen friend. "Oh my God, David!" She saw the blood and the bullets in his chest. He must have died instantly. She could feel no pulse. She slowly closed his eyes and dropped her head in anguish. She rushed over to help Doctor Shapiro, but she could see he too was dead. She felt his pulse and closed his eyes. When Christine looked up, she saw a Vietnamese man with bitter, dark eyes aiming a M-16 rifle at her head. Fear flowed through every vein in her body. It was as if her life had just stopped.

Another Viet Cong came into the Triage unit. He was carrying two knapsacks. He dropped them on the floor and quickly began to fill the knapsacks with the needed medical supplies. He seemed to be an expert. He knew exactly what he was looking for. As soon as he was done, he tied Christine's hands behind her back. The Vietnamese men talked for a moment. The man with the rifle picked up the full knapsack and strapped it onto his back. Afterwards, the other Viet Cong strapped on a heavy knapsack as well. The Viet Cong with the bitter eyes motioned to Christine to follow the second Viet Cong and they left the compound with Christine between them.

Finding the way out of the camp without being blown to pieces by a landmine was the hardest part of the attack. Christine could feel that both Viet Cong were very tense. The Viet Cong had attacked just before sunrise so there was now a slight glow on the horizon.

Somehow, they made it. They all made it. All the Viet Cong disappeared as quickly as they had come. They split up into small groups and headed into the jungle with their heavy loads. Christine was *now* with the enemy!

Christine did not know where they were going. She was in shock from what she had seen. Both Doctors were dead. They had been her friends. They had worked together for a year and now they were dead. In an instant, in a moment; life became death. Everything had happened so suddenly. Christine was numb. She couldn't cry. Right now, she was just trying to survive. She was trying not to stumble, she was trying to keep up with the Vietnamese men, and she was trying not to imagine what lay ahead. She did not have a chance to think. She was just responding. She was moving her legs, she was running, she was trying to keep her balance, and she was scared. The men were intent on moving quickly. Any time she slowed down, she could feel the heavy barrel of the metal rifle go deep into her back, and she would experience a violent shove forward.

The men were relentless. There was no stopping them. By early morning, they were well on their way up the mountain. The rains had finally moved in and everything was wet. The Viet Cong took out their ponchos and rain gear. A thick mist descended upon the mountain. This is what they had hoped for. With the cloud bank so close to the ground, the helicopters were unable to fly. Great Mother Earth had protected them once again!

The Viet Cong were tough, fit, and determined. There were few rest breaks that day as they ascended the mountainous terrain. The Viet Cong were happy and victorious, but they would not celebrate. This was just one skirmish, and there would be many more battles until the Americans left their Country.

The Viet Cong and the NFL were fighting for their Homeland. They were a communal culture. It was a village culture, and it was concerned about the community—the whole community. The Vietnamese would pay a high price for their beliefs as would the Americans. After all,

95

Vietnam was the Vietnamese's Country and just like the United States, they wanted self-determination. The USA should have studied Vietnamese history, but they did not. They preferred to send a generation of young men to their deaths and create havoc and destruction to Vietnam and the people they were trying to help. And were the Vietnamese grateful? No, they threw out the Americans and soundly defeated them! So much for the Dominos Theory.

Late in the afternoon, this little band permitted themselves a rest near a fast-moving mountain stream. There was something soothing and eternal about the water splashing down the mountainside. The water immediately raised Christine's spirits. She was out of breath and she needed the rest. Her body ached. She was scared and she was miserable. Branches and thorns had torn her clothes and grazed her skin. Vines had whipped across her face like stinging slaps. The mosquitoes and the flies were around her constantly. Her hair and her clothes were wet from the rain and clung to her body.

As she sat alone on the warm rocks near the river, she could hear the Vietnamese men talk rapidly in low voices. It was the kind of low-tone that made one nervous. She had stumbled several times and had been dragged to her feet. Was she too much of a burden? A terrible foreboding was in her heart. Would they get tired of her presence and shoot her here in the middle of the jungle? She did not know. She could not see their faces or read their emotions. The important thing was to keep moving no matter how tired she was.

The Viet Cong untied her hands. They gave her water and shared their rice cakes with her. They filled their canteens with water from the mountain stream. This was the hottest part of the day. Both captors and captive dangled their feet in the chilly mountain stream and let the water mend their aching feet. In this they were all equals. Rest, eternal rest!

Never had Christine been so exhausted. If she could only stay here. Stay here forever! But the Viet Cong were ready to go. They stood up and pointed a rifle to her head until she had her socks and combat boots on. The Viet Cong picked up their heavy knapsacks, and headed out with Christine in the middle again. But her hands were no longer tied. She had just experienced one small freedom.

Instead of heading North as Christine had thought, they turned and headed West toward the sun. There was still a dense cloud cover as they walked along the mountain ridges. Both Viet Cong were swift and very agile as they hurried on their way.

Christine had not realized how beautiful Vietnam was. They hiked through stately teak forests and went further up into the mountains. Christine looked at the spectacular views where she could see the rugged peaks and the distant emerald valleys of the Annamite Mountains. She felt that if the Viet Cong were going to kill her, they would have done it by now. But she was still afraid. There was a deep foreboding in her heart. Anxiety filled every inch of her body.

It was the twilight hour. The sky was turning the clouds a brilliant color. They hiked past steep cliffs and ledges. One of the Viet Cong made a haunting sound and that sound was returned. They approached a mountain stream and walked alongside it. The stream brought them to a camp that was occupied by many soldiers. This was the *enemy's* camp!

CHAPTER 13

The Viet Cong brought Christine into a cave. The cave was dim. One of the Viet Cong turned on a Coleman lantern. The light gave the cavern an odd, surrealistic look. The cave was about the size of a good-sized bedroom. It had high ceilings and the walls were made of solid gray rock glistening with moisture. It was cool in the cave, but after the long march through the sweltering heat of the jungle, the cave was paradise. On the opposite side of the cave, Christine could see a rolled up sleeping bag and some knapsacks and blankets neatly arranged on the cave floor. There was also another inner cave opening that looked dark and forbidding.

The bitter-eyed Viet Cong motioned to Christine to sit down. Her eyes filled with fear. Her heart started to pound. She was ready for flight. She was not sure what to do. She sat down on the cold cave floor. The bitter-eyed Viet Cong knelt down beside her and tied her hands and feet with rope again. He stood up. Both men looked down at her. They said something to each other, laughed, and left the cave.

Christine was now alone. She felt almost safe. This cold mountainous cave was like a sanctuary to her. There were no more mosquitoes or flies to bother or bite her, she could rest her tired body, and no one was behind her with a rifle constantly threatening to shoot her. She knew full well any misstep today in the jungle and her life would have been over. She was exhausted and emotionally drained. She could feel the cold of the cave floor penetrate her body. Her muscles ached. She bent her head forward and closed her eyes.

Christine thought about her two friends who had been killed. Why kill the Doctors? They had only been there to help the wounded. She thought how difficult the news would be for their families. They were good men. They had spent years studying to become Doctors. Now in an instant, they were died. It was hard for her to believe; and why had she survived? She just let her body rest, but the guilt was there. She was alive; they were dead. The guilt would always be there.

Yuri came bounding into the cave. He was a very masculine man with dancing blue eyes. He was handsome and he had a presence that was arresting. Christine looked up at him and he looked down at her. Both were equally startled.

Yuri gave out a loud Russian expletive and scrambled out of the cave.

The Vietnamese fighters had gathered around to watch the show. They were laughing wildly as he came out.

"She's yours!" Someone shouted to him in French.

There was more laughter. Everyone was having a good time. Yuri laughed too. He needed to laugh. They all did. He talked with one of his companions and went back into the cave smiling. But he knew she was going to be a problem; a big problem. Yuri knelt down and untied Christine's feet. Then he gently untied her hands. Christine watched him in the soft light. He had a strong forehead and commanding eyes. He turned both her hands over. He could see where the rope had rubbed against her skin and had left open sores.

Yuri got up again and left the cave. When he returned, he brought a sleeping bag, some bananas, and a stem of an aloe plant. He placed the sleeping bag and the bananas beside her. He looked down at her Military black boots, her sweat filled Army fatigues, and her matted blonde hair. She was a sorry sight. But she was pretty; very pretty.

"What is your name?" He asked in perfect English.

Christine looked at him but she did not reply. Their eyes met.

Yuri was a trim and fit Russian with high cheekbones and a radiating smile. He opened the aloe stem with his knife and rubbed the salve into her wounds.

"What Division are you from?" He asked in his low, velvet voice.

Christine said nothing.

"You are in a very bad spot. Do you realize that?"

Christine stopped looking at him and dropped her eyes.

"Well, maybe we can barter you off for a cow and some rice or maybe the Americans will swap you for an armored tank. Ha! There is wishful thinking!"

Christine looked at him in a hateful manner.

"Usually when I sleep with a woman, I like to know her name." Yuri said.

Christine's muscles tightened. She said nothing.

"My name is Yuri. It used to be Count Yuri, but now they just call me plain old Yuri. Welcome to my private chambers, my sleeping quarters, my suite/sweet." He said smiling expansively.

Christine did not say a word.

Yuri could see he was not making progress. "What do we know?" He said standing up. "We know you are an American, we know you are a woman, and we know you do not have a sense of humor."

He stood before her an all powerful man—strong, healthy, and intensely masculine.

"You have been given to me. You will stay here. But your life will be far easier for you if you cooperate." He looked into her eyes and she looked fiercely back into his. He did not like the hostility in her eyes. It was unpleasant.

"You will have the freedom of the camp, but if you abuse that freedom upon my word, you will be shot. Is that clear?"

She said nothing.

Yuri's straight nose gave vent to brooding, powerful lips. You could only mistrust the lips. They were sensual yet very firm. They spoke of hardness. They spoke of tenderness. They gave way to all of the inner workings of the man. They were part of his laughter, his dark humor, and his wide grins. If you were a woman, he held a power over you. If you were a man, you would stand ready or you were a fool.

"Let us understand each other completely." Yuri continued. "You will do my bidding and you will obey me. If you cooperate, your life will be far more pleasant."

Christine quickly got to her feet and raised her head high. Her body stiffened.

Yuri could see the fear in her eyes.

"You need not worry. I will not touch you." He said sarcastically. "I sleep here." He pointed to his bedroll on the opposite side of the cave. "You sleep there." He said pointing to the sleeping bag he had brought for her.

There was a tension in his voice.

"And do not expect any favors from me because I never grant favors! Now get into your sleeping bag and go to sleep." Yuri said and he left the cave.

For Yuri the day had been long, and she was being very difficult. He was not so sure he wanted to be around this defiant American woman. Whatever happened to sweetness and grace? Maybe he could send her to Hanoi; but she would be locked up. Perhaps they would send her to Moscow, but there again, she would be imprisoned. She was a huge security breach and that made her future not too bright.

Christine watched Yuri leave the cave. The light from the lantern danced on the cave walls. It was true that she had invaded his space. He seemed like a decent man. He appeared to be amicable and non-threatening. Must she be so hard on him? But then again, he was on the side that had killed David and Noah and all the American soldiers. How could she accept that? How could she forgive the loss of her friends?

Could she trust him? He was the enemy! But he seemed sincere. Was he capable of murder? Would he hurt her? Was she safe? She did not know. But somehow, they needed to co-exist. This was a very small space. If they could not get along here, where else could she go? Back into the jungle? That did not sound too appealing or would they just consider her too much of a bother? She did not like that idea either. She knew that if they were going to kill her, they would have done it by now. Only the anxiety of not knowing her fate continued to plague her.

Christine was exhausted. She took off her heavy black Army boots and unrolled her sleeping bag. It looked American made. She ate one of the bananas and climbed into the sleeping bag fully clothed. After her long day, it was nice to be in this warm, protective enclosure. It was as if the sleeping bag was there to protect and hold her. Maybe it had mystical powers to keep her safe. She hoped so. She thought about her family and friends. Her parents must know by now that she was missing. It must be very hard on them. She seemed to be an imposition on everyone. She wished Yuri had not gone away so irritated. She closed her eyes. There was still a dim light coming from the Coleman lantern. Please let sleep take me away from here. She thought to herself. Please let sleep take me far away.

Later Yuri came back into the cave. He looked at Christine. She was asleep. She looked peaceful. He took off his boots and shirt, unrolled his sleeping bag and went to sleep. He was tired also and he went to sleep with ease.

Both Yuri and Christine slept late. For Yuri it had been an intense week of planning, logistics, and reconnaissance. For Christine, it had been a traumatizing two days. For the dead American soldiers, they were now resting also.

Christine woke up first. The cave must have faced Easterly as the sunshine poured through the cave opening. Christine lay in her sleeping bag and watched Yuri sleeping. His eyes opened and he looked at her watching him. He did not want to think about her today. She was very feisty and willful, and he did not want to deal with another problem. He rolled over on his side and went back to sleep.

Christine felt empty and hollow. She was alone in a world she did not understand. How long would she be here? Would she ever see her family again? It was hard not knowing. But right now, she was feeling the call of nature and she needed to use the latrine. She had no other choice but to wake Yuri. She put on her boots and went over to him. She lightly put her hand on his shoulder.

"I need to use the latriine." She whispered into his ear.

Yuri awoke with a start and instantly reached for his gun. Then he relaxed back down onto his sleeping bag with a thud. Woman! Yuri thought to himself. But he dutifully got out of his warm sleeping bag. Still half asleep, he put on his socks and boots, tucked in his shirt, and tried to straighten his hair. They emerged together from the cave. Yuri took Christine's hand. His hand felt warm. The whole camp was alive. They passed people who were smiling and nodding, and a couple of Viet Cong gave Yuri the American thumbs up. Yuri smiled too.

He led Christine down a well-used path to the latrines. There was a men's and a women's latrine. Yuri showed Christine the women's latrine and he pointed out the Vietnamese symbol for women.

"Do not even think of escaping." He warned her. "There are tigers and large snakes that can kill you instantly."

Christine went into the latrine. She was impressed by the sanitation and the cleanliness of the latrine. As a nurse, she respected that greatly. She knew the havoc that bad germs could create. She was happy to be here. She had been very uncomfortable. Now she had the opportunity to wash and feel clean again. She looked at herself in the small mirror that hung in the latrine. Her hair was matted and snarled. There was mud on her cheeks. She was not a pretty sight. No wonder he did not want to look at her. How wonderful it was to feel the water on her face and to wash her hands! It was almost as if it was some sort of luxurious gift!

Yuri used the latrine also. He washed and looked into the small mirror in the men's latrine. His hand went up to his cheek. When he grew a beard, he had the ability to scare even a wooly Mammoth. Clearly, he needed to shave. He looked severe and unkempt with the stubble on his face. His cheeks felt very rough. Yuri liked shaving. It made him feel civilized and more appealing to women. But he had forgotten his shaver back at the cave. Christine had certainly destroyed his morning rituals.

When Christine was done, Yuri took her hand and they walked slowly back to the cave. When she tugged on his hand to be free, he held her hand tighter. As soon as they were in the cave, Yuri instantly dropped her hand. He went over to his knapsack, and pulled out his battery run shaver and began to shave. When he was done, he straightened out his bedding and made his little part of the cave more orderly.

"I am going to get some breakfast for us. I want you to behave yourself." He looked at her doubtfully. He was not sure how much he could trust her. Yesterday she had been very unruly and defiant. He never liked those traits in women.

Yuri was gone a long time. Christine sat on her sleeping bag and tried to untangle her long blonde hair. Life was going to be very difficult without a comb. Christine thought. It is amazing how it is the little things that one misses. Yuri came back with some rice cakes, bananas, and some mountain grapes that grew everywhere. He shared them with Christine and sat down on the cave floor beside her. They began to eat.

"So now we know you can talk! Ah latrines, the great leveler! What is your name?"

"Christine." She said softly.

"You mean Christine Blakely from Great Fish, Montana. Where the Hell is Great Fish, Montana?" Yuri wanted to know.

"How do you know that?" Christine asked in amazement.

"I know everything about you. Saigon is like a giant sieve. There are spies everywhere. Do you really think there are any secrets in the US Military? You grew up on Harvest Lane. I love that! Harvest Lane." He repeated. "It sounds so bountiful! Like wheat fields of plenty bending in the wind! I know your rank. I know where you completed your nurse's training, and I know your Father owns a hardware store in Great Fish, Montana. I know everything." Yuri said.

"Then can I go home now?" Christine asked softly. "I have nothing to do with the killing of people."

Yuri was not ready for that. He looked down at the cave floor.

"No, you are not able to go home right now. I am sorry. I will try to keep you entertained, healthy, well fed, and sheltered. But I am not able to get you back to the other side. Not now."

All of Christine's hopes vanished. She could feel reality knocking at her door, but she did not want to hear what he was saying.

"You look so much better when you are not glaring at me. I am not the enemy." He said.

"You are keeping me here against my will!"

Yuri shrugged. That was true he had to admit.

"You killed two of the best Doctors I have ever worked with and all the soldiers in the camp." Christine said angrily.

"You forget that we are at War and that they are trying to kill us!"

"David and Noah were only there to save the wounded." She said bitterly.

"Yes, I agree, it was unfortunate that their lives had to be taken, but no one could predict how they would react and time was of the essence. No one wanted to fight these Doctors if they chose to fight."

"They were good men!"

"You are the Occupiers!" he accused her. "The Vietnamese are fighting for their Country. They want you foreigners out! If you were in their place, you would do the same thing." Yuri said with distain. As a Russian, he knew the fear of invasion far too well. His Father had given his life fighting the Nazi invasion of the Soviet Union in the Second World War. In the end, the Germans were defeated and all that was gained was mayhem and destruction and many dead on both sides.

"You and I are going to be here for a while. Can we not respect each other and live in peace?" Yuri asked.

"I saw all of my Countrymen and friends killed yesterday. We are on different sides. How can we respect each other?"

"We will find a way." Yuri said.

"I do not think so."

Yuri did not like conflict. "I am going back to bed. Please do not stab me as I sleep."

"I have nothing to stab you with."

"Ah! Then you have been contemplating it! You American women are so opportunistic!" Yuri said as he climbed back into his sleeping bag and went to sleep. Christine could not sleep. She got back into her sleeping bag and replayed the events of the last couple of days in her mind. The Americans would find the massacre. They would know she was there, but they would not find her body. Would they come looking for her? Would she ever see her home again? It was a frightening thought. Right now, her sleeping bag was her only friend. It kept her warm and safe. It protected her. When Christine first joined the Army, she never thought she would be in any danger. Now she was in a lot of danger!

Later Yuri woke up refreshed. He rolled up his sleeping bag.

"Do you swim?" He asked Christine.

Christine nodded.

"I will show you where there is a pool where you can wash if you like. It is large enough to swim in."

"Thank you." She said softly.

They left the cave. Again, Yuri took Christine's hand and they walked through the camp down to a swift moving stream. There was a deep eddy in the stream that had created a rounded pool over the centuries. The rock was smooth, and it had a beautiful chiseled curve to it. Low lying boulders surrounded the deep basin. Yuri started to undress.

"What are you doing!" Christine asked in alarm.

"I am going swimming." Yuri said.

"You are not going in naked, are you?"

"No, but I am not going swimming fully clothed. You have seen men in shorts, have you not? You are a nurse. I am sure you have seen a lot more than this." Yuri stripped down to his boxer shorts and jumped into the water. His body had taken a great deal of abuse over the last couple of days and the water felt rejuvenating! Yuri surfaced grinning.

Christine sat on the smooth rocks and dangled her feet in the cold mountain stream. The water soothed her aching feet. It was nice not to have on her heavy black Army boots. There was a dragonfly sunning itself on the rocks. Life once again seemed almost pleasant in the late morning sunshine.

Yuri was splashing about and moving closer.

"Why do you not come in? The water is great!" He inched his way closer to Christine like a stealth hunter.

"I do not want to take my clothes off, and I do not have anything else to wear."

Yuri moved closer to her. "Oh, that is too bad!" He said. Very slowly he was coming up next to her. In an instant, his arm went around her waist and he pulled her into the clear, fast-moving water. Her body went deep down into the depths of the mountain pool. She could feel her long hair streaming behind her. All the heat, sweat, long march, filth, dirt and fear flowed away from her. She rose quickly and gasped for air. She was smiling.

"It's fantastic!" She cried out. The sunlight glistened off of her hair. She felt that sensuous feeling of having water flowing all over her body. She felt clean and pure. The cold, tingling water made her feel whole again. She splashed water at Yuri.

"You are so devious!"

Yuri swam away from her. He smiled. His white teeth flashed.

"You said you can swim, and you swim very well." He smiled again. They swam and floated and let the cool water release the tension from their tired muscles. Yuri got out and extended his hand to help Christine onto the warm rocks. He had a very beautiful body and Christine tried not to look at him.

"Lie down on the rocks and the sun will bake you dry." Yuri said and he stood up.

Christine always loved hearing her heart pound and the feeling of the sun ravishing her body. It was like a lover; and when the sun went behind a cloud, she would call out to it and plead with it to come back. She was like a well-exercised animal, content and rested. It seemed both Yuri and Christine were 19 again. They were at the quarries and a long, long way from here. Each of them was in their own world. It was a good reprieve. One in which they both needed. What had happened at the base camp was not easy for either of them.

Yuri dressed and they went back to the cave. Christine's fatigues were still damp. Yuri found a nightshirt in his knapsack and he give it to her. She accepted it gracefully. Yuri turned away and spent a great deal of time trying to find something in his knapsack.

"Don't look." Christine said as she quickly took off her wet fatigues and put on the nightshirt. It came down to her knees and sagged at the shoulders, but she was elated to have a change of clothes! Yuri gave up on his knapsack and turned around.

"You look very good. I will take your clothes outside to dry and get us some lunch. If the cave is too cold, there is a sweater somewhere in my knapsack."

"Thank you." Christine said gratefully.

It had been a good day, much better than the previous days. They began a ritual of eating, sleeping, and swimming. There was a distance between them, but they were respectful of each other. Christine liked Yuri. He teased her, but he had been good to her. He provided her with food, he took care of her, and he made the days less lonely. Little by little she began to trust him. In two weeks time Yuri began to pack his knapsack.

"You are leaving?" Christine asked.

"Will you miss me?" Yuri replied facetiously.

"I feel better when you are here."

"I will be gone for several days. Will you behave yourself while I am gone?"

"Yes."

"Do not try to explore this cave. It is very dangerous. There are steep cliffs and rock ledges and you could easily be hurt if not killed. There is no exit there. The cave has been thoroughly searched so do not even attempt it. You can use the latrines, and you can go down to the stream, but I suggest you keep yourself out of sight. The Vietnamese can be just as trigger happy as you Americans. And remember, just because I have cut off your ropes, does not mean that you are free. Behave yourself!" Those were his last words.

Yuri picked up his knapsack. He nodded to her and left.

CHAPTER 14

With Yuri gone, the days were very long for Christine. The
monsoons had moved in and it rained continually. A thick cloud settled
over the land. Christine would sit near the cave entrance with a blanket
around her and watch the rain fall. It came down in steady sheets.
Outside, it was hot and humid. Inside the cave, it was cold and damp.
In the beginning, the rain seemed wonderful. It was cleansing and
gentle; but as it continued every day, it became tiresome and gloomy.
Each time she went to the latrine, she came back totally soaked. Each
time she went to breakfast or dinner in the Great Cooking Hall, she
would end up with wet hair, wet clothes, and wet feet. During the day
a soaking was not so bad, but in the early morning or the late evening,
once you got wet, the cold mountain air penetrated deeply into your
bones, and it would be a long time before you ever got warm again.

Late one evening, Christine was wrapped in a blanket watching
an explosive thunderstorm from the cave entrance. The sky was filled
with amazing lightning displays. Far off in the distance, Christine could
hear the thunder crashing amongst the trees as if the earth was breaking
in two. There was a huge explosive sound. In an instant Yuri came
leaping into the cave. He threw off his wet American made poncho and
dripping American made rain gear and thrust them against the cavern
walls.

"Those are bombs." He shouted as he scooped Christine up
and whisked her to the back of the cave.

"Get down." He commanded. They fell to the floor and Yuri
covered her with his body. His body felt warm and protective. Christine

could feel his strong muscles touch every part of her body. She was scared. Her heart was pounding. She closed her eyes tightly and pressed her body to his. Yuri moved on to his side after the thunder had stopped and watched her.

Christine opened her eyes and saw him smiling at her. There was a moment of silence.

"Those were not bombs, were they?" She said.

"No, thunder." Yuri said grinning broadly.

"You are so bad!" Christine said as she scrambled to her feet. She tugged at her fatigues and straightened them.

"You scared me half to death."

Yuri roared with laughter. "An American scared of her own bombs! Oh, that is good! Now you know how the Vietnamese feel when you continually bomb their homes, factories, and their Country!"

"You are so bad!" Christine said again and she went over to her side of the cave.

"Now, now there I was coming up the trail weary and dead tired. Lightning shattered the sky, and there you were cuddled up in the cave entrance like a little dog waiting for its Master."

"I am not a little dog and you are not my Master!" Christine said curtly.

"As always, my playful little bitch." Yuri said mockingly.

Christine gasped. She could not believe the insult! She picked up a tin cup that was next to her sleeping bag and threw it at Yuri. The cup landed far off of its mark. It bounced off the cave wall making a ringing sound that echoed around the cavern walls and clambered to the cave floor. Yuri went over and retrieved the cup. He brought it over to Christine and presented it to her.

"Your aim is about par for an American." He said with merriment in his eyes. He turned and went over to his side of the cave. He spread out his American made poncho so it would dry.

"You'll excuse me while I get out of these wet clothes." Yuri undressed in front of Christine down to his waist. She could see his strong chest.

"Ah! No peeking. Because if you can peek at me then I can peek at you."

"You are intolerable!" She said.

"But you were peeking."

"I was not peeking." But she knew that she had been. Yuri had a beautiful, masculine body and it was hard not to look.

"All is fair in love and War, and if you can peek at me, then I can peek at you; and I can assure you, my dear, it would not be a little peek."

Yuri smiled to himself. He had always had his way with women. He had always enjoyed being the dominant one. Half-naked, he climbed into his sleeping bag.

"Good night, my sweet. I am glad you survived."

"Good night." Christine said curtly. She could hear the rain falling heavily outside of the cave, and the thunder continued to crack and shake the earth apart. Nature was turning violent. Christine wished Yuri was still close. Even though he teased her relentlessly, she was still glad for his presence.

CHAPTER 15

Both Yuri and Christine were up early.

"Good morning." Yuri said.

"Good morning." Christine replied coolly.

"Would you like to go down to the stream and swim?" Yuri asked.

"No, I think I will stay here."

"Are you still angry with me for last night?"

"No, but you did scare me!"

"Yuri is bad." He said.

She smiled at him.

"Yuri is very bad." He said again. He brought Christine some breakfast and left for the day. Christine had the cave all to herself. She sat against the cave wall and thought about her life. The day was long. Yuri did not come back. Christine was sorry she had rebuffed his invitation to go swimming. The cave was making her feel enclosed and isolated. She looked at the inner cave opening and wondered what the next cave chamber was like. It frightened her. She always imagined some terrible monster with giant legs coming out of the forbidding cave opening surrounded by mist and darkness. There was a tremendous draft that came from the inner cave opening, and it swept past her and out into the jungle night like a raging beast. The inner cave was a mystery. Christine wondered what it would be like to explore it.

The sun went down and Yuri came bounding into the cave with dinner. They ate quietly.

"There is a full moon tonight. I want to show you the most beautiful Indochina moon you have ever seen!" Yuri said enthusiastically.

"OK." She replied half-heartedly.

They went through the cave entrance and Yuri took Christine's hand. They walked down the trail to the flowing mountain stream.

"Why do you always hold my hand when we are outside of the cave?" Christine asked.

"Because I do not want to hunt you down in the jungle if you try to escape." Yuri said. But he knew it was more than that. He liked being near Christine. He liked the warmth of her hand and the comfort it gave him.

"Do you consider me a prisoner?"

"Yes, I consider you a member of the Red Cross and I will respect that. But you are still in my care."

That was delicately put. Christine thought. She wondered about her fate. She depended upon Yuri a great deal.

They sat down on their favorite swimming rocks. Each looked up at the night time sky. The moon was golden and it was huge. It looked so big that at any moment it might fall from the sky.

"I doubt they have moons like that in Great Fish, Montana!"

"It is amazing. I think I could almost reach out and touch it!" Christine said as she looked up at the full moon and wondered how it ever stayed in place. The moonlight showered down upon them.

"Why does America fight this War?" Yuri asked.

The night sky was all around them, and the harvest moon was magnificent and overwhelmingly beautiful.

"We are here fighting to win freedom for the Vietnamese people."

"Yes, the United States talks about freedom. That is so laughable! Look at Kent State University where students protested this War. They were asking your Government to listen to them. 'We do not want this War'! They said. And what happened to the students? Your

115

Government shot them dead. The students were evoking their right to free speech, and the Government killed them. Democracy? What a farce! And the War is still going on. Now the Corporations have been given the right to free speech. Next, Corporations will be given the right to vote. It is just a ragged, vicious abuse of power. Are you not concerned that so many people in your Country oppose this brutal War and yet it continues?"

"Yuri, I did not come here out of patriotism or to help our troops. I came to escape a painful relationship. That is all. I just want a home and a family and a loving husband like my Father who gave us a good life and who loved my Mother. I want a secure life, and I want people around me who I love. I am not here to save the world."

"But that is exactly what the Vietnamese want. They just want to enjoy their lives and take care of their families and harvest their crops and practice their beliefs. They do not want your helicopters flying over their homes and fields day and night. They do not want your soldiers entering their villages and breaking into their houses. They just want to live in peace. The Vietnamese are Buddhists. They want to live in harmony with the land. Why does not your Country understand that? Why can you not respect that?

The Vietnamese have their own values and way of life. They do not want to imitate the United States. They just want to be Vietnamese. Would you want a foreign Army on the Great Plains of Montana surrounding your towns and flying helicopters over your homes with their ever-present machine guns ready to shoot at anything that moves? Would you like B-52 Bombers coming toward your family's ranch, and wiping out your Mother's prize horses and maybe your house with your family in it? I just marvel at you Americans! What if it was your

116

town, what if it was your family? Why don't you Americans care about anything except yourselves and your damn ideology?

Do Americans have any compassion at all? And the amount of money that you have poured into mass destruction is truly amazing! The money is all borrowed money! How are you ever going to pay it back! How are you going to pay for all the death and destruction that you have caused? It is a tragedy! It is an incredible tragedy!"

There was a silence.

"Anytime you want to accomplish defeat, just try invading and occupying another Country, and all of a sudden you have every malcontent in that Country standing up and fighting for what is his. That is what the United States does not understand. Every time the US invades another Country, it just creates more hatred; and someday your warlike behavior will drive your Country into poverty, and make it the most hated Country on earth! It has happened again and again in history, yet the United States goes down the same corrupted path. And once you take that path, you create whole new institutions that do nothing but promote the War purely for economic reasons until your Country has spent its last dollar on defense and it crumbles from within. That is the direction the United States is going in."

Christine said nothing.

"You do not care about this, do you?" Yuri asked her.

"No, it has nothing to do with me."

"You are not going to win this War." Yuri said. "Once you Americans leave, everything will revert back to its mean."

"Of course, we are going to win!" Christine said. "Look at our vast Military power. We can easily overtake this small Country. They are nothing against all of our machinery and technology. How could they ever hope to win this War?"

"What you have is nothing. Just a lot of cold metal and empty circuit boards." Yuri said.

There was a silence. Yuri got up and took Christine's hand. They slowly walked back to the cave in the soft moonlight. Each went to their respective part of the cave. Neither spoke. There was an immense space between them; a divide.

CHAPTER 16

The next day when Christine entered the cave, she saw Yuri on the cave floor cleaning his gun. He always carried a Colt 45 pistol on his hip, and now it lay in pieces on a cloth on the cave floor. Yuri was oiling the gun, and the tart smell of the oil reminded her of her Father's motorboat.

"If you are a man of peace, why do you always wear that gun and holster on your hip?" Christine asked.

"Because I am not above defending myself against American soldiers, jungle tigers, or the charms of beautiful American women." Yuri said as he continued to oil his gun. "I hate to tell you this, I know you will be sad, but I will be leaving tomorrow for two weeks." He continued.

"Two weeks! Why so long?" Christine asked in alarm.

"Are those tears in your eyes? How sweet."

"Can't you ever be serious?" Christine asked.

"Have I not been serious with you?"

Christine did not know what to say. She had missed him and now he seemed only to taunt her.

"What will I do when you are gone?"

"Maybe you can practice your shot." He suggested.

"Oh, very funny."

Yuri thought it was. His grin was a mile wide.

In two weeks time, the sun was out and Yuri was back. He returned from a forced march with two weeks of harassment and constant movement. How nice to feel safe once again. To know that he could sleep in peace and wake up completely rested and whole. But right now, he was hot and grimy and not too happy. The stress of the last two weeks was immense. Playing cat and mouse with the enemy had not been fun. Every inch of his body was sore and he needed to relax. He came into the cave.

Christine looked up. Yuri was back! It was so good to have him back! It was a feeling that followed her around like a shadow. She knew she needed to be careful. She needed to stop relying on him. When he was gone, she needed to stop missing him. After all, he was the enemy, wasn't he?

Yuri dropped his gear. "Come with me."

"Where are we going?" Christine asked.

"You are going to wash my back."

"Oh no I am not." She said as she continued to follow him.

"Oh yes, you are." He said and he had a tight grip of her hand.

It was twilight. It was still warm out and the earth was soft and glowing. Yuri was tired and his temper was short. Christine looked at him defiantly as he stripped down to his waist and walked into the water.

"I want my back washed and I want it washed now!" Yuri said and he reached out his hand and pulled her into the water. "I have been tramping through the jungle for days, and I am not about to take any more American flak!"

He held her tightly with one hand and reached out for the soap with his other hand. Yuri was very strong. He gave her the soap. Christine took it ungraciously. Yuri turned from her. She was left looking at his strong, muscular back. Yuri had broad shoulders that tapered down to his waist. Christine lathered the soap and spread it across his back. It had been a long time since she had touched a man in this way. She could feel his muscles and the curve of his body as her hand went down the small of his back.

"You do that very well. Now the front." Yuri commanded.

Christine hesitated. Then she went ahead. She put her hand on his breast and moved it across his chest bringing the lathered soap down to his waist then back up again and then down. Suddenly she turned her back to him.

"Are men that repulsive to you or is it just me?" Yuri said rinsing himself off.

Do men not think that women have sexual desires of their own? Christine had not forgotten the passion she had known so long ago.

Yuri got out of the water and walked up the path alone. Sex was the last thing on his mind. He was exhausted and mentally drained. Christine was still in the water with her head in her hands.

The twilight was slowly fading. Christine got out of the water and walked up the path by herself. She entered the cave.

"So you have come back." Yuri said as he lay on his sleeping bag with his back against the cave wall.

"Yes, I have come back."

"Christine, why do we always have our missiles trained on each other?"

"I do not know."

"Let us try to get along."

"I would like that."

"I am sorry about today. I am very tired and I am badly in need of rest. I want you to know that I am truly sorry for my behavior."

"Thank you." She said.

"Let us eat and then I must go to sleep."

121

In the middle of the night, Christine heard Yuri talk erratically. She was not sure what was happening. She felt her way over to the Coleman lantern and lit it. The light danced on the cave walls. Yuri was turning from side to side saying something she could not understand. She knelt down beside him and softly touched his arm.

"Yuri." She whispered. "Yuri."

Yuri woke up with a start and reached for his weapon.

"Yuri!" Christine cried out.

He saw Christine and settled back down on his sleeping bag.

"What is it?" He asked.

"You had a bad dream. You were talking in your sleep."

"What did I say?"

"I don't know. It was all in Russian."

He closed his eyes.

"Are you all right?" Christine asked.

"I am fine. Go back to bed."

"Are you sure?"

"Yes." He said.

She put out the Coleman lantern and went back to bed.

"Good night."

"Good night." Yuri said in his deep masculine voice.

The next day it was raining and they were forced to stay inside. Yuri used the day to write memorandums and dispatches and to rest. Christine sat by the cave entrance and watched the rain. She was becoming restless. She came over to Yuri.

"Are you writing about me?"

"Oh yes, it is all about you. It says how well you wash tired backs, how pretty you are, and how sweet you look when you are asleep."

"Does it say what a good prisoner I have been, and how much I want to go home?"

He looked at her for a moment. "No, it does not say that." He said in a very serious tone.

They looked at each other. The reality struck both of them.

"What will happen to me?" Christine asked.

"I do not know."

"Yuri, I want to go home so badly!"

"Do not worry Christine, we will get you back; but as long as you are here, you will be safe."

That evening they ate in the cave. Yuri ate very slowly and watched her carefully.

"Why do you look at me so?" Christine asked.

Yuri smiled. "I was just thinking how nice you would look in a dress and a pair of beautiful shoes."

"You are not impressed with my Army fatigues and boots?"

"No." Yuri answered curtly.

There was a silence. "I will be leaving tomorrow." He said.

"Leaving!"

"Does that upset you?"

"I feel better when you are here. I do not like being in this cave alone."

"It is only for a couple of days."

"But the weather is so bad."

"This is the best weather for Vietnamese operations, and I have my American made poncho. God bless America!"

"Where do you go when you are away?"

"We visit other base camps, and sometimes we survey American Military outposts. The Vietnamese are trying to draw the American

Military up into the mountains where the fight will be more even and away from the civilian populations."

"Are you involved in the fighting?"

"No, we try to avoid contact with the enemy at all costs."

"Who will win this War?"

"We will. There is no doubt in my mind."

CHAPTER 17

Yuri had packed and was gone again. Christine tried to stay in the cave as much as possible. She lay on her sleeping bag feeling sad and alone. There was a lump in her throat. She wanted to cry but instead her whole body was full of sorrow. Sorrow for her fallen friends, sorrow for her captivity, sorrow for what would become of her.

She only felt despair. The kind of despair that comes when there is no future, and everything you thought about and dreamed about was gone. She was fragile and broken and she felt desperately alone. How did she ever land in this cold mountainous cave with this smiling Russian who loved to tease and taunt her, and who was always gone? She wanted so much to go home. She missed her parents. She missed her friends. She missed her work. She wanted only to be home! Why can't they just let her go? Then the sobs started and they did not stop.

In the morning Christine had formed a plan. She would save her rice cakes, and tomorrow morning she would take her poncho and rain hat that Yuri had given her, and she would go down to the stream as if she were exploring the flowing water as it headed down to the Sea. Surely if she walked far enough, she would find a village where she could seek help. It sounded like a good plan. All streams ended up at the Sea, didn't they?

She went to bed early excited about her escape. In the morning she wrapped up her rice cakes, folded the poncho Yuri had given her to protect her from the mountain rains. It looked American made. Little did she know that America was funding both sides of the War. The

Vietnamese loved the American flak vests, ponchos, mosquito netting, watches, and weaponry. They were all the booty of War. Either they were stolen from the American warehouses, bought on the Black Market, or taken from the dead.

In the morning Christine went straight to the mountain pool where the water ran swiftly down the mountainside. She continued her routine washing. In the distance she saw a butterfly darting amongst the rocks. This was her chance! She decided to follow it. She swallowed hard. Soon she had left the butterfly far behind. She knew she must watch her step. Sometimes the rocks could be slippery. She could not afford to fall or break a bone. She carefully picked her way amongst the tumbled rocks and headed downstream. She could hear a chorus of bullfrogs. Were they laughing at her or cheering her on?

Christine did not see anyone. She kept to the edge of the rainforest so that if she saw any human movement, she could quickly move into the jungle for cover. It had been several hours. Her heart had been pounding. The adrenalin was flowing throughout her body, but she was resolute. She was not going back!

Christine was hopping from rock to rock. She was free! She was going to make it! The water sparkled in the morning sunlight. There was no one in sight. She thought she had evaded everyone. She had heard animal calls in the jungle that frightened her, and one time she saw a large snake sunning itself on the warm rocks, but other that this, her escape seemed effortless. It seemed so easy! She was making good progress. She prayed by nightfall that she would find a village or a human settlement. She kept her head down and carefully worked her way around the large boulders that bordered the fast-moving stream. Out of the silence, she heard a voice. She looked up.

CHAPTER 18

"Where are you going, Christine?" He called out.

Christine could see a figure ahead of her. It was Yuri! Christine stopped. She was frozen to a rock. He had come out of nowhere.

"I am going home!" She cried out. She could feel her throat becoming tight and her emotions rising to the surface. She could hear the rushing water gargling and splashing against the rocks. She wanted to rush along with it. She did not want to be here anymore!

"You cannot go home, Christine." Yuri said. He was moving closer to her. He did not want her to flee so he kept talking to her, and very slowly he inched his way toward her.

"Please Yuri, I want to go home!" Christine pleaded with him.

"I cannot let you go. I am sorry." Yuri replied.

"Please Yuri, I beg of you. Please let me go!" Tears began to fill her eyes and they flowed down her cheeks.

"Christine, if I could let you go, I would; but I cannot." He was so close to her now that he was in reach of her.

"You mean I have to go back?"

"Yes." He said as he reached out for her arm.

"But I am so homesick here." She sobbed. The tears came fast and hard. She dropped to her knees and took his hand and placed it on her cheek imploring him. "Please Yuri, Please! Please let me go home!" She began crying fitfully.

Yuri sat down on the boulder beside her. He placed his hand on her shoulder and let her cry. Sometimes it is important to cry. It is best to flush out all of the ache inside.

"You are not happy here?" Yuri asked her when she had quieted herself and the weeping had subsided.

"I need to go home."

"Am I making you unhappy?" He asked.

"No."

"Then why do you want to leave?"

"You know why, Yuri. I do not belong here. I belong with my own people; on my own side."

Yuri softly placed his hand under her chin and looked into her red, swollen eyes. "I cannot let you go right now." He said as sternly as he could for that was the truth.

As much as she did not want to believe it, it was reality. Christine had free access to the camp, but she was not free. This became very clear to her. She was a prisoner, held here against her will, and there was nothing she could do about it.

"Come now, Christine. We have a long journey back to the camp." He said as he helped her to her feet. "You did a good job finding your way amongst the rocks. Let us see how well you do going back." He said as he urged her forward.

Christine could have resisted him. She could have fled into the jungle. But what good would that do? It would only make matters worse. She slowly got up and they started back up the stream. Yuri let her lead the way. When she stumbled or slipped, he was there to catch her or brace her fall. They walked a long way upon the rocks of the stream bed. The sun was going down. It was twilight. The earth was quiet. The sky was immense, and it was filled with flaming pink and scarlet colors. It was another breath-taking Vietnamese sunset.

"We can rest here." Yuri said. He had chosen a large, smooth boulder that faced West. The rock was still warm from the heat of the day. The jungle was now quiet. The land was very peaceful and serene in the soft evening light. They sat down on the rock and looked at the magnificent sky.

The sitting felt good. They had been walking a long while. They were both tired.

"God has given mankind such a beautiful world. I often marvel why mankind doe not appreciate this world and all of its gifts." Yuri said.

"Do you believe in God?"

"No, not really. I believe in a Maker of heaven and earth, but I do not believe in a personal God. My Grandmother does. She is Russian Orthodox. She is very devout."

"Why are you here?" Christine asked.

"I am here only because my Government has sent me here. I do not believe in War."

"Why did the Viet Cong kill everyone at the base camp, but spared me?" Christine wondered.

Yuri thought for a minute. "The Vietnamese are very thoughtful people and they did not want me to be alone."

"You mean I was a gift?"

Yuri was quiet for a moment.

"Yes, you were a gift." He said softly.

"I think not." Christine said coolly.

Both were silent again. It was nice just to sit here and enjoy the evening sky.

Yuri and Christine sat side by side. Both were at peace. Christine brought out her rice cakes and shared them with Yuri. They ate slowly and watched the flaming sky.

"I hate to get back to reality, but I need to tell you that you are always being watched. There are five Viet Cong watching your every step, and they are excellent scouts. One of them was sent to get me, but if he had not found me, you could have been in great peril. I am trying to be a compassionate and caring prison guard, but you are not making this easy. I have given you free reign of the camp, but if you try to escape again, there will be serious consequences. Do you understand what I am saying?"

"Yes."

"And when you go down to the pool and strip naked to wash, you are not alone. You are being watched. I am trying to protect you and keep you safe, but you are making it very difficult."

"I am sorry, Yuri." She said sincerely. Why had she been so stupid to think she was totally free? Why had she been so naive to think she was not being watched? She thought to herself.

"Do we understand each other?"

"Yes."

"It is time to go." Yuri helped Christine up, and they went back to the camp and into their cave.

CHAPTER 19

"I am going to go and get us some dinner. Promise me you will not make another daring escape."

"I promise."

"And rest. You have had a long day."

"I will sit quietly." Christine said. She was tired. The deep sadness was still inside of her. She had never known emotion like this. She did not know why or where it came from. She only knew it possessed her and made her very unhappy. It was like a steep wave that overtook her and held her and would not let her go. The emotions rose up from deep within her body and bubbled, and twisted, and controlled her. They had affected her profoundly.

Yuri came back carrying two bowls of rice and a little bit of pickled fish. The food smelled very good and she was hungry. She was sad and hungry. Yuri handed her a bowl and sat down Indian style beside her. Yuri was hungry also. He was relieved that he had found Christine before nightfall and that she was safe in the cave again. She seemed quieter now and not so distraught. But her eyes were still red, and her chest heaved a bit every once in a while as if the sorrow would not leave her. Maybe if Christine talked about her family, she would let go of some of this sadness. Yuri thought to himself.

"Tell me about your family." He said softly.

Christine looked at Yuri and thought about home.

"Great Fish, Montana is in a large valley that is surrounded by mountains. There are several large lakes nearby. My Father owns a hardware store in town, but we lived on a ranch outside of Great Fish because my Mother raises horses. I have wonderful parents and they love each other very much. My Father is quiet and takes care of us, and my Mother is outgoing and keeps everything running. I miss them! I miss the valley, I miss the ranch, I miss Great Fish! But it is very odd. For several years I have lived in Minneapolis, Minnesota, and I was never lonely like I am lonely here."

"Do I make you feel lonely?" Yuri asked. He watched her closely.

"No, it is not you. It is just a deep longing to be free and to be home with my friends and family. I cannot explain it."

They were both silent while they ate their food.

"Why did you leave the valley and go to Minneapolis, Minnesota?"

"I have two older sisters who were very mean to me. They were horsewomen and they were very controlling and hurtful. I like horses, but not the way they liked horses. They lived and breathed horses. I was always a very sensitive child. I am not sure why. I was just born that way, I guess. They loved to make me cry. They would tell me I was ugly or that I was adopted, and I would run away crying. They would just laugh. They loved to see me cry. For some reason that would make them happy. I also have a younger brother who excelled in sports. So between my sisters and my brother, I was the lost child. It made me very vulnerable."

"Do you think of yourself as ugly?"

"Yes, I do."

"You are not ugly. You are beautiful!" Yuri said.

Christine smiled. "You are very sweet for a captor. But when you hear so often that you are ugly and you are vulnerable and always beaten down, then that becomes your reality.

132

"I cannot believe that. Sometimes when I think of your beauty, I become weak!"

Christine flashed her beautiful smile. "You are such a flirt!"

Yuri grinned also. He had always been flirtatious.

"Why did you go into nursing?" He asked.

"I used to volunteer at the local hospital in Great Fish, Montana when I was a teenager. I knew what pain was, and I wanted to help people who were experiencing pain. Once I graduated from high school, I was accepted into the Nursing program at the University of Minnesota. Minnesota is known as a World-Class Medical Center.

There is a train called the Great Empire Builder that runs through Great Fish, Montana and on into Minneapolis, Minnesota. It was built by a hard-driving St. Paul Irish businessman with amazing vision. The Great Empire Builder linked the Continent and for better or worse, it opened up the Western United States.

My leaving the valley is so vivid to me as if it was yesterday! I remember the train coming slowly down out of the mountains and crossing deep gorges that were so frightening it would make your heart pound. Once over the gorges, the train would hug the side of the mountain for dear life as it made its slow descent into the foothills of the Rocky Mountains.

Almost immediately we were on the Great Prairie. The sun was just setting. The sky was huge and the land was endless. There was so much open water on the prairie and so many birds! Thousands of birds filled the sky! On the prairie you could see forever. There was nothing to stop me now! There were no mountains blocking my way. The sunset was golden. It was truly magnificent! I had my whole life ahead of me. This was a new beginning! I was so hopeful and my expectations were overflowing. I could not wait for tomorrow! I fell asleep thinking of my future.

In the morning the Empire Builder pulled into the Minneapolis Train Station. I took a cab over to the University of Minnesota campus, and I was dropped off in front of the dormitory where I lived until I graduated from Nursing school. I had only one suitcase and a strong belief in my future! I was so young and so naive!

Once I graduated from Nursing school, I got my first job at a well-known Hospital in Minneapolis. I majored in Intensive Care and I was in the Surgical Department."

"You must love blood!" Yuri said and flashed his white teeth.

"No, I just had a compassion for people who were hurting."

"I wish you had compassion for me." Yuri said.

"For you?"

"Yes, if I could just see a tiny smile on your face or see the slightest amount of warmth in your eyes, it would mean the world to me."

"You forget I am a prisoner, and I am being kept here against my will."

"Yes that is true, Christine. But we must get along. We cannot be enemies forever. I am not the one who brought you here. I have tried very hard to keep you safe and healthy and to protect you."

"If you wanted to, you would help me get back to the other side." She said.

"The security of this camp is much too important to be breached. I am sorry, Christine; right now, I cannot help you. The best I can do is to share my humble abode with you. But we must be civil to each other; we must get along! No more silences and unhappy faces."

"I want so much to go home." Christine said.

"I know you do. I want to go home too, but right now that is not possible. We need to live together in peace and put away our differences. Can you do that?" Yuri asked.

Christine looked at Yuri. She knew he was right. There was no sense being hostile to him. He had been good to her, and it was not his fault that she was here. He was respectful of her and she appreciated that, but it was not easy being a prisoner. It was not easy not knowing your fate. She wanted to be free again. She wanted that so much!

"Can we live in peace, Christine?" Yuri asked.

"Yes, I will try to be a model prisoner." She said, but there was some bitterness in her words.

"I will give you as much freedom as I can but in return, I need detente. Can you do that?" Yuri asked.

"Yes, I will try to be a happy prisoner, but it is not always easy."

Yuri understood her dilemma, but there was nothing he could do about it. For now they needed to get along. Life in this mountainous camp was too perilous and difficult as it was, and the Americans were moving ever closer in flushing the Viet Cong out of their jungle retreat. To add constant conflict and emotion into the mix was more than anyone should bear.

Yuri and Christine were at the fault line of two huge superpowers trying to fight each other in distant, tiny skirmishes. And for what? What could ever justify so much slaughter and destruction?

"It is late, Christine. We have had a long, eventful day. We must rest."

Yuri picked up the bowls and brought them back to the Great Cooking Hall. When he came back, Christine was already in her sleeping bag. Yuri went over to his side of the cave and turned off the Coleman lantern. He undressed and sought sleep and rest as well.

CHAPTER 20

In the morning Yuri was up early. He could see Christine sleeping peacefully. He went about his morning rituals. Afterwards, he went out of the cave to find breakfast. When he returned, Christine was up and dressed in her fatigues. Yuri went over to her side of the cave and handed her a bowl of fruit and a rice cake. They sat together eating.

"Are you better?" He asked.

"Yes, I am sorry I am such a problem."

"You are a handful." Yuri smiled his beautiful smile and his eyes were dancing. He had some sort of inner light that radiated.

"Where does your family live? Are you married?" Christine wanted to know.

"No, I am not married. My family originally came from Saint Petersburg. It is a City to the Northwest of Moscow. Years ago, my family had a great deal of property and an estate outside of Saint Petersburg, but after the Revolution, the Soviet State took over the land, the houses, our wealth and our possessions—everything!

My Grandfather fought the Bolsheviks. He outfitted the men on his estate with uniforms and weaponry, and they all went off to fight in the Revolution. My Grandfather had a beautiful white horse. We still have photographs of him sitting on this magnificent horse! He rode the horse with a saber in his hand as he charged the enemy. But the Bolsheviks had some sort of new automatic weaponry, and the whole line of soldiers fighting for the Czar was cut down instantly. It was a slaughter. Eventually the Bolsheviks did win and then all of society changed.

136

My Grandmother had two children. My Father and my Aunt. My Grandmother lost everything in the Revolution—her husband, her estate, her title, her land, her wealth. All she had left were her two children and two trusted servants. Together they buried the silver, gold, expensive china, candelabras, hand cut glass—everything so it would not be confiscated and taken.

The family had a summer home in the Ural Mountains and my Grandmother's brother helped move the family out there. Our dear servant, Ivan, made many trips out to the Ural Mountains trying to salvage as many of our personal possessions as possible. Grandmother called him 'Ivan the wonderful'! She and my Mother though felt their servants, Ivan and Petra, were the lucky ones. They did not have the gold and the silver; they had each other! Both of these women, my Grandmother and Mother, have grieved so for their fallen men. You ask me do I believe in War? I do not. We must find another way to settle our differences."

"I am sorry, Yuri."

"There was an enclave of Russian nobility who had retreated to their Summer homes in the Ural mountains. Everyone was afraid that the Soviet State would confiscate these homes, but no one ever did. Mostly the families in the Ural Mountains were made up of women, children, and the elderly.

I grew up in a house full of women. My Father as a young man was killed in World War II defending the Soviet Union from the Nazi invasion of Russia. I was five years old and my Mother was pregnant with my sister, Natasha, when my Father was killed. So my Grandmother has known nothing but loss in her life. I do not believe I have ever heard her laugh, and rarely have I seen her smile. She has witnessed the total collapse of society where all the rules had been rewritten. She has experienced hardship, suffering and the fear of tomorrow. All the men in her life have been brutally taken from her. She is petrified of having anyone come to her house for fear word might get out that she has beautiful possessions and wealth in her home.

But my Grandmother's wealth did not last. One by one, Ivan took the beautiful sterling silver pieces of the grand banquet silverware and sold them to the Turkish trader in town. We sold a fork or a spoon or a serving plate so we could buy food and mittens and shoes! That is how we survived.

My Grandmother has lived a quiet and solitary life never knowing security or well-being. She is always in constant fear of the knock on the door telling us we must vacate our home or that they must take away the family clock or other personal property.

My Mother and my sister and I have always lived with my Grandmother in the Ural Mountains. I, like you, grew up in the mountains. I miss my family also. My Grandmother is an aristocratic and a handsome women. She is very regal looking. She still wears her jewels and pearls in the house. She still has her family possessions around her, and she still has her religion. But all she really has is her memories.

My Mother was a part of that Russian group that had retreated to their Summer homes in the Ural Mountains from Saint Petersburg. She and my Father grew up together. They were a handsome couple from the pictures, and they looked so happy! My Mother tried to make the best of her situation, but she never remarried. She just dedicated her life to bringing up my sister and me and to consoling my Grandmother.

Have you ever lost something? Lost your keys, lost your way, lost your heart? My life is all about loss. But some day I will regain those losses and drop them in front of my Grandmother's feet and say: 'Here they are. I have brought everything back for you'! But I am not going to go head on into the fray like my Father and Grandfather. They could never change. They could not adjust. They lived in a world that they refused to accept. I will not be like them. The Soviet system may not be the best system in the world, but if you are smart, you can make the system work for you. You cannot breathe life into the past. You cannot go back. You can only move forward! I want my wealth and position back, and I intend to get it!"

"Are you a Communist?"

"No, I am just Yuri. But the smartest thing my Mother ever did was to send me to the Communist Youth Camps every Summer. This was the only disagreement my Grandmother and my Mother ever had. Mother wanted me to go to camp because she felt I was always around women, and that I needed to be with young boys my own age, and that I needed male companionship as if it would somehow substitute for my Father.

My Grandmother was outraged that I was to be sent away to the Party machinery. But my Mother won out, and it proved to be a wise decision. In the Soviet Union, it is all about who you know and what alliances you can make. I know so many people across Russia who will be our Country's future leaders. It was a good decision on my Mother's part. A very good decision."

"Where were you before you came here?" Christine asked.

"Oddly enough, I have spent the last three years attached to the Soviet Embassy in Washington DC. What a change!"

"I was in Virginia very close by completing my basic training before I was sent to Vietnam."

They looked at each other for a moment.

"It is extraordinary that we would be in the same place then and now.

Life can so perplexing! It is hard to believe in predestination. On the other hand….." Yuri just shrugged.

"Is that why you speak such excellent English?"

"No, I began to study English when I was eight years old."

"What do you think of the United States?" Christine asked.

"It is truly amazing. The first time I went into an American grocery store, it blew up my mind! I have never seen so much food and so many options! In the Soviet Union we have two choices. Beans or beans. How do you ever make decisions?" Yuri asked.

Christine broke down into uncontrollable laughter. It was a deep emotional laughter that comes from nowhere and sometimes just erupts. She was choking and laughing and she could not stop.

Yuri looked at her.

Finally, Christine regained her composure and wiped the tears from her eyes.

"No, Yuri." She said trying to talk but she was still having gasps of laughter. "In American slang it is not 'blew up my mind'!" She demonstrated this with her hands flying over her head like an explosion. "American slang is: 'It blew my mind.'"

Yuri smiled. "Did we break open the ice?" He asked.

Christine dissolved into another fit of laughter. She fell over on her side and she could not stop laughing. It felt so good!

"You are laughing at me." Yuri said quietly.

"No, no! I am not laughing at you. You try so hard!" Christine said as she was gasping for air. She sat back up. "American slang is: Did we break the ice?" She tried to say.

"Did we break the ice?" Yuri repeated slowly and carefully once Christine had recovered. His look was open and direct. Their eyes met.

"Yes, we broke the ice." She said softly.

"We had a hard day yesterday. Shall we go for a swim?" Yuri asked. He was going to try to spend more time with Christine to see if he could lift her out of her melancholy.

"Yes, I would like that."

They both had small towels and they brought along the soap. The morning light was exquisite and the day was exceptionally warm. Yuri held Christine's hand as usual as they walked down the well-used trail to the rushing mountain stream.

There was a bright orange bird that was singing to them. Yuri pointed him out to Christine and she smiled. They were content and happy as they went down the mountain trail. When they arrived at their mountain pool, they sat on their towels and watched the rushing water flow. The morning light was making the fast-moving water sparkle. Delicate dragonflies were sunning themselves on the boulders along the stream.

"What do you think of the War?" Yuri asked.

"It makes me sad."

"You Americans are much too aggressive. You are alienating the world for your own misguided purposes. The Government and business interests that are leading you down this road will be your undoing. So much of America's talent and wealth and resources are going into self-preservation that your inner core is crumbling. Do you not worry about this?"

"No, I don't think about it." Christine said. Yuri could be so intense at times. Christine thought.

"You have sent a whole generation of men to an early death. And what about the investment? All the dollars your Nation has squandered on nasty chemicals, bombs, guns, tanks, and every conceivable manner of destruction when you could have invested that money into schools,

141

bridges, health care, non-polluting factories, railroads, research that would make the world so much better."

"Yes, the money is being badly spent and so many young men and women have lost their lives or have been badly wounded."

"Your Government is determined to fight this brutal War to the end. The Vietnamese are just pawns and they know it. So when you win this War and you pull out, what have you gained? You defeated a struggling third world Country trying to defend their Homeland. How great is that? So let us say you win the Cold War and you defeat the Soviet Union. What do you gain by that? What do you really gain by going to War?

You destroyed over 58,000 of your young men and women, and you spent billions of dollars much of which is borrowed money. Was it really worth it? Believe me, your Country will only collapse under the heavy weight of your huge Military financial burden! And when you spend so much of your Nation's wealth on the Military, it is only a matter of time before the paranoid Fringe Right will press that Military into action again; and the world sees more deadly conflict. It is a vicious cycle. And in the end, you will become the target."

"Yuri, I am just one person; and sometimes my world is so complicated that I struggle only to manage my own life. How can I ever hope to influence the fate of my Nation?"

"Yes, everyone just wants to live in their own little world and pretty soon the machinery will run over all of us, and there will be no world left. Christina and all of her beautiful children will have no world to live in. Is that really what you want?"

"I just want to be happy." Christine said.

"Yes, we all want to be happy and safe. But must we pay such a high price? We are at the edge of two competing forces that want to destroy each other, and my question is why? Why can we not accept each other's differences?" Yuri asked.

"Yuri, I care for you very much. Even though we come from different parts of the world and different cultures and different governing bodies, we have been able to become friends and care about each other. You have been very good to me, and I appreciate that so much. Let us not speak of War."

Yuri was good at changing gears. He immediately changed the subject. "Good! Let us talk about Christina! Do they have little fishes in Great Fish, Montana?" Yuri asked in a playfully serious tone.

Christine broke into laughter again. Sometimes in life, one needs to laugh long and hard and in a crazed, out of control manner.

"Yuri stop! You make me laugh so."

Yuri beamed. "It is good to hear you laugh, Christine!" Yuri said and his eyes radiated goodwill.

They were smiling at each other. The sky was happy; the earth was happy. They had found a bridge and they crossed it.

"It is time to swim." Yuri said.

The sky was crystal blue and the day was beginning to heat up. They both entered the water together. It felt divine! They washed themselves and swam. Yuri got out of the water first. He turned his head slightly. There was something he heard in the distance.

"Christine, come here." He said.

Christine swam over to the low-lying rocks. "What is it?" She asked.

"Get out of the water." He said in a low voice. He took her hand and helped her out of the cold mountain stream.

"Take your towel and soap and clothes." He said as he picked up his own towel and clothes.

Now he could hear the planes clearly. Christine looked at him as if he were crazy. He led her deep into the jungle where the jungle canopy was protective and it shaded the ground from the glaring sun. Yuri held Christine's hand as he sat on the jungle floor with his back against a huge teak tree. He placed Christine between his legs.

This was odd for Yuri. Christine thought. He always kept his distance from her except when he was holding her hand.

"Yuri, what are you doing? I will get you all wet!"

"Just relax, Christine and lean yourself against my chest."

Christine sat down and Yuri tightly closed his thighs against Christine's as if she was some high-strung race horse. She could feel the strong muscles in his legs. It was as if they were made of steel. Yuri wrapped his arms around her shoulders and held her tightly. Christine could feel the warmth of Yuri's body against hers.

Christine and Yuri were in the shade and because of the mountain stream, they had a clear view of the cloudless sky. A moment later Christine also heard the noise. Now she understood why Yuri had so tactfully guided her into the jungle. They both saw the planes flying low in a tight V formation. They were black ugly planes. They were death planes. They were loud and they were frightening. As the planes came closer, Yuri held Christine even tighter. She could feel his heart pounding.

"What are they?" Christine asked.

"B-52 bombers. The United States has dropped more bombs on Vietnam than all of the bombs dropped in World War II. Your taxes at work, my dear." Yuri whispered into her ear.

They both watched the evil planes coming closer. The planes were flying low. They could hear the loud, whining sound. It was as if the Military was beating its chest: 'Fear us for we are fierce. We respect and honor no one; not even the children or the newborns or the women or the elderly or life or the animals in the field, and clearly not the earth; the clean sweet earth that gave us all life'! Yuri held Christine as if his life depended upon it.

The planes passed by with no mishap. They were in the clear, but Yuri was not happy with their presence on that mountain top today. He released Christine.

"It is time to go back to the cave." He said. The happiness he had felt before was gone. It had all vanished.

When they had entered the cave, Christine looked up at Yuri. Their eyes met.

"When you are gone Yuri, I miss you so much." Christine wanted him to know.

"You miss me? No, you miss me pampering you and waiting on you hand and foot. That is what you miss!" He teased her.

"No, I miss you and I worry about you." Christine said.

Yuri looked down at Christine. His eyes softened "Christine, if anything ever happens to me, trust the Vietnamese. They are good people. They will take care of you."

Christine looked at Yuri. He seemed so serious. He was so unlike himself today. Christine felt hurt. She had tried to express her feelings to him, but he did not acknowledge them. It was as if he did not want to hear what she had to say.

They both separated and went to their own part of the cave.

CHAPTER 21

After the planes had flown overhead, Yuri had stayed close to camp for several days. One evening he said: "Come with me."

"Where are we going?"

"I want to show you the stars." Yuri took Christine's hand, and they left the cave and walked through the camp and deep into the jungle. Yuri took Christine to an outcropping of rock that even the jungle could not penetrate. The rock ledge had a steep drop and a wide view of the jungle below. From a distance, you could see the river winding its way to the Sea and reflecting the last golden rays of the sunset. Soon it was dark and the stars began to come out. Yuri and Christine sat on the rocks and looked at the heavens above. The immense sky was full of twinkling stars.

It was cool on the rocky ledge, and the cold night-time air seemed to make the stars appear even brighter. It was amazing to look up and see the whole universe before them!

"Does man ever gaze at the stars anymore and ponder life?" Yuri asked.

"The sky is beautiful. The heavens always seem so friendly and kind. I love the way the stars twinkle in the night sky!" Christine said. She was happy and felt a measure of well-being.

"When you see the magnificence of the universe, it is hard to understand why man must go to War. Why can't mankind be inspired by the heavens to be more peaceful?" Yuri paused. "The Vietnamese people have fought off invaders for centuries. First the Chinese, then the Japanese, then the French, and now the Americans. You Americans think the Vietnamese are Communists, but they are only patriots fighting for their Country and their way of life."

"We are here to help the Vietnamese." Christine said.

"No, you are only here for ideological reasons, and your Country is so brutal with your bombs, and your high-powered weaponry and your lethal chemicals. You will not win this War. The Vietnamese are smart, they have outstanding leadership, and they are dedicated to their cause. These people are Buddhists. They believe in compassion and non-violence, but they will fight you to the bitter end in order to take back their Country!

There are thousands of Vietnamese who are carrying supplies down from North Vietnam. On their backs they carry explosives, food, ammunition, cloth, medical supplies, footwear, guns. They are the human supply chain and they endure the heat, the jungle, the rain, the snakes, mosquitoes, discomfort and constant fear of the US bombings. But they do this so that their Country can be free. They are a mighty force, and they are far more powerful than all of your guns and planes and battleships. Why does not the United States understand this?"

"I don't know." Christine said lamely.

"Have you ever read 'War and Peace'?" Yuri asked.

"No."

"Have you ever read 'All Quiet on the Western Front'?"

"No."

"Have you ever read 'A Farewell to Arms'?"

"No."

"Have you ever read 'Gone With The Wind'?"

"No."

"Have you ever read 'The Red Badge of Courage'?"

"No."

"The great writers throughout time have pointed out again and again the great fallacy of War. Its destruction, its devastation, its brutality, its pointlessness; and yet we continue to go to War. Why? What does it ever solve? World War I just brought us World War II. Now the US continues to carry on the French War in Vietnam. The Vietnamese people do not even know where the United States is. They do not care about democracy. They care about their own lives and their own Country. Why can not the United States respect that? Why can not America understand that different cultures have different ways of viewing the world?"

"I don't know. I wish we were a more peaceful Nation. Please Yuri, you must calm yourself." Christine said.

Both looked up at the heavens. They were silent for a while.

"What do you know of the Soviet Union?" Yuri asked.

"Well that your life is drab and dreary and that you are a backward Nation."

"Are you saying we have no culture? Have you ever listened to Tchaikovsky?"

"No."

"Have you ever seen the Swan Lake Ballet?"

"No."

"Have you ever been to a Chekov play?"

"No,"

"Who put the first man into space?"

"You did."

"Thank you! Someday I am going to take you to Saint Petersburg and then you can tell me that we are drab and dreary and backward. What do they teach you in school? Yes, we have problems, but War and revolution are not the solutions. We need to change and we will change, but the only way is through peaceful and thoughtful change." Yuri was quiet for a moment.

"What do Americans do when they are not working?" Yuri wanted to know.

"We go to football and hockey games, and we have bonfires and we drive fast cars. Everyone has cars in America, and sometimes they have several cars. And we have music. Everyone loves hard rock music!"

"What do woman in America do when they have time?"

"They go shopping. They buy make-up and clothes and do dads."

"What is a do dad?"

"It is something that is absolutely worthless."

"Why do they buy it?"

"They fancy it. I do not know why, but it runs our economy."

"Is that why the United States invaded Vietnam? For do dads?"

"No, for freedom."

"Freedom? This is their Country. Do you not think that the Vietnamese should decide that? You Americans are so incredibly arrogant! You have your own problems and injustices to look after. Do you not?"

Christine was silent. Sometimes Yuri was so passionate about his beliefs. She liked his playful side better.

"Please let's not argue, Yuri. Couldn't we just enjoy the evening, the night-time air, and this magnificent sky! It is as if we have our own private collection of stars, and whenever we want to, we can come and visit them. They seem so friendly and happy, don't they?" She said smiling.

Yuri leaned over and kissed her on the cheek. "You are my happy star." He said.

Christine was astounded. Yuri had always maintained a correct distance from her. She did not know what to say. There was a prolonged silence.

"Why did you come to Vietnam?" He asked.

Why had she come? That was a painful question.

"I came to escape a very hurtful relationship." Christine paused. "I had fallen in love with a man who used me very badly and who broke my heart. I was such a fool; such a ridiculous and utter fool!" Christine was silent for a time as she thought back to the past.

"It was like being on an uneven playing field where you are so in love, so enmeshed in love, and the other person feels nothing and uses you as if you were a little toy to be played with. You were not a person with thoughts or feelings. You were just there to be used and enjoyed." She stopped again.

"I have always felt somewhat worthless. My Father said I was naive. And I was! I was stupid and naive! I was a fool; just a simpleminded, trusting fool looking for love."

The deep feelings started to pour from Christine's heart.

Yuri kept silent.

"He was a surgeon that I worked with at the Hospital in Minneapolis. I was so in love with him. I thought we would spend our whole life together! I did not realize that what I thought was love, was not love; and that he was just using me for his own pleasure. What I wanted was a home and family, and all I got was heartbreak and pain. In the end all I did was cry. The pain was so horrible, I do not think I could be close to anyone ever again."

Yuri listened quietly.

"First it started with lunches. He would say: 'Christine, you did such a great job! Let me buy you lunch'. When you are young and vulnerable, those words are so important to you. He was known as an excellent surgeon at the Hospital, and I basked in his praise and attention. Then it became dinner: 'Christine, let us celebrate the Simpson operation. You did such a wonderful job. I will pick you up at 7:00 o'clock'. I knew he was married, but I truly thought he was in love with me because I was so in love with him. He was heaven and earth to me and he was always so anxious to be with me. I was such a fool! I was just a young little fool from Montana who only wanted to be loved."

Christine stopped again. Did she want to continue? No, but she did. Perhaps because for so long this needed to come out.

Like an expert on human emotions, Yuri waited quietly for Christine to continue.

"There were several dinners. Then he asked if he could come up to my apartment. We had such a lovely dinner, and I had been drinking such lovely wine and of course I cared for him intensely. He came up to my apartment. He started to kiss me and I kissed him passionately also. In seconds my panties were down and it was over.

We became lovers, and we no longer went out for lovely dinners. When you know nothing and have nothing and find something so exquisite as deep and passionate love, it is hard to let it go. He was everything to me! He was my life!"

There was a long silence.

"When I became pregnant, he asked me to destroy the child. He said he could never leave his wife, and that there was nothing between us. I did what I was told. When I destroyed that child, my heart broke into a thousand pieces. I could hardly function. After work, I would come home and draw a hot bath. For hours I would lie in the warm water trying to soothe my pain. I would not cry, but endless tears rolled down my cheeks. It was such an incredibly deep sorrow. It is the wound that never heals. There will be no lifetime of love and happiness for me. Everything I loved and cherished had been taken from me."

Christine hated herself for loving and caring so deeply and with so much of her heart.

"I do not have feelings anymore. Sometimes I think I am incapable of ever loving again. Everything inside of me was destroyed."

"Is that why you are so hard on poor Yuri?" He asked.

"Am I hard on you?"

"You run away and make me find you, you make me worry about you all of the time, and sometimes your eyes are so cold and hostile that I think you are the descendant of some prehistoric reptile!"

Christine made a sharp gasp. "I am sorry. I am not trying to make your life difficult. You have been good to me, you have been respectful, and I depend on you. I do not want to make you miserable. I don't!"

"That is good." Yuri said.

"But sometimes I think I no longer have a heart. It was torn from me a long time ago."

"No heart?" Yuri looked perplexed. He reached out and put his hand just above her left breast.

"Yuri!" Christine cried out and her face became flushed.

Yuri smiled in a kindly manner. "Yuri feels faint heart beat." He said and he withdrew his hand. His smile was glowing.

"Now you are laughing at me." Christine said.

"No, inside I am crying for you. I am crying for your heartache and your anguish. And if ever I meet your Surgeon friend, I will smash him with both my fists! But I did not create your pain nor do I want to be a recipient of that pain." He said with emotion.

Yes, Christine thought. Yuri is right. He was entitled to be free of my pain and my anger!

"It is late. We should be getting back." Yuri said.

"And leave our stars and beautiful sky?" Christine said smiling.

"Yes, we must." Perhaps it was not such a good idea our coming here tonight. Yuri thought to himself as he took Christine's hand. He helped her down, and they walked back to the cave under the starry night.

CHAPTER 22

Life had fallen into a routine for Christine. In the beginning it had been very awkward and bitter, but Yuri and Christine had learned to adjust. Christine was grateful for being sheltered and fed and not having a rifle pointed at her head. Yuri was respectful, and at times he could be very sweet. With the coming of the planes, Christine became more curious about the camp, and she tried to make herself more useful. Now she understood the fear the Vietnamese people lived under. Now she understood why they were so united. She became curious about the camp and the Vietnamese fighters.

In the camp area, all the underbrush of the rainforest had been removed so that the jungle floor had been exposed. There were many cave openings on the mountainside of the ledge and they opened onto the jungle clearing. Hammocks hung from the trees. Knapsacks lay here and there.

The camp was fascinating to Christine. The camp was a rest area and a supply depot. It had a hospital and a training area. It served as a factory and a repair center. There were sewing machines that worked with pedals for sewing uniforms. There was an area for making rope sandals and repairing footwear. There was another area for making mosquito netting and for repairing hammocks. This was a village where people knew each other and who shared a common bond. They were a tough, dedicated people and a disciplined group of people; and they had a will and a powerful determination to win!

Viet Cong were coming and going all of the time. This was part of the Ho Chi Minh Trail that skirted the mountain tops and penetrated deep into South Vietnam. The Americans bombed the Ho Chi Minh Trail regularly. Ho Chi Minh was the spiritual leader of Vietnam. He had been fighting the French for years. Now he had to battle the Americans. He was affectionately known as Uncle Ho. This was his trail. Time was on his side.

The camp area was a hotbed of activity. The Vietnamese shared their food, they ate together, they lived together. They were a communal society, and they placed a premium on cooperating and conforming and helping each other. These were Eastern values. It was part of their heritage and their beliefs. They shared their common fears, hardship, and suffering together. They fought off mosquitoes, infections, fear, exhaustion, tigers, snakes, and the enemy because they were devoted to their cause. They walked the length of the Ho Chi Minh Trail carrying supplies and ammunition because they believed in their leadership. They believed in their mission. Everyone, both men and women, knew their role and their duty; and they contributed their part with all of their hearts to the War and to defeating the Americans!

Christine wandered around the camp. There had been a warm rain and the air was soft and it smelled clean and new. People were either working or relaxing. Christine could hear their sing song chatter. They watched Christine walk by. She either smiled or waved to them as she walked past.

A beautiful Vietnamese woman with long raven black hair by the name of Leli came up to Christine. She had lovely brown eyes, but they were cold and blank. She was like a breathe from the earth that came out and haunted you at night. It seemed her delicate face was hardened and made of granite. She gave Christine a cold and wintry smile as if her heart was made of stone. She said something to Christine in

Vietnamese and she motioned for Christine to follow her. She wanted to show Christine something. Christine followed her.

There was a medical bag on the ground. The Vietnamese woman wanted to show Christine something in the bag. Christine got down on her hands and knees and started to look through the bag. Suddenly, there were five men from all sides of the camp sprinting, dashing, hurtling over baskets and bolts of material to try to reach Christine. Yuri had gotten there first. He had watched the whole procession of events.

As Christine looked through the medical bag, the Vietnamese woman had raised a large knife over her head and was about to stab Christine in the back. Yuri had gotten there just in time to wrestle the knife from Leli's hand. Christine had turned in that instant and saw the two struggling for the knife. Yuri took the knife from Leli's hand. Five men stood in a circle and watched Leli fall to her knees and burst out crying. They were mournful sobs. Her head was held between her hands and she wailed with anguish.

"Go to the cave." Yuri told Christine harshly.

Christine quickly got to her feet and walked swiftly toward the cave. There were people gathering now, and they watched Leli on her knees buried in her own tears. Yuri stayed with her and placed his hand on her shoulder. A tall Vietnamese man came to her and slowly lifted her up and placed his arms around her. Christine looked back only once. Yuri watched them go.

Everyone was silent.

Yuri went back to the cave. His face looked tense.

"Are you all right?" He asked.

"Yes."

"You must not judge her."

"Not judge her? She almost killed me! I looked back just in time to see the knife coming at me. It is my sisters all over again. What did I ever do to her?" Christine was emotionally shaken.

"I am sorry, Christine. I did not realize the depth of Leli's pain. She hates Americans!" Yuri said flatly.

"What have I ever done to her? I was trying to help her!" Christine was upset. She could not understand why Yuri did not know how she felt and why he would take this women's side.

"Christine, I know you are upset, but I want to tell you about Leli, the woman who tried to kill you." Yuri paused as he sat down beside Christine. He looked at her directly and spoke softly.

"Leli was once married and she had four children. They lived on a plateau on the Highlands and their village overlooked the South China Sea. It was a beautiful village. Everyone knew each other. Families had lived there for decades. Everyone got along. Leli's husband already had been killed in the War, and this was a great heartache for her. She continued to live in the village with her parents.

One evening she left the village to get water. When she came back, the village was in flames. The Americans had dropped bombs and napalm on the village. She watched as her house went up in flames with all of her children and her parents in it. The whole village was in flames. No one was spared. The heat was so intense. People, children, the frail—everyone was burnt alive. All Leli could do was watch near a bamboo bush with her little pail of water beside her and scream in anguish.

Right there and then, she became a fervent Viet Cong. Her soul had hardened. She would do anything and everything to defeat the United States of America. Her anger against America is frightening. It is so deep and so strong that she alone could win this War.

They say that she was half crazy for a year. Then her mind recovered, and the United States had a new Viet Cong convert on their hands. She is a product of your War. She is lethal and she is unstoppable."

"Why didn't you tell me about her?" Christine asked in a softer tone.

"Because she is the norm here. There are so many like her."

"Yuri, you are not giving me much comfort."

"Leli has been up and down the Ho Chi Minh Trail four times. She always volunteers for the most dangerous missions. She has the deepest vengeance. Not for you, not for your Country, but for your Government and its brutal, amoral conduct. I am saying this to you so that you will understand the depth of her pain."

"Why didn't you tell me this before?"

"Leli for many days has expressed her anger for you, and she has said that she wanted to kill you."

"She came very close to doing that!" Christine said. "I think you had a duty to tell me!"

"The Vietnamese have been watching over you. They are your protectors. It is complicated. We have tried to keep you apart. Let us leave it at that."

That was easy for Yuri to say. He was not the one that had nearly been stabbed to death. Christine thought. Sometimes she had such a difficult time understanding him.

CHAPTER 23

Several weeks had passed. Christine and Yuri were both in the cave when a lean, young man came through the cave opening. He was deeply tanned and had a graceful, strong body. Yuri looked up.

"Misha!" Yuri roared.

"Hello Yuri! I have brought you some vodka to keep you Russian!" Misha had a huge grin on his face. Immediately the bottle went flying through the air. Yuri caught it with one hand.

"Misha, you are a saint!" Yuri said as he kissed the bottle of vodka and laid it on the cave floor. Both men embraced each other warmly. You could see that they had an enormous regard for each other.

"It is so good to see you, Misha!" Yuri said.

Christine had never seen Yuri display so much affection.

"Christine, this is Misha. He is a long-time childhood friend. He is my great ally and my brother! Together, we plan to change the face of the Soviet Union! Misha is a bell ringer and he has many friends! He is our great agent of change!" Yuri said proudly.

Misha was a tall, muscular man. He had a gigantic presence. His eyes were intelligent and he had brown dark hair. He had the same high cheek bones and sensuous lips as Yuri. He was strong and youthfully energetic. Any woman would have been proud to stand by his side.

Misha stretched out his hand to Christine. He held Christine's hand and brought it to his lips. He kissed her hand with bravado and smiled at her gently.

"So, this is your captive. We have been hearing about her!" Misha spoke perfect English.

Yuri put his hand to his forehead and grimaced. "She does not like to be called that. She tells me she has no Masters!"

"Really? She sounds rather Godless."

"Oh, she is a heathen all right, but we are straightening her out."

"She is very pretty. You must be having a fine time." Misha said to Yuri in Russian.

Yuri tossed him a smile. "She is a big problem." Yuri replied in Russian.

"Send her North to Hanoi."

"I cannot do that."

"Why?"

Yuri looked at him oddly.

Misha exploded in laughter. "You and an American woman! Oh, that is good! Where are your Communist morals? We had better open up some Vodka for you tonight!" Misha said in Russian, and he went into another roar of laughter.

Christine watched these two virile men. She wished they would speak English so she could understand what they were saying. She had no idea how to speak Russian.

"Christine, Misha is the son of Stalin."

"The son of Stalin?" Christine repeated in amazement.

"No." Misha said in English. "Yuri is teasing you at my expense because he thinks that I am a hard core Party man. But I am only an opportunist looking for an opportunity." Misha's eyes radiated light.

"Yuri teases me relentlessly!" Christine said.

"Doe he? I would be careful of him. He has many charms!"

Misha's body was a golden bronze color from the sun. He had grin lines around his mouth, and he had a smile that could light up the sky.

"What about a little go around before lunch? Are you man enough to take me on?" Yuri asked Misha.

"A light-weight like you? Of course! But remember, you are a doomed man!"

Yuri went out and brought back two poles. He tossed a pole to Misha and Misha caught it. Both men faced each other smiling. They approached each other and started to fight. They swung at each other hard and braced off of each other's blows; blunting their power as they protected themselves. Christine could not believe the viciousness of how they attacked each other. She thought they were madmen.

Why must men always have to pit strength against strength and show their valor? But whatever blow came, it was always blocked by the other person. They moved around the cave like agile dancers.

Christine backed away from them as she watched in terror.

"I think Christine is afraid of us." Yuri said.

"I hope she likes the color red."

"No, I think white is her favorite color. She is a nurse, you know."

"Good! Then we are both in luck!"

The two men fought on with Yuri taking the advantage.

"Misha, you are a marked man. What are your last words?"

"Veni, vidi, vici." Misha said weakly.

The tide turned and now Yuri was in trouble.

"And so Yuri, what are your last words?"

"Bienvenido a mi casa."

Yuri dislodged Misha's pole and the two started wrestling on the cave floor like little boys.

"Ok Misha, you win." Yuri said.

"Thank you." Misha said with great dignity and got up off of the cave floor.

Yuri lunged at him and put him into a bear hold.

"You rotten scoundrel!" Misha cried out.

"You fell for it. Now say you are sorry."

"I am not sorry!" Misha said defiantly.

"Say you are sorry or I will pound you one more time!"

"Ok, I am sorry." Misha said.

Yuri got off of Misha and helped him up. They smiled at each other, shook hands and embraced each other. They put their hands on each other's shoulders, and they both smiled happily at Christine.

Christine looked at them speechless. Men and women are so different. She thought to herself.

The two friends started to sing Russian songs, and they marched out of the cave singing loudly in their deep Russian voices.

"We will be back after lunch." Yuri called out.

Yuri and Misha sat down under the forest canopy and ate rice and sweet potatoes together.

"Christine is a very attractive women, although I am not taken with her Army fatigues. Do you care for her?" Misha spoke in Russian.

"Yes, I care for her very much. Too much." Yuri replied in Russian.

"You and an American women? That is hysterically funny!" And Misha roared with laughter. "Don't you know the Americans are our arch enemy?"

"Are they?" Yuri asked rhetorically.

"Yes! They want to destroy us, and any other Country that does not have the same cultural values and government institutions. They want the whole world to be exactly like them. What a farce!"

Yuri only shrugged. "We have problems; they have problems. Why can't we just work for a better world?"

"Ah yes, it is like currencies. We all have different currencies. But ours work for us. Why can't they just accept that?" Misha shook his head and went on. "Back to Christine. I could see instantly that there was some kind of electricity between the two of you. Does she care for you?"

"No."

"You two have lived together for five months. Surely by sheer physical instinct there must be something there?"

"On a pleasant basis, we are friends. But it is a delicate balance. I am the captor; she is the captive. Where does the trueness lie in that?"

"Why not send her to Hanoi. Certainly the Red Cross could get her out."

"No, that is impossible. The trip would be too hard and very dangerous."

"But don't you realize how dangerous it is for her to stay here?"

"Yes, yes. But at least here, I can watch over her."

"Does she know you are leaving today?"

"No, I never tell her where I am going or what I am doing or when I will be back. At some point this will all be over, and I will get her back to the other side."

The men finished their lunch and went back to the cave. As they entered, Christine smiled and waved to them. "Are you always so nice to each other?" She inquired.

"Yuri picks on me and then I have to defend myself." Misha said smiling.

Yuri got his knapsack and placed something in it. "I will be back in a moment." Yuri said.

Misha and Christine were alone in the cave. There was an awkward silence.

"Is he good to you?" Misha asked.

"Yes."

"He needs to be pampered and adored. That is what he is used to. Do not forget that! He is a very disciplined man. He does not let his passions flow freely, but they are just below the surface. He can be difficult at times, but he is a good man. He will take care of you."

Yuri came back into the cave. There was an abrupt silence.

"Did I miss something?" Yuri asked.

"No, we were just talking about the weather." Misha replied.

Yuri picked up his knapsack. "I will be gone for a couple of days." Yuri said to Christine.

"That was a very cold and cavalier parting!" Misha said to Yuri in Russian.

Yuri shrugged.

Christine was standing near Misha. He took her hand and held it in both of his hands. He was friendly and warm. "It has been my great pleasure to meet you. I know I will be seeing you again!" He said with great courtesy.

Christine smiled at Misha. "Thank you." She said graciously. She liked Misha very much.

"Travel safely!" She said to both of them.

They waved to her and went out into the hot, sultry air.

CHAPTER 24

Christine had gotten use to Yuri leaving. She never knew when he was going or when he would return. She did not like being alone in the cave, but there was nothing she could do about it. She worried about the inner cave opening, and the rushing air that came from it. She worried about snakes or wild animals entering the cave, and she worried about Yuri.

When Yuri had been gone for several days, for some reason Christine woke up in the middle of the night. In the shadows of the cave, she could see Yuri standing unsteadily in front of the cave entrance as the moonlight shone down behind him. He was watching her. A frozen shiver went down through her spine. His eyes were dark and furious. They looked evil. He was swaying slightly as he moved toward her. He stopped and looked down at her. The look in his eyes seemed inhuman, yet at the same time deathly human. An instinctive fear shot through her.

He came toward her and slowly unbuckled his belt. The moonlight reflected the great hammer and sickle on his belt buckle. He stared at her and dropped his pants. He was as erect as any rocket ready for its final thrust into the unknown. He picked up one end of Christine's sleeping bag, and she came tumbling out like a sack of potatoes. She tried to move away from his grasp. She fought him, but he came down upon her and pinned her to the cold cave floor.

In seconds, it was over. He was still. There was no more movement. He was done. One hundred and eighty pounds of male flesh was on top of her sleeping happily. She could feel him slowly parting from her. His head lay on her shoulder, and his massive arm was draped over her chest. He was snoring heavily. There was a stillness in the cave; a sad and poignant stillness.

Christine could not move. She felt hollow and empty like a used vessel standing alone and unwanted. He had taken all of the pleasure from her, and left her with nothing except humiliation and rage. The rage that comes from being taken against one's will. She felt inwardly tarnished and repulsed by the invasion of her body. His steel thighs bore down on hers, but there was nothing she could do about it. She was helpless and angry. She did not want to be near him.

Hour upon hour she lay awake with her shoulder blade pinned on the moist cave floor. The freezing draft made half of her body shiver. There were tears of sadness and despair in her eyes. Yuri was asleep snoring happily. Christine squirmed, wiggled, and inched herself from under Yuri's heavy body.

She stood up. Her nightshirt was open with her breasts exposed. She felt broken and full of shame. Last night was violent. It all seemed like a nightmare. Tears began to roll down her cheeks as she looked at her half naked body. She wanted to hide. She wanted to go some place dark where she would not be so vulnerable and exposed. A torrent of tears rushed down her cheeks as she entered the cave's inner chamber.

She was crying hysterically now. She did not know where she was going. She just walked slowly into the darkness. It was drafty in the inner chamber of the cave, and she could feel the cool air against her body. Some parts of the cave were colder than others as if some evil spirit dwelled there. At one point, Christine sank to her knees and cried convulsively. But she got up and walked on. She went deeper and deeper into the interior of the cave.

Somehow, she tripped and fell four feet down. All the wind had been knocked out of her. She could barely breathe. Her knee was sore and her leg hurt. She was frightened. She tried desperately to breathe. She lay quietly on the rock floor. She was stunned like a bird that flies into a window and is knocked to the ground not knowing what had ever happened.

Slowly her breathing came back. She felt everything around her as she could not see. At arms-length as she extended her hand, there was a drop. She felt all along the edge with her hand. She must be on a small ledge because beyond the ledge, there was nothing. She could not go down because she did not know how far the drop was. Christine tried to stand up, but she could not hoist herself up over the ledge. The ledge wall was moist and slippery. She sank back down and began to cry.

Yuri woke up in the morning. Sunlight was shooting through the cave entrance. He saw Christine's rumpled sleeping bag. His pants were down and his head hurt. From the interior of the cave, he could hear a faint whimpering sound. A deep fear flashed through his body. Had Christine gone deeper into the cave? Had she been so fearful of him that she wanted to destroy herself? He had warned her of the inner chamber of the cave. It was a dangerous maze with many sharp drops that fell sixty feet to the bottom. One wrong move and she would be gone. There would be no way to even remove her body.

Yuri sat up and tried to think. He must remain calm. He pulled up his trousers and buckled his massive belt. He still had on his boots. He picked up the Coleman lantern and entered the inner cave chamber. Yuri could still hear Christine's faint crying. He hurried as fast as he could go. He came upon one of the most dangerous parts of the cave. On a narrow ledge four feet below, he could see Christine. Beyond the ledge, there was a sheer fifty-foot drop. Yuri knew he had to control the panic in his voice.

"Christine, you are going to be all right." He said in a steady voice. "Move as close as you can to the ledge wall."

Yuri got down on his chest and lay prone.

"Christine, I am going to reach out my hand, and I want you to touch it so I know that you are all right. No one is going to hurt you."

In the flickering light, Christine saw for the first time how close she had come to disaster. She kept looking down at the rock floor fifty feet below. The faltering light made the sharp drop look hard and grotesque and even more frightening. Her body edged closer to the ledge wall.

"Christine, please take my hand. It is very dangerous here, and I have got to know you are all right. Christine, here is my hand—please!"

He slowly extended his hand as far as he could reach.

"You are all right, Christine. No one will harm you." His voice was controlled and measured, but his breathing was shallow and his body was tightly clinched.

The tears were caked on Christine's face. Her body was shivering. Slowly she reached out and grasped his hand. Yuri closed his eyes and took a deep breath. Thank God! The hardest part was over.

"Christine, I want you to hold my hand and move as close to the ledge wall as possible. Can you do that? Good. Now steady yourself for a moment."

Yuri could see her moving. He could see her head and her hair, but she did not look up at him. He held her hand tightly. If she was going over the cliff, they were going together!

"Trust me, Christine. You have got to trust me." He waited a moment so that she would have time to think on what he had said. Every so often, he could hear a little sob.

"Christine, can you stand up? Whatever you do, do not look down."

Christine slowly raised herself up to the ledge wall. She could feel the cold rock against her breasts and the soreness and pain in her leg. Yuri leveraged himself and put his strong hands under her armpits. He hauled her up as one hauls up a marlin onto a boat in the turbulent Florida Keys.

Yuri quickly took Christine away from the ledge and over to the cave wall. She was crying hysterically now; partly from fear; partly from relief. Yuri held her in his arms and let her cry. He stroked her hair tenderly.

"Christine, I am so sorry! You are safe now. Please do not cry." Her arms went around him and he held her tightly. She clung to him as a non-swimmer frantically clings to a rescuer in the water. The wetness of her tears covered Yuri's hands as he rocked her gently. When she had quieted down, he asked if she could walk. She nodded her head. He helped her up and picked up the lantern. Together they limped back to the cave entrance with Yuri's arm around her. He helped her into her bedroll.

"Try to rest, Christine. I will be here, but I will not hurt you." Yuri said. Christine slept for a long time. Yuri watched her sleep, and he wondered how he could ever regain her trust. He knew he had crossed a definitive, age-old line, and that it was something he would always regret.

When Christine woke up, Yuri was across the cave on the other side watching her.

"Good morning." He said and smiled at her. "Although it is afternoon. Let us go down to the stream and wash."

Christine was still in a disheveled state. She knew she needed to wash. They walked down to the stream although this time Yuri did not take Christine's hand. They brought their small towels and soap. It was mid-afternoon and the heat of the day was intense. They both quickly went into the water and shared the soap. When they got out of the water, they sat on the rocks to warm themselves. Yuri again tried to apologize.

"Christine, I want you to know how sorry I am for what happened. If I could take back the dark deeds in my life, this would be one of them." Yuri paused. There was a silence.

"Misha was killed 2 days ago by a cluster bomb. It totally mutilated his whole body. His legs were severed. His face was crushed. He was cut up into terrible bloody pieces."

"Misha dead?" Christine said, She could not believe it. He was such a beautiful man! He was so vibrant and full of life!

"I am sorry, Yuri." She could see the pain on Yuri's face.

"I collected his remains and buried his body. Misha had a wife and children. I wish to God it had been me!" Yuri said with deep emotion.

Misha dead? Christine thought to herself. What an ugly War. What a truly ugly War.

Yuri was quiet for a long time.

"I have always wanted you. I will not deny that; but lust, desire and anger are very bad combinations. You know that I was drunk. I know that is no excuse for what I did. I drank and drank and drank to numb the pain from Misha's death. I was very drunk and very angry, and I took that anger out on you; and for that I am very sorry. I hope you can forgive me." Yuri said sincerely.

Christine did not know what to say. She was always so protective of herself and so easily hurt. She did not understand her own feelings. She still felt violated and used. She nodded her head, but she did not look up at Yuri. They walked back to the cave. Yuri got them some dinner and they ate together. Both were silent. Yuri moved his sleeping bag in front of the inner cave opening just in case Christine tried to enter the inner cave again.

"I am going to sleep with you tonight, but I am going to sleep here. I will not touch you." He assured her.

They got into their separate sleeping bags. Christine wanted only to sleep. She wanted to go far away—far, far away and rest. She definitely did not want to be here anymore!

In the days ahead, Yuri watched over Christine. She became distant and withdrawn. Her anger was relentless as the breakers on a rough sea. Her rage reverberated throughout her body, and made her lash out or descend into a troubling quiet. She began to shut down and sink into the darkness. She did not know how to put her feelings into words. She only knew she was sinking deeper and deeper into despair and there was nothing she could do about it.

Now she avoided Yuri at all costs. She stayed away from the cave all day and returned only at sunset. Many times Christine would seek out the babbling stream. She wished the flowing waters would wash away her pain. Yuri had been her one ounce of security in a very insecure world, and now that ounce of security was gone. He had been her sword and her shield. He had been her protector. She depended upon him. Now she could not forgive him. Inwardly, she felt so diminished. There was shame, there was anger, and she felt so worthless! No, no matter what Yuri said, she could not forgive him. How could she?

Yuri could see the change that had come over her. He resented her disappearances and her sullen ways. He had brought her extra food. He had apologized and asked for forgiveness, but she continued to sink deeper and deeper into the darkness as if a black veil had descended down upon her and would not lift. She became totally unresponsive to the point where Yuri had to leave. Despite all of his efforts, he was being pushed away. The tension was everywhere. This was his space and he was being forced out.

Now they never spent time together. There was no swimming in their favorite pool or long talks on their mountain perch late at night as the clouds drifted across the moon, and the stars shone down upon them, and gentle breezes caressed them. Why didn't Yuri realize how violated she felt? How she could never stop thinking of herself as something used and soiled, and how ugly she felt inside. She had trusted him. She had depended upon him, and now that deep trust had been broken. There was a gulf between them a thousand miles wide.

One morning Christine woke up and saw Yuri packing. Yuri saw that she was awake.

"Christine, I am going away for a month. I want you to promise me that you will not enter the interior of the cave again."

"No, I will not go in there."

"And please do not try to escape again because I will not be here to save you."

She just looked at him steadily.

"Christine, they will track you down. They will not let you escape. Please promise me that you will be good."

"Yes, I will be good. I will be a model prisoner."

But Yuri was skeptical. Maybe the privacy would be good for her to heal herself. He knew he had hurt her deeply, and he was not sure if he could ever repair the damage. Maybe his absence would be healing for her. Maybe it would help her to recover. After all, she had trusted him once and now there was no trust. Maybe if he was gone, she could find it in her heart to forgive him.

"Goodbye." He said, and he left the cave with his knapsack and his heavy burden.

CHAPTER 25

Christine was now alone in the drafty cave and the days went by slowly. She was free to wander the camp, but she knew she was being carefully watched. In the beginning she stayed in her sleeping bag and slept long hours. She thought of Yuri; his strong body, his intense masculinity, his beautiful smile, his playfulness and his kindnesses. Yet she still felt angry and hurt. When he was here, she had withdrawn into herself, and there was a divide between them. It was as if the strong foundation of their relationship had been shattered. She still did not understand her own feelings or even know how to express them. It was just a crushing rock that she carried on her shoulder and of which she could not let go of.

In the beginning, Christine was glad Yuri was gone. She was glad she was alone. But after so much time had passed and still he did not return, she thought of him often. What had happened to him? Would he ever come back? Was he hurt? Had he been killed like Misha? It was so hard to understand her emotions. She still had the anger pent up inside of her, but she also missed him.

Christine thought too about Leli, the woman who had tried to stab her. She could understand Leli's pain as Christine had also lost a child and had suffered greatly for it. But to watch your own children and family burn to death; to see the red flames shooting high into the sky and feel the intense heat, and to be completely helpless. How does anyone cope with something like that? How does anyone ever forgive, or forget, or let go of after that? She did not know. Christine could understand Leli's anguish. She could understand her pain and her bitterness and her remorse. She could clearly understand her anger and her rage! Christine wished she could reach out to Leli and tell her how sorry she was about her family. How truly sorry she was! No one should endure such heartache and pain.

Christine felt abandoned. She felt cold and free and totally unattached. She did not care what happened to herself anymore. But slowly the black veil began to lift and she became more active. They say time heals all wounds. Maybe.

Christine decided to explore the camp. There was a great deal of movement that came down the Trail from the North. People would arrive with their heavy loads and then depart. The Trail was the Ho Chi Minh Trail. It started far up in the North, and it worked its way through a thousand paths into the South of Vietnam. Hundreds of volunteers toiled southward carrying War materials and supplies. Their goal was to unify their Country. Their determination was profound. Their motto: 'Born in the North, die in the South.' They knew reunification would be difficult, but they were willing to pay the price. Christine wanted to understand their world.

The camp was very large. It bordered the mountain stream, and it had many trails leading off to where? Christine knew the location of the Great Cooking Hall. It was a large cavern in a cave along the mountainside where the Viet Cong did all of their cooking. The Viet Cong did not want to cook outside in the open air for fear the US surveillance planes would see the smoke in the mountains and decide to investigate further. But inside the Great Cooking Hall, there were always 8 to 10 cooking kettles in use.

They cooked wonderful food with sweet potatoes, rice, fish, peppers, cinnamon, and cardamom. Sometimes there was fish pickled in brine or sometimes there was mashed fish in peanut pesto. The tea was always on because when the Viet Cong carried their burdens for so many miles; delicious food, hot tea, and a warm welcome helped to cheer them and raise their morale in spite of their fatigue and exhaustion. There were sacks of rice, potatoes, tea, whatever the Villagers around the Region had to spare. The Viet Cong would bring these food staples back to camp. They would live off of the land. They fished, they hunted, they collected wild grapes, bananas, pineapples, coconuts—whatever was available.

The Great Cooking Hall was also a popular place to come and socialize, hear the news or the latest joke or War story. The Viet Cong warriors especially enjoyed the stories of how the US aid and Military supplies would mysteriously leave the US warehouses by the cunning efforts of their daring Viet Cong brothers and sisters.

The Great Cooking Hall was cool and it was free of pesky flies and mosquitoes that so often plagued them and followed them everywhere. The strong air movements in the cave drew the smoke deep into the interior of the cave so that what was left were smiling cooks, hot tea, and the marvelous smells of wonderful food slowly cooking!

When Yuri was gone, Christine would stop by the Great Cooking Hall to pick up small portions of food. People were always friendly to her although she did not know what they were saying, but she appreciated their smiles and she liked going to the Great Cooking Hall. It was a hotbed of activity, and it seemed everyone knew she was the guest of Ho Chi Minh!

Christine was ready to explore the camp. Yuri was gone. There was no concern or caring there. Yuri had hurt her, and he had left her so now she was free. But what do you do when you are free? Where do you go? She was not sure. She only knew she wanted to understand the other side of the War. She was not afraid of Leli anymore. In fact, Christine was hoping to find Leli in the camp.

Christine started walking through the camp clearing. She could see people working, relaxing, exercising, joking, laughing. The camp was a holding area where people came to rest or help with producing items needed for the War effort. They made bandages, baskets, packaged medicines, manufactured uniforms, footwear, and ammunition. The camp was part factory, part workshop, part training center, part hospital, part rest area. Life was highly organized and disciplined. Christine respected these people. They were tough and dedicated and they stood together. They were a united front!

Christine aimlessly wandered down a well-worn path. She came upon a clearing in the jungle with benches and posters and red banners. There was a platform and a table overlooking the benches. Tung was sitting at the table looking at Military maps and writing in his log. He saw Christine as she entered the meeting area.

"Hello." He said in perfect English.

"Hello." Christine said. She recognized him as the man who so tenderly had taken Leli away. Small beams of sunlight floated down upon him through the thick forest canopy.

"Come and sit." he said.

Like walking through a Salvadore Dali painting, Christine went down the long aisle past the many empty benches. She stood in front of the Vietnamese man. He had jet-black hair with wisps of gray at each temple. He had beautiful brown eyes. They were expressive eyes. They were intelligent eyes with a shining light full of wisdom and sorrow and joy and eternity and an unstoppable determination that was wider than the Mekong Delta.

"You are Christine." He said.

"Yes."

"Yuri has spoken of you often." Tung said. "I am sorry for what happened to you with Leli. She has experienced a very hard and difficult life. She is possessed of a hatred that she cannot let go of. It is poisoning her."

"Do you know her well?" Christine asked.

"I am in love with her." Tung said. "I am also responsible for your being here."

"Why is that?" Christine wanted to know.

"It is so." Tung said. That is all he would say. That was an odd answer. Christine thought to herself.

"Where did you learn such excellent English?" Christine asked.

"I was educated in France and in Berkley, California. Please sit down." Tung stood up and motioned her to a bench.

"My name is Tung. Are you getting enough to eat?"

"Yes." Christine said. He seemed very thoughtful, and he had a kind look in his eyes. Christine thought to herself. She liked him immediately.

"We are all thin up here." He said and smiled. "We have a great threshold of pain. We have a strong inner strength, resiliency and an iron determination to win! Those are our strong points. You have your bombs, we have the strength of the Vietnamese people behind us.

The United States has employed the most massive bombing attacks on Vietnam known to mankind. Your Country has employed the deadliest anti-personnel assault ever invented to kill and maim. You have released massive chemicals onto our land, on our people, and even on your own soldiers. You have destroyed the ecology of our land that will affect my Nation for decades. You shoot our livestock, destroy our crops, burn our villages, and uproot our villagers from their ancestral lands. How can you ever hope to win this War?"

"I came to Vietnam to help the wounded. I do not condone the actions of my Government. I have experienced fear from both sides. I have crawled under my bed at night when you launched mortars at my Hospital. I have watched US bomber planes fly over me not knowing if they planned to drop a 500-pound bomb upon me. I have seen beautiful, young men shot to pieces. I have seen their blood. I have heard their cries. I too have experienced sorrow and grief." Christine said.

"We are fighting for our Country. The United States Military does not belong here!"

Christine nodded. There was a silence.

"Why do you stay up in the mountains away from the fighting?" Christine asked.

Slowly Tung replied. "Our strategy is to attack the US in both the urban and rural areas so that we compel the United States Military to spread out its forces over a wide area. We continually attack the US everywhere and at any time. We create chaos for the enemy and we direct powerful blows at them. Right now, we are trying to draw your Military into the mountains where we fight best.

Our goal is for every Vietnamese no matter what age, sex, or status to become a fighter on one of these fronts: military, economic, political, or cultural. Our password is resistance. Every act, every poem, every song must be a bullet shot directly at the enemy. You will not win this War. As long as there is one of us left, we will continue to fight on.

'Nothing is more important than independence and freedom'. Those are the words from our leader, Ho Chi Minh. We are following his lead. This is known as a protracted War. Time is on our side. We are guerrillas. We engage in guerrilla warfare. 'When the enemy advances, we retreat. When the enemy tires, we attack'. These are the words of Mao Se Tung. The US soldiers call us cowards; the Chinese call us brilliant!" Tung smiled. "We are always looking for the enemy's weak spots. Your bombs, your cold heartless metal, your swift bullets are nothing to my people. Yes, time is on our side. It is our greatest asset!"

"But don't you miss your family and home?" Christine asked.

"Yes, we in the mountains all miss our families. I lost my wife and daughter in the Hanoi bombings. I lost my son on the Ho Chi Minh Trail. I lost another child at childbirth. Now I love Leli, but she cannot love so we go down this long treacherous path together. We want only to recover what is ours. That is our goal."

"I am sorry." Christine told him with compassion.

"Do you have any requests?"

"I want very much to go home!" Christine said earnestly.

"We will all go home soon." There was a faraway look in Tung's eyes. Both were silent.

"What do you think of the Vietnamese mountains?" He asked.

"I think they are beautiful! I love the way the trees grow all the way down the the steep gorges to the fast-moving river. Everything is so green and tall here. And I love when the clouds turn into mist and float amongst the trees like spirits wandering the land!" She smiled at Tung. He had a quiet presence and an unmistakable charisma about him.

"In my land, we believe in spirits. We call them lost souls."

"Why are they lost?" Christine asked.

"They have been taken from their ancestral homes, and they are trying very hard to find their way back home. My Country has known War for more than 20 years. We aspire to peace. But 'It is better to stand on your feet than to live on your knees'. We have a right to be independent and free!" He said with unshakable force.

"I want you to be free and to live in peace too." Christine said sincerely. She could see that what she had been through was nothing compared to the sorrows these people had endured.

Tung nodded a thank you. There was a silence again.

"Why does Yuri leave so often?" Christine asked.

"He helps us with logistics and surveillance. He is very brave. We are fortunate to have him here."

"Could he be hurt?"

"We are all at risk here."

"Could I meet with Leli? I would like very much to talk with her and tell her how sorry I am about her family."

Tung raised an eyebrow. He did not think their meeting would be a wise decision.

"Leli carries many burdens inside of her. I will let you know."

"I never knew this area was here." Christine said after a pause.

"This is our Meeting Hall in the forest. This is where we meet, train, sing, and gather. We are united and we have one goal." He looked at her with an intensity that was inspiring.

Christine stood up. "I am very glad that I met you. I hope that we can be friends." Christine said earnestly.

Tung stood up also. "We are friends." He said with goodwill in his voice and he bowed in Buddhist fashion.

Christine smiled at Tung. "Goodbye." She said and she walked slowly up the aisle past the many empty benches.

CHAPTER 26

Several days later when Christine was in the Great Cooking Hall for breakfast, a NFL cadre gave her a small white note. She opened it up. It was from Tung. In beautiful penmanship he wrote her a note in English asking her if she would visit with him at the Meeting Hall after her breakfast. She folded the note and put it in her pocket.

Army fatigues were designed for infantry on the move. Her fatigues had pockets everywhere! She had two pockets above her breasts, two pockets on her hips and two big pockets all the way down her pant legs. She put the note in her thigh pocket and got some breakfast. She brought the bowl outside and ate under a large banyan tree. When she was done, she headed for her meeting with Tung.

Tung was at his platform desk working. He saw Christine as she entered the meeting area.

"Good morning." He said pleasantly.

"Good morning." Christine said and smiled.

"Please sit down." Tung said and he stood up.

Christine sat on a bench and looked up at Tung.

"Do you know what the National Liberation Front is?" He asked.

"No."

"It is the force that is liberating our Country. This is the National Liberation Front's creed: 'Let us not be seduced by wealth, let us not be discouraged by poverty, let us not submit to force, let us suffer hardship now in order to enjoy happiness in the future'. We in the jungle are here to educate, mobilize, and organize the whole population in order that they may take part in the resistance. Do you know of General Giap?"

"No."

"He is our great Vietnamese General who follows Mao Se Tung's teachings: 'Is the enemy strong? One avoids him. Is the enemy weak? One attacks him'. General Giap tells us: 'Be secret, rapid, active; now in the East, now in the West; arrive unseen, leave unnoticed'." Tung smiled. "You have not heard of him?"

"No."

"General Giap believes that a Revolutionist must always be patient, calm, vigilant as he believes our heroic spirit, our huge sacrifices, and our will to win distinguishes our troops from all the others. He knows that neither difficulties, enemy bombings, and artillery fire can shake the iron will of the fighting National Liberation Front men and women. In fact the more we fight, the stronger we become!

Why do we fight? You ask. We are fighting to eliminate the inequities between the rich and the poor, we fight to expand educational opportunities for those who want it, we fight to improve health facilities, we fight to clothe and feed our people, we fight to push out the foreigners so we can reclaim Vietnam for the Vietnamese. What is wrong with this?" Tung asked.

"I cannot see anything wrong with it. It makes perfect sense." Christine said.

Tung smiled at her. "We are determined to win."

"I hope the War ends so we can all go home and lead happy and secure lives." Christine said.

"I wish this also." Tung replied. "Leli would like to meet with you."

"She does! I am so glad!" Christine said with joy. "When?"

"We will meet you down by the river where you and Yuri swim. I will send you a note tomorrow after breakfast."

"Thank you! Thank you so much, Tung!" Christine stood up. "I cannot tell you how grateful I am! I will see you tomorrow!" She said happily. She waved and walked up the long row of empty benches. There was a slight breeze. It was as if all the trees were nodding their approval in the Summer wind.

The note came the next day, and Christine went directly down to the river to her special swimming hole. Tung was standing apart from Leli as if he wanted to give both women plenty of space. As Christine approached them, Leli did not look up at Christine but stared down at the ground. She looked very delicate like fine porcelain. The two women faced each other.

Christine took a deep breathe. She knew this was not going to be easy. Leli had every right to spit in her face. This was a long shot; a gamble. But Christine had to take it. She did not want to live her life without at least trying.

"Tung, will you translate my words for me?" Christine asked softly. Tung nodded quietly.

"Leli," Christine began. "I want you to know how sorry I am about your family. It is a terrible story. One of which I am not proud."

Christine looked at Tung as he translated her words.

"Many Americans oppose this War. Many Americans at home are protesting and calling for an end to this terrible, terrible War. But those in charge keep prolonging it." Christine took Leli's hand. "From the bottom of my heart, I cannot tell you how sad I am about your family. What happened should happen to no one, and I am so sorry! I hope you can forgive my Country, and I hope you will let me be your friend." Christine asked her imploringly.

Leli looked up at Christine. "I sorry too." She said in broken English. Leli turned to Tung and said more in Vietnamese.

"She says she has suffered much and that she misses her family greatly and the smiles of her children, but it was wrong to try to hurt you and she too would like to be friends."

Christine still held Leli's hand with both of her hands. "Friends!" Christine said smiling at Leli. "I too would like to be friends! Thank you! Thank you so much!"

Christine gave Leli a quick hug. "Thank you!" Christine said again. She let go of Leli's hand. "Could we see each other again?" Christine asked Leli.

"Leli says yes." Tung said after Leli replied.

"Good."

Christine smiled and waved. She walked back to the cave. She did not want to overstay her welcome, but she went away happy and hopeful. She looked back only once, and she saw Tung embrace Leli and hold her tightly in his arms with the flowing mountain waters behind them rushing mightily to the Sea.

This was good. Christine thought. This was right. She felt so much better as she went up the mountain path.

CHAPTER 27

A week later another note was given to Christine at breakfast in the Great Cooking Hall. She opened it up. 'Leli would like to see you again. Would you meet us down by the swimming hole after breakfast'. The note was written beautifully in Tung's neat handwriting. Christine put the note in her breast pocket and headed down to the stream. Tung and Leli were both sitting by the river watching the water rush to the Sea.

"Hello!" Christine called out and waved.

Both Tung and Leli got up and smiled and waved back. They all stood together. Leli had something in her hand and she gave it to Christine. It was wrapped in the black cloth that the Viet Cong used to make their uniforms.

Christine took the bundle and unwrapped the cloth. In the middle of the cloth was a beautiful comb made out of seashells. At the top of the comb, several delicate seashells were attached in the shape of flowers. It was a lovely piece! Leli looked at Christine. Leli's eyes were happy. They were beaming.

"These are popular combs with the Vietnamese ladies. One of our cadres was near a coastal village on his duties, and he was able to purchase this comb for Leli. She wanted to give it to you as a gift." Tung said.

"It is so beautiful! I love it! Thank you so much, Leli. You are so sweet!" Christine said smiling at her. "You are right. I have so needed a comb. Yuri must think me an abomination with my hair always so tangled!"

Leli took the comb and started to comb through Christine's tangled blonde hair.

"Have you ever braided hair?" Christine asked.

Tung looked at Leli and translated.

"No." He said.

"Do you think you could braid my hair?" Christine asked.

Tung translated. Leli looked at Tung and replied.

"She said she would try."

"Good! So what we want to do is divide half of my hair on each side. Can you do that? Tung, I need some string or twine. Do you have any?"

"I will try to find some." Tung said and he went up the mountain trail.

Christine smiled at Leli. "Thank you for the comb. I love it!" Christine said. She knew Leli did not know what she had said. So Christine picked up the comb and placed it on her heart. "Thank you!" She said again. They both smiled at each other.

Tung came back with the twine. He watched the women carefully. They seemed happy and at ease with each other. Christine asked Leli to part her hair in the back. Then Christine tried to show her how to section the hair into three parts and braid it. But it was hard to show her with her own hair.

"Wait!" Christine said. "Let me braid your hair!" So Christine parted Leli's hair in the back, and separated it into three parts. She showed Tung so he could see what she was doing. Leli sat quietly as Christine braided one side of her long beautiful black hair. Tung watched carefully and nodded. Christine tied the braid at the end with twine. She braided both sides. When done, Leli's braids were thick and black and beautiful!

"Now we will braid your hair." Tung said and he showed Leli how Christine had braided her hair. Leli tried this way and that way, and Tung tried to help, but they both started laughing and could not stop. Christine could hear them laughing as they braided and unbraided her hair, and she started to laugh also so they were all breaking down with laughter.

"This is very hard." Tung said. Needless to say, he was not used to braiding hair especially blonde hair. He was the Chief Military Commander of all the National Liberation Front operations in South Vietnam. What did he know of braiding women's hair? But his desire to please Leli was enormous. Finally, they finished braiding Christine's hair. Both women looked at each other. The braids were fun and new and helped them move one step closer.

"Thank you for the comb and my new braids!" Christine said with her eyes glowing.

"We thank you." Tung said. A patch of sunlight showered down upon them. A little bird was singing in the trees. The soft sensuous air surrounded them. Christine could see Tung had enjoyed himself and he was happy for Leli. He liked seeing her laugh. He liked to see her eyes shine with joy and happiness. He was bursting and beaming inside. He wanted Leli to discover the beauty of life again. He wanted this so much!

"Take our picture, Tung!" Christine said.

"I have no camera." Tung looked confused.

"It is OK, just pretend." Christine said.

The two girls stood together each with their braided hair. They put their hands around each other's waist. Tung stepped back. He pretended to hold up the camera. Both women were smiling their glorious smiles. Tung clicked the camera.

"Got it!" Tung said and they all laughed gaily. That picture would forever be captured in their memories.

Christine wrapped up the comb in the black cloth. "Thank you so much! This is a wonderful present. Will we see each other again?" She asked.

Tung looked at Leli and asked her.

"Leli says that she would like that very much. You have made us very happy." Tung said.

"I am glad. I am very glad! You have made me happy too! Goodbye. I hope to see you soon!" Christine said. She waved and walked up the path.

Several days later, Christine went down to the Meeting Hall. Tung was at his desk working. Christine walked up the rows of empty benches.

Tung looked up.

"Good morning." He said pleased to see Christine. "We enjoyed being with you."

"I had such a nice time and thank you for the comb! I love it!" Christine said. "I would like to give Leli a present also. Would you help me?" Christine asked.

"I will try." Tung said.

"Could your cadre purchase some pink silk material in the town by the coast? I love the ao dais dresses that the Vietnamese women wear. They are so free and flowing. I would like to make two ao dais pink dresses so Leli and I can be sisters! Can you help me? I have a $20 American bill in my pocket. Please use this money to buy the silk. Will you?"

"Yes, I can try to do this for you. Our seamstresses can make the dresses. I am sure they would like to work on something other than Military uniforms."

"That would be wonderful! I need raspberry pink silk. Do you know what color of the inside of a watermelon looks like?"

"Yes."

"That is the color I need. I will need six yards of raspberry pink silk. Could you find that for me?"

"We will try our best."

"Thank you!" Christine said. "I can't wait! I think they will be beautiful. Bye, Tung. You are wonderful!"

Tung smiled. What men do for love. Tung thought and shook his head. But he also smiled broadly. He wanted so much to make Leli happy. Tung and Christine waved to each other and Christine left the Meeting Hall intent upon her plan.

In a weeks time, the silk arrived with great fanfare. It was a shimmering bolt of cloth and the pink color of the evening sky was beautiful! Christine loved to touch the silky fabric. The color was perfect! She could not wait!

Tung introduced her to the head seamstress of the National Liberation Force camp. She was an elderly Vietnamese woman with driving energy, flashing white teeth, and keen eyes. She wore a measuring tape around her neck, and she measured every inch of Christine.

The seamstress and Tung discussed the dresses at great length. They thought that Leli would be about the same size as Christine only a bit thinner and a bit shorter. The seamstress had made many ao dais in her day, and she was very pleased to be working on these dresses. The petite Vietnamese seamstress had very quick movements and she had an aura of professionalism about her. Tung told Christine that this elderly

Vietnamese woman loved the silk material, and she was confident she could make two beautiful dresses for them.

Christine was elated also! The soft, free moving dress would make her feel like a woman again. She was so tired of her dreary and very unattractive Army fatigues with their heavy material and baggy pants. Christine wanted to feel feminine, and she so wanted Leli to have a soft, free-flowing dress that was soft and feminine as well. She wanted Leli to be happy too!

The Vietnamese seamstress with the sharp eyes was very skilled. In two days time a note was given to Christine to meet Tung by the sewing machines after breakfast. When Christine arrived at the sewing area, Tung was already there.

There were five antique sewing machines in the jungle clearing under a huge banyan tree. The sewing machines were black and finely decorated with gold trim detail. The sewing machines came from a different era, and they looked like fine pieces of art. Each sewing machine was run by pedals. The Vietnamese could pedal forward if they wanted to sew; and they could pedal backward if they wanted to reinforce an area. Little cans of oil were placed here and there to make sure the machinery ran smoothly.

There were many bolts of light-weight, fast-drying black material stacked in baskets. The jungle thorny plants and tangled thickets snapped and ripped the Viet Cong's clothing. The sewing machines were always kept busy.

There were five seamstresses talking gaily in a sing song manner. Each had their own sewing machine. A group of ponchos hung from the trees as a changing area, and there was a large tarp that covered up everything when it rained. The seamstress with the flashing white teeth brought out the dress to show Christine. It was gently based together for the fitting. Christine smiled at this industrious woman. The elderly seamstress smiled back. She was proud of her work.

Tung showed Christine the ponchos where she could change. Christine went there and put on the dress. It felt so soft and light. She was jubilant! She came back out into the clearing radiant and happy! Both Tung and the seamstress studied the ao dais dress. They discussed it at great length. The seamstress would gather the seams of the dress and say something. Then Tung would take hold of the seams and say something else. Another discussion ensued. Tung was a perfectionist. He was a technician! It was as if he was planning one of his strategic operations!

Now the seamstress was kneeling on the ground trying to get the dress length correct. The head seamstress pinned the dress and Tung stepped back. No, that was not exactly right. Another long discussion ensued. Christine stood very still. She had no idea what they were saying. She was only the mannequin. But she loved the dress and she hoped Leli would love hers also.

"Tung, will you thank your seamstress for me, and tell her I think the dress is beautiful and I am so pleased!"

Tung translated everything and all parties were satisfied.

The great day had arrived. Tung sent word to Christine that the dresses were done and to meet he and Leli down by the river. Christine stopped by the Sewing Center and found the wonderful seamstress. The elderly Vietnamese woman brought out the two dresses and showed them to Christine with considerable pride. Christine loved them! The seamstress urged Christine to try on her new ao dais. Christine went behind the ponchos and put on the dress. It fit perfectly. Christine could not be happier! She came out to where the Vietnamese woman was standing and smiled. The elderly seamstress came up to Christine and inspected the dress. She ran her hand down the back and smoothed out the material. She checked the seams and the length, and she was delighted with the dress as well.

"Thank you!" Christine said. "Thank you! I love it!" Christine turned around in a circle and felt the shimmering material move easily about her. Christine pointed to herself and embraced herself so the Vietnamese woman would know how much she liked the dress. Christine picked up the other pink ao dais and headed for the river.

"Thank you!" She said again. "Thank you so much!" Christine said and waved.

Christine saw Tung and Leli near the river. Christine had on her beautiful ao dais and she carried Leli's dress on her arm. The sky was very blue, and the sensuous heat was warm and inviting. Christine smiled and waved and said hello to them as she came closer.

"I have brought you a present, Leli." Christine said and Tung translated for her. Christine held up the pink ao dais.

Leli touched the beautiful material and a glorious smile appeared on her face. She could not believe the dress was for her.

"Yes, this dress is for you. You see, it matches my dress. Now we can be sisters!" Christine exclaimed. "Try it on." Christine gave the dress to Leli with great excitement.

"Try it on behind the bamboo thicket." Tung suggested.

Leli looked at Tung. Then she looked at Christine. She could not believe her good fortune! She went over to the thicket.

"Thank you, Tung. You have made this all possible." Christine said.

"Leli likes the dress very much. It is good to see her smile." Tung said. "I thank you. The dress becomes you also." He added.

Christine looked down at the dress. It felt wonderful to wear.

"Your staff does excellent work!"

"Yes, they work very hard for our cause." Tung said and smiled.

Leli came back sparkling with happiness. She was overflowing with smiles. Leli gave Tung the most loving, caring, enduring look that Christine had ever seen. Tung was a very lucky man. Christine thought.

"Now we are alike." Christine said. "Tung take our picture again!"

Tung translated and everybody laughed. The girls hugged each other and smiled as Tung stepped back and took their picture.

"I hope you keep this dress always. It is a friendship dress so you know that all Americans do not believe in death and destruction." Christine squeezed Leli's hand and smiled while Tung translated what she had said.

"Leli says she thanks you, and that she will always keep the dress; and when she wears it, she will think of you."

"Thank you, Tung! Will I see you again?"

"Yes, yes!" Tung said and he smiled his gentle smile.

CHAPTER 28

The two women became friends. They would do wash together, they would prepare food together. Today they were sitting on the jungle floor wrapping bandages. Yuri came bounding up the trail. He had been away a long time. He was sunburned, his lips were chapped, he needed a haircut, he was thirsty, his uniform was torn, he was exhausted by the tension and the need for constant surveillance and deception.

Leli saw him coming along the trail.

"Hi Yuri!" She called out to him smiling and happy as she waved to him.

Yuri waved back and continued on his way. In an instant he stopped dead in his tracks and walked backwards. He halted again, and looked down at the two women in disbelief. He could not believe that they were laughing and giggling with each other as if they were the best of friends. Do fish fly? Maybe this War was made in heaven if two rivals could become friends? He thought to himself and he continued on his way.

Yuri, however, had noticed that Christine did not smile or wave to him. He had hoped that time would heal her. Apparently, it had not. He was not looking forward to his homecoming. He was not looking forward to it at all! He needed to wash, he needed to shave, he needed to eat, he needed to sleep, but most of all he needed peace.

When Christine walked into the cave, Yuri watched her carefully. His look was soft and searching but all he got back was hardness. There was no warmth or joy in her eyes. They were cold and bitter. He could see the loathing in her eyes. In his heart he had hoped for a reconciliation.

"Did you behave yourself?" He asked.

"Yes."

"And did you miss me while I was gone?" He asked factiously.

"No, I didn't." She said in a contemptuous manner and a little too quickly. It was the age-old game of wounds. You hurt me, so I will hurt you back. Yuri had been playing with her, but her words caused him pain, and they found their way deep into a spot where he was afraid to enter. He had tried for so long to control his emotions. Now they were raw and bruised and painfully in the open.

"Fine! Then we can maintain this distance that is continually between us." He said in disgust. He picked up his towel and soap and abruptly left the cave.

So he was back and now they both must endure this hell. Christine thought. Yuri had always been a gentleman, he had such excellent manners, he was compassionate, he was a good listener, he was always in good humor, and then all of a sudden he had turned into a monster. How could she trust him again? She wanted to, but how could she? And how could she ever forgive him? Did it matter? Did anything matter?

It was starting to turn dark outside and a slight drizzle was falling. Christine was confused and angry. She would tell him. She thought. When he came back, she would tell him how mean and brutal he had been, and how much she hated him! He had taken everything from her —her security, her trust, her caring; and he had left her used and humiliated. She would shout at him and throw that in his face. The cave was cold and damp. She just wanted to sleep. She wanted to sleep for a thousand years. But Yuri came back into the cave.

"Christine, we must have a truce. We cannot live this way in tension and hatred." He said.

Their eyes locked She said nothing. She did not want to talk to him. She did not want to look at him. She just wanted to be alone. She just wanted to sleep. She wanted only to shut out the world.

Yuri waited for Christine to say something, but she only looked at him with cold, frigid eyes full of contempt and distain. Yuri came towards her, and clasped her arm tightly almost dragging her to her feet. His eyes always so playful were now frozen like the great steppes of Russia under a hard winter snow.

"I will not have this!" He said fiercely. "You can take your hostile stares and your cold, boney fingers and live outside with the insects and the wild animals where you belong!" He grabbed her roughly by the arm and almost dragged her from the cave. He took her out to a bamboo cage that had always stood empty in the jungle.

Yuri did not realize how strong he was. He opened the door of the cage and flung her in. A heavy rain was beginning to fall as he slammed the cage door and walked angrily back into the cave. It was dark now. Christine had stumbled, and her knees and her fingers went deep into the mud of the cage floor as she tried to brace herself from the fall. The rain was coming down all around her as if to humiliate her even further. Her head was bent downward. She slowly got to her feet and wiped her muddy hands on the back of her Army fatigues.

Christine looked at her surroundings. She had often seen this cage and had wondered what it was for. Now she knew. The cage was six feet long, six feet high, and six feet wide. It was solidly made of bamboo. There was no roof only the strong bamboo poles on top and the stars to cover her. But there were no stars out tonight. There was just a cold, relentless rain. Christine had wanted to be alone. Now she had gotten her wish.

The bamboo cage was just long enough to string a hammock from end to end. The hammock stood empty. Christine climbed into it. Right now, she felt she was at the edge of the world. The air was cold. She moved into the fetal position, and tucked her knees up to her stomach. She tried to rock herself as she lay awake. She hoped sleep would take her away from this. She was cold and miserable and more than that, she was alone. She felt more alone than she had ever felt before. All she could do was just close her eyes and feel the rain pound every inch of her body.

But she was not alone! How many War-weary Viet Cong were moving along the Ho Chi Minh Trail carrying their War burdens for the Fatherland, and how many Viet Cong had been caught in this rain as well? And they would endure the rain knowing that they would have to traverse another twelve miles tomorrow along a very rough and dangerous terrain that would be slippery and wet. Their loads would be heavy, and all the while they had the US Calvary bearing down upon them.

And then there was Yuri; safe and warm in his cave. She had not realized what a powerful force he was. He could do anything he wanted with her. Prisoner of love, prisoner of War, it was all the same. He had total control over her. She had never realized how good her life had been.

Before she had the freedom of the camp, she could go to the stream, she could go to the cave; but now she was locked in this small bamboo cage with no protection from the elements. She knew when the rain stopped, the sun would be her next enemy. It would beat down upon her harshly and the the insects would continually plague her.

She now saw Yuri in a totally different light. He had been her redeemer, he allowed her to share his quarters, he had given her his protection, he had shared his meals with her, he gave her the freedom of the camp, he supplied her with clean water and bedding, he gave her the shelter of the cave, he made her smile. He had eased the pain of her captivity. He had tried to help her through her loneliness. Why had she been so mean to him? She had always missed him when he was gone, and now she was alone; totally and completely alone.

She had brought this all upon herself. She had been contemptuous and hateful. He had apologized, and had asked for forgiveness, and she had spurned him and threw it in his face. How hurtful that must have been. And of course, she could not stop. Her cold and hostile eyes said everything. Had she been Yuri, could she have withstood such treatment? No, she was the one who was wrong! Did he not rescue her from the inner cave? Did he not apologize several times for the pain he had caused her? Did he not make amends for his actions? And she, like a hard-hearted shrew, a malicious and hateful shrew; could not even say: 'Yes Yuri, I forgive you. Let us live in peace. Let us find a better way'!

Now look where she was. She had lost everything only because she could not reach out to him half way. What a fool she was! Yuri had always been so happy, amicable, playful. He had always had abundant energy and relentless optimism. She had never seen the fierce anger in his eyes as she saw last night. She had always thought of him as caring and protective, but he had a dark side that was truly frightening.

She tried to rock herself in the hammock to soothe her pain. She was wet, she was hungry, she was cold, she was alone in a hostile land; and she knew now how lucky she had been. Why did she think that total destruction could resolve all of her problems? She was a fool. She was such a fool! She had gambled, and now she had lost everything! Even

Yuri's affections. Yes, she knew Yuri cared for her. How many times did he come out from nowhere to protect her, and all she could do was give him the back of her hand and a cold, forbidding look. She was good at that. She was the frozen one; the cold-hearted Christine. She knew how to dish out the anger. She was an expert at it!

Christine started to think about the wild horses in Montana. How magnificent they were! What a great feeling it was to be free! She looked longingly at the cave entrance. In the dark, she could see the faint glow of Yuri's lantern. That was odd. Yuri was always so good at using his lantern sparingly. Christine rocked herself and closed her eyes. Now and then she would fall asleep, but she would always wake up with a jerk. She was startled at her surroundings until she became fully awake and remembered that she was an unwanted outcast.

The sky began to lighten and turn a coral pink. Christine was now fully awake, and she knew she needed to go to Yuri. She carefully watched the cave opening in hopes of seeing him. Christine got out of the hammock and went to the door of the bamboo cage. She was going to call out to anyone. But when she put her hand on the bamboo door, it opened. It had never been locked! Yuri had never locked the door. He had let her make her own decisions. She could have tried to escape again. She could have stayed in the cage and refused to leave, or she could go to Yuri and ask him to forgive her.

She knew what she needed to do. She knew her hair was wet, and her fatigues were soaked and dirty, and that she looked a fright, but she had no reservations about her appearance or what she would say to Yuri.

CHAPTER 29

Christine headed directly for the cave. She entered the cave opening slowly. Yuri was dressed, and he was sitting on his sleeping bag with his back against the wall. His feet were crossed in front of him. He was writing in his Military journal. When Christine entered the cave, he looked up coolly.

"May I come in?" She asked.

"Yes."

"May I speak with you?"

"Yes. Sit here." He made room for her on his sleeping bag.

"I am very wet."

"It does not matter. Sit." Yuri pointed palm down to his sleeping bag and touched it.

Christine sat down with her back against the wall. Their shoulders almost touched each other. Yuri's long legs were spread out before him. Christine looked directly at him.

"I am sorry for the way I have treated you." Christine said. "I just felt so used and humiliated by what happened, and my anger prevented me from even hearing your apologies. I have made life very difficult for you, and for that I am truly sorry! You have given me so many things that I have taken for granted. I know that you did not ask for me to be here, and that you are not the one who is keeping me here. I only wish that I had a larger and more gracious heart so that I could have accepted your apologies."

Christine paused. This was so hard! What if he threw this back in her face? What if he said no!

"May I come back?" She asked.

"Is that what you want?"

"Yes."

"Will you be civil?"

"Yes, I will."

"No more long and angry faces."

"No."

"I have fed you, protected you, and I have tried to keep you safe. What I did was very wrong, and I cannot tell you how sorry I am. I never meant to hurt you." Yuri said earnestly. "I am weary of War. I am tired of seeing the destruction and mayhem, the young men being blown to pieces, the children and the elderly screaming for their lives, the countryside and the culture being ripped to shreds, people's lives being torn apart and destroyed, and I am very angry over Misha's death.

I was out of my mind with drink and rage. I remember dropping my pants and being as erect as erect can be and wanting you as I have wanted you for so long. I had absolutely no right to violate you and take my anger out on you as I did. That is something I will always regret. Lust, drink, rage are all very bad combinations. Can you forgive me as well?" Yuri asked.

"Yes, I can and I will."

"Can we repair our friendship, and live in harmony for the time we have left together?"

"Yes." Christine said because that was what she wanted.

"Good. Then you can come back. I will do everything I can to respect you." Yuri affirmed to himself as well as to Christine. "But the moment you become distant and unruly, then we will need to make other arrangements." Yuri was firm on that.

201

Over time the ice began to thaw. Every once in a while Yuri would just look at Christine and smile, and she would smile back. Yuri was overly attentive to Christine. He would bring her bouquets of flowers from the jungle and interesting rocks that he found along the way. They tried to be polite and considerate of each other. They both wanted to repair their broken relationship. They began to swim and eat together again. And sometimes they would take short hikes into the jungle.

"Come with me." Yuri said one evening.

"Where are we going?"

"Up to our perch to watch the sunset."

They climbed the steep rocks and sat down on the limestone ledge that overlooked the whole valley. The jungle was growing dark and the sky was flaming with radiant colors. The river below reflected the sky, and it became a pink coral river that twisted its way along the valley floor. It was peaceful on the mountain ledge. Yuri and Christine sat in silence and drew in the magnificent evening sky.

"How did you meet Tung?" Yuri asked.

"I accidentally ran into him. He is very polite."

"He is very much in love with Leli." Yuri said.

"Yes, he told me that. He also told me that he was responsible for my being here. Why is that?" Christine asked.

"How well do you know men?" Yuri asked her.

"Not very well. Men are so difficult to understand. Why did the man I was so in love with need to be with me? He had a wife who slept next to him in his bed every night. Why must he have me as well? Why did he have to drag me through the dirt? Why did he have to break my heart?" Christine asked wearily.

There was a long silence.

"I will try to explain the dilemma Tung was in. Tung felt that Leli was favoring me with too much attention so he tried to provide a distraction; something that would totally preoccupy me while I was in the camp. You were part of the solution to his problem. This is known as camp politics." Yuri tried to explain the situation delicately.

"Do you have feelings for Leli?"

"No. I hardly know Leli, and she is still half crazy with grief. The loss of her family hangs around her neck like a giant weight. It is the heaviest of anchors. She is not fully recovered. But Tung loves her, and he will do anything for her!

I also work very closely with Tung. He is one of the top people in the Vietnamese National Liberation Front for all of Vietnam. He plays a key role in the fate of his Nation. I would never do anything to endanger that relationship. Tung has nothing to fear from me. I think he realizes that now and he also understands the difficulty of your situation.

The Viet Cong had been watching your base camp for many weeks. When the US Army sent in the surgical unit and all of the medical supplies, Tung knew he had to strike. He desperately needed those medical supplies. The Viet Cong watched you in particular for several days. No one wanted to kill you. It was Tung who decided to spare your life. That one decision solved two of his problems."

"In America we would call that using one stone to kill two birds." Christine said.

"Exactly!"

"I think that sounds rather cold-hearted and calculating."

"That, my dear, is what War is. No one can afford to be nice in War. You owe your life to Tung."

"I like Tung very much!"

"Do you have feelings for him?" Yuri smiled at her playfully.

"No, he works very closely with a sweet Russian, and I would never ever endanger that relationship! I have worked too hard to be this dear Russian's friend and to build his respect."

"That is good."

"Will this War ever end?" Christine asked in a more serious tone.

"Yes. it will come to an end. It is a War that cannot last forever. You Americans will either run out of money or men. You have already sent your best and your brightest men, and someday people will stop lending you money because your Country will have become bankrupt. There will be a small footnote in the history books: 'They were once a great Nation, but they spent all of their wealth on death and destruction'."

"I hate the bloodshed." Christine said.

"We all do; I, Tung, the Vietnamese people! It is time for the United States to go home!"

"Yes. It is time."

"How did you make friends with Leli?" Yuri asked.

"I thought about what you said. I thought about what Leli had gone through. I tried to put myself in her place, and I just wanted her to know how sorry I was for her family and for the enormous, long-lasting pain. So I asked Tung if I could meet her. He was skeptical at first, but I think they talked it over, and Tung set up a meeting. I am so glad he did!"

"I am proud of you, Christine. I know you felt very threatened."

"I turned just when the knife blade was coming down upon me. If you had not been there, I would have been dead!"

"I am glad you extended your hand and took that enormous step. It takes a very strong and courageous person to do that."

"Yuri, I am so glad I had the opportunity to apologize to Leli. I am so ashamed of my Country. I am so sorry she has gone through so much agony and hurt!"

"Yes, but she is doing better now. I understand Leli gave you a beautiful comb."

"Yes! I was so touched! And I had some money in my pocket from when I was captured. I gave the money to Tung and asked him if he could secure a bolt of fine silk for me. His cadre came back with the most beautiful silk material I have ever seen, and the seamstress in the camp was able to make matching ao dais dresses for Leli and me so we could be twins. So we could be sisters!"

"Tung told me that." Yuri said.

Women think that men do not talk. But Tung gave Yuri a complete and detailed rendition of everything that happened between the two women.

"Tung was somewhat torn because North Vietnam looks on the ao dais garment as a symbol of the ruling classes." Yuri said.

"They do? But the dresses are so feminine and so flowing and graceful!"

"Tung came from an upper-class family in Vietnam so he knows and appreciates the finer things in life. He has always loved the ladies in their beautiful ao dais and he wanted that for Leli. It reminds him of a time when life in Vietnam was secure and pleasant and good.

Tung's Father was a plantation owner. He was very entrepreneurial. He became, shall we day, French. He even turned Catholic. When the French colonized Vietnam, they imported rice from aboard and destroyed the Vietnamese rice market. At the same time, the French heavily taxed the Vietnamese rice farmers. The rice farmers could no longer afford to live on their land due to the low prices they were getting for their rice, and they could not afford to pay their taxes. Eventually, the Vietnamese rice farmers were forced to sell their land.

Tung's Father and the French were right there buying up the land at an enormously discounted price. You might say the French and market forces helped to destroy the village life of Vietnam. The rice farmers were forced to work on French plantations and French mines for almost nothing.

Tung was sent to France to study. He learned about liberty, self-determination, and equality for all. But when Tung looked at the Vietnamese population, he did not see the French rulers practicing the same French ideals. Tung only saw the hardship and the pain of the Vietnamese people. So Tung came back to Vietnam a true radical. He was determined to make Vietnam free again and to let the Vietnamese people decide their own fate.

It is not that Tung hated his Father. It is just that he had a wider view of life than just self, family, and wealth. Tung wants the Vietnamese to have a secure life again. He wants his people to be educated, to have healthcare, and to have a just and fair legal system. He wants the Vietnamese to be free of hunger, to be adequately clothed, and to be free from aggression. This is his life struggle. This is his cause. 'Conquer famine, conquer ignorance, conquer the enemy'! For now, that is what Tung and Leli live for."

"We are not helping them, are we?" Christine said.

"No, you and I are using him and he is using us."

"Will we ever get off of this odd merry-go-round?"

"Let us just concentrate on making things better between Christine and Yuri."

"I would like that. I would like that very much!" Christine said.

The soft light had come and gone. The moon was elegant in the sky and shone down upon them. They walked back hand in hand. Peace and harmony flowed between them.

The next evening huge storms came rolling in from the Sea. The monsoon season had started. Mighty thunderbolts shook the earth and the sound was frightening. It was as if the earth was breaking in two from the booming crash of the thunder.

"If you are afraid, Christine. You can come over here. I will not hurt you."

The crashing thunder was frightening. Christine did not hesitate. She picked up her sleeping bag and brought it over to Yuri's side of the cave, and they listened to the thunderstorm together. Both were sitting on their sleeping bags with their backs against the cave wall watching the sheets of torrential rain come down in front of the cave opening. Lightning bolts shot across the dark sky in an amazing display of jagged electricity. A huge thunderbolt cracked over them. Christine leaped into Yuri's arms and he held her tightly. Every time the thunder roared, they held each other tighter.

They sat quietly watching the rain, and they felt warm and secure in each other's arms as they watched the lightning dance across the cavern walls. Both were lost in their own worlds while they watched the storm move through. They both knew Mother Nature would not harm them. But of mankind? Of that they were not so sure.

The storm began to die down.

"If you are still frightened, you can sleep here tonight. I will behave myself." Yuri said.

Christine was too tired to move. "Thank you." She said, and she got into her sleeping bag. She went to sleep instantly.

In the morning when Christine awoke, she saw Yuri watching her. She smiled at him and he smiled back. Something special had been exchanged. They spent a carefree day together, and in the evening, they shared a wonderful meal with hot green tea. But the next morning when Christine woke up, she saw Yuri packing. She drew her sleeping bag around her shoulders and leaned her back against the cold cave wall. Yuri was standing by the cave opening.

"Why do you linger?" She asked him.

Yuri's head was bowed. "I will be gone a long time. I was hoping for a kiss."

Their eyes met. Christine had on her nightie but her feet and legs were bare. When she laid back the covers, she could feel the cold, piercing air clamp down upon her, but she didn't care. She moved swiftly towards Yuri and their lips met. He kissed her softly and beautifully. It was a kiss she would never forget. Their eyes held each other for a long time. Yuri put his hand softly on Christine's cheek.

He gave her a goodbye kiss and picked up his knapsack. He was gone again. Once the cave had been warm and alive. Now it was cold and empty.

CHAPTER 30

The days moved very slowly. Christine and Yuri had worked hard to rebuild their withered relationship. Now Yuri was gone. Christine did not know where he was or when he would return. She remembered the warm Summer nights when they would sit on their mountain perch and look out over the vast valley below. They would talk intimately of their lives and their thoughts. They would look up at the moon and the stars. Softly, the mountain breezes would caress them.

Christine missed Yuri. She depended on him and he always made her smile. When she kissed him, it came from deep within her heart. It was a force that was urgent and unstoppable. Now he was gone.

Sometimes Christine would catch herself waiting for Yuri. At times she would feel a bitter disappointment on coming into the cave and finding it dark and empty. She missed his big stretches in the morning, and the way he rubbed his cheeks after a long march which always produced a sandpapery sound; and she knew that meant his battery-powered shaver would soon be coming out of his knapsack. She remembered the odd faces he would make while shaving, and how tidy and neat he always was on his side of the cave. But the days turned into weeks and still he did not return.

Christine would go down to the river. The stream was wild up in the mountains and it swiftly cut past the rocks on its way downstream. Christine loved to watch it flow by. She remembered how unsure and afraid she was of Yuri. In the beginning, she had an ice-cold heart that was wrapped in barbed wire. But somehow Yuri was able to break through her steel mantel. He had become a friend and now...admit it, she thought to herself, her feelings for him ran deep. Her feelings were strong and overwhelming. There was some physical force that kept propelling her toward him. In the night, in the day, it was a constant drum beat. Is that what one kiss can do? Do you continue to go on a lifetime of wanting? She wondered.

She knew she needed to stop relying on him, she needed to stop missing him, she needed to stop caring for him. She was losing herself to him. She was becoming trapped and entangled and lost. Lost in an intensity and an emotional depth that was hard to navigate and difficult to let go of. Now she was always on edge. It was the constant wanting that was so unsettling. But she was afraid too. She knew how vulnerable she was. She feared being crushed and broken and shattered. Could she bear such pain and torment again?

The camp had thinned out. Even Leli was on a mission somewhere carrying supplies. In the past, the Viet Cong were good to Christine. They smiled and nodded to her. They gave her food. They did not hurt her. They seemed like a peaceful people. She saw them resting in their hammocks, sitting together playing cards or swimming or fishing or just relaxing under the hot Indochina sun. Christine was not afraid of them anymore. There were guns all over the camp, but no one seemed to be hostile towards her. There were both men and women Viet Cong in the camp. Either they were sleeping or they were working. Everyone played a role. They were on a mission for Uncle Ho and they were focused on their goal! This was the other side of the War. The side that held the collective pain.

Night after night, Christine sat at the cave opening waiting for Yuri's return. Then one night he did return with all the others. It was dark out and Christine could hear men talking rapidly. There were shouts and distant wailing. Flashlights were moving around in the dark. Christine crept outside. She could see the remnants of a fierce battle come crawling and limping into the camp. The night air was clear, and there was a brisk wind blowing, but no one noticed. As the Viet Cong fighters reached the safety of the camp, they would sink to the ground. The soldier's clothes were torn and caked with blood.

They had been severely beaten. Guns were lying on the ground, bloodstained bandages were everywhere, medicine bottles lay fallen and empty. Tired and exhausted men staggered passed her. They were soaked and cold and defeated. Everywhere she looked, she was surrounded by torment. Men were holding their wounds and groaning. They were crying out for help. They were calling for their families.

Christine rushed to the camp hospital for a medical bag and a flashlight. She helped the nearest fighters to her. She opened up their shirts, cleaned and packed their wounds, generously applied disinfectants and antibodies, and bandaged the men's injuries. She gave them water and tried to make them comfortable. She moved on as quickly as she could. There were so many wounded, so many in pain.

She had never seen a battle like this. Usually, the Viet Cong attacked and slipped away. This offensive must have been planned for weeks. Is that why Yuri was gone? Christine couldn't think of that now. She tried to help those most in need. There were Viet Cong medics working with her throughout the night. They struggled to help everyone.

When the dawn had arrived and Christine was totally exhausted from the night, she saw from the corner of her eye four Viet Cong carrying a stretcher into her cave. A laser beam of fear shot through her body.

"Oh my God, not Yuri! Please not Yuri!" She cried, and she quickly picked up her medical bag. She hurried to the cave entrance and entered.

CHAPTER 31

When Christine entered the cave, she stopped immediately. Oh my God, it was Yuri! Beautiful Yuri, strong invincible Yuri! How could this be? He was wounded. His skin was yellow and his lips were blue. Was he breathing? Was he dead? Christine quickly took his vital signs. She picked up two wool US Army blankets from a corner of the cave and folded them in half. She wanted to make sure the cold stone floor of the cave would not chill Yuri's broken body. She placed his sleeping bag on top of the blankets and motioned to the Vietnamese men to lift Yuri's body onto the sleeping bag. They took the heavy body off of the stretcher and laid it on the makeshift bed.

Yuri had lost a great deal of blood. The Viet Cong and Christine looked down at Yuri's lifeless body. Christine's heart was melting in two. Why of all men, Yuri? The grief she felt was overwhelming! Christine thanked and waved to the three Vietnamese men as she gently held the sleeve of the fourth man. The men left the cave with the simple stretcher. Christine motioned to the fourth Vietnamese man to help her undress Yuri. They took off his trousers. There were no wounds or marks on his lower body just massive amounts of dried blood. Christine gently unbuttoned Yuri's shirt. It was caked with blood and glued to his skin.

With the help of the Vietnamese man, they were able to gently remove Yuri's shirt. Yuri did not move. Dried blood was all over his chest. The bandage over his wound was red and bloody. The Vietnamese man helped Christine move Yuri's body to his side. She could see where the powerful bullet had exited his back. That was good!

She would not have to enter his body and probe for the bullet. But had the bullet caught a lung or broken a bone? She could not tell. She could see the pain had been intense and that Yuri had lost a lot of blood. His pulse was very weak. Could Yuri die? That was impossible! That was unthinkable. No, please God, don't let him die!

Once the Vietnamese man and Christine had moved Yuri onto his back, she thanked the Viet Cong fighter with all of her heart. He bowed to her out of respect and left the cave with dignity. Now Christine was alone with the fallen Yuri. His face was ashen and his lips were still blue. As the light flickered on the cave wall, there was an eerie presence in the room. Was Yuri that close to dying? Was death circling over him and waiting to lift up his spirit to the heavens above? Christine knelt beside him and took his hand.

"You must fight for your life, Yuri. Everything is up to you." Christine pleaded. Christine looked down at Yuri's wounded body. His eyes were closed and his breathing was shallow. Christine tucked his hand in and covered him. She knew she must have hot water to wash and clean her hands first, and wash and clean his wounds.

"Please, Yuri stay strong! I am not leaving you. I will be back. I need hot water for your wounds." Christine said and she rushed to the Great Cooking Hall. Christine thought of all the times she had been unkind to Yuri and how difficult she had been. She was the frozen Madonna; the cold one, and he had walked right into her heart and had opened it up. Now he lay dying.

"Please let him live, God. Please!" Christine begged.

Once back in the cave with the hot water beside her, she gently washed Yuri's body. Now she could see his large, gaping wound. Why must mankind be so brutal? She wondered. It was so difficult to understand. Christine softly rubbed his wounds with disinfectant and

213

bandaged both sides of his body. She gently washed and dried his face. He did not stir. Christine slipped her hand into his and pressed it.

"Yuri, you must continue to fight throughout the night!" She implored, and she placed his hand gently down. Christine covered up his clean body with the warm sleeping bag and placed another warm blanket on top of him. She placed both of her hands on him and closed her eyes.

"Everything is up to you now, Yuri. You must fight for your life, my dearest one. You must not give up! I have come to love you, to care for you. Please Yuri, please! I beg of you with all my heart, you must will yourself to live!" She would watch over him. She would pray for him, but in the end, it was his will and his spirit and his drive to live that would get him through these most difficult hours.

There was no response from Yuri. He lay as a dead man lays. There was nothing more that Christine could do. She had been up all night tending to the others. She brought her sleeping bag over from the other side of the cave and placed it next to Yuri. She would watch over him. She would stay by his side, but right now she needed to sleep. She must remain strong.

She placed water and a canister near him. She left the lantern on because she did not want Yuri to wake up in the dark. Not now! He had become precious to her and she had always taken him for granted. There was a foreboding in her heart as she got into her sleeping bag. Would Yuri make it through the day? She did not know. If he called out, she would be close to him. But he was far from that. How far? She had no way of knowing.

Christine woke up in the late afternoon. She looked at Yuri. He did not move, but he was still alive! She could hear his troubled breathing. She got up and made sure his covers were securely around him and that he was warm. Tung came slowly into the cave. Christine looked up. She was surprised to see him. He was carrying some Vietnamese soup in a US made thermos. The United States was fighting three wars. One on the battlefield, one for the fight for supplies and weaponry, and one fighting the corruption of the South Vietnamese Government. Tung handed the soup to Christine. She could see the strain and worry in his eyes.

"How is he?" Tung asked quietly.

"The wound is ugly. The bullet went through him cleanly, but he has lost a great deal of blood. He is very weak, and I do not know if there was any damage internally."

"I have brought some Vietnamese soup. It is medicinal and very healing."

"Thank you, Tung. You are so sweet!"

"Thank you for helping our wounded. I know you worked throughout the night."

"I do not take sides in War. I am here only to help the wounded. That is my oath." Christine said. But Christine did not tell Tung how difficult it was to nurse these men back to good health so that they could go back out and slaughter each other. This was the cruelest of fates and the supreme irony of War.

"We thank you all the same. So many of my people are hurting. I thank you again." Tung said and left abruptly.

Christine thought how difficult this must be for Tung. He had planned everything, and it was he who had sent his fellow Vietnamese to their final destinies. Christine went over to Yuri and laid back the covers. She wanted to make sure that there was no more bleeding coming from his wounds. No, all of the bandages were clean and white. She carefully laid the sleeping bag around him again.

Yuri opened his eyes.

"Yuri, oh my God, Yuri!" She cried. Christine was elated! She was overjoyed! Just to see him open his eyes! She touched his hair and stroked his forehead. "Oh Yuri!" She smiled at him. "I am so happy!"

Yuri blinked at her in response. He hadn't even the strength to smile.

"Tung brought you some wonderful, healing medicinal soup that has magical powers to make you well. Do you think you could swallow some?" Christine asked.

Yuri nodded.

Christine quickly turned his knapsack into a fluffy pillow and gently raised his head. She poured a little bit of soup into the thermos cup, and she tasted it first to make sure it was not too hot. Christine moved very close to Yuri, and tenderly held his head. She tipped the cup very slowly so just a bit of soup went into his mouth. He swallowed it. It went well! She tried for more. That too went down. Good! She thought to herself; he can take liquids! How the smallest things can bring so much joy! Christine was able to get four swallows into Yuri. Then he drifted off to sleep again. Let him sleep she thought. He needs to sleep! I can go and help the others. She knew he had crossed one tiny milestone. She was so happy!

Christine went straight to the Meeting Hall to tell Tung that Yuri had opened his eyes, and had taken some of the soup. She was jubilant! She turned down the path to the meeting area. When she arrived, she saw Tung sitting at his desk in the open air with his head in his hands. This must be so hard on Tung. Christine thought. She felt for him. It must be so difficult to see the decimation of your troops brought about by your planning and decision making. It must be so hard to feel defeat! Her heart went out to him. She so callously had been thinking only of

216

her own concerns today. She had not given any thought to Tung and the tremendous sense of responsibility and failure he must feel since his loss. Christine went quickly to him and gently placed her hand on his shoulder. He knew she was there.

"My people have suffered so much."

"I know Tung. Soon this will be over and we can all go home." How War-weary theVietnamese people must be. Christine thought.

"Leli has not returned." He said.

A chill went through Christine's body. She had only thought of how hard it must be for a leader to see the devastating results from a decision that he had made. She had not even given a thought that Leli was also in danger, and how difficult this must be personally for Tung.

"Leli is brave. She is very resourceful! We must have heart. You and I must be strong for them!" She told him. She tried to comfort Tung. From his back, she put her arms around his shoulders and hugged him tenderly.

"Everything will turn out well. I came to tell you that Yuri opened his eyes!"

Tung dropped his hands and slowly raised his head. The determination came back into his eyes. "We will fight on. We must repair and rise again." He said quietly. Those were difficult words to say after so much slaughter and destruction. He was tired, he was weary, but he could not and would not give up. Not now!

"Yuri is resting, Tung. I am going to make my nurse's rounds. How can I keep my hands clean?"

"I will find someone to bring you hot water and soap. After you wash with each wounded soldier, he can throw out the water and bring fresh warm water back to you. Do you have enough antibodies and disinfectants?"

"Yes." Christine said and she paused for a moment. "We must remain strong, Tung. We must not lose hope. We must have faith!" She placed her hand on his hand.

Tung quietly nodded.

This must be one of Tung's darkest hours. Christine thought to herself as she left the long row of empty benches. He seemed so disheartened and in such distress.

Christine came back to the cave after helping the other wounded. It was now dark out and she had stopped at the Great Cooking Hall to pick up something to eat. When she entered the cave, Yuri was still asleep. She ate and went to bed. In the morning when Christine awoke, Yuri was awake.

"How can I help you, Yuri? Would you like some water or some soup?"

"Water." Yuri said faintly.

Christine got out of her sleeping bag and went over to his knapsack. It had worked well before. She gently raised his head and tipped the cup up slowly to his lips. He was able to take several swallows of the water. Christine caressed his hair.

"Yuri, I think the soup did wonders for you. Could you try some more? I am sure it is still warm."

Yuri nodded. Christine opened the thermos of soup and poured some of it into the cup. She tipped it slowly to Yuri's lips. He took several swallows again and she let him rest.

"Your color is looking so much better, my darling one! I am overjoyed that you are awake!" Christine told him, and she softly stroked his hair.

Yuri closed his eyes but he was not asleep.

"Shall I turn down the lantern?" Christine asked him.

Yuri shook his head. He reached out and took her hand. He brought her hand to his lips and kissed it. "Thank you." He said weakly.

"Oh my God, Yuri! Please get better! I will be good! I will do anything you want, only please, you must make yourself strong again!" She implored him. But Yuri's eyes closed and he had drifted away.

Christine looked briefly at his bandages and covered him up again so that he was warm. She had to remind herself that our bodies are miraculous creations, and they have amazing powers to heal themselves. She knew Yuri was strong. She knew he would come through this. She must have faith. She must believe!

But later when Christine was gone, Yuri woke up again. The Coleman lantern was lit and he was alone in the cave. The pain made everything clear. He could see the textured lines in the rocks and the dark moisture of the cave walls. Then Yuri saw the whole room in its entirety. It seemed like a death tomb. He followed the edges of the light with his eyes. He was fighting now; he was fighting for his life.

A warm sea washed over him. His mind kept delving back to the past. He was in Russia. He could see the cherry trees. They were in full bloom along the river. The trees were so fragrant! Why must he leave now? The night was alive with the songs of nightingales and the melting of the Winter snows. The whole mountainside was covered with tiny white cherry blossoms. The smell was delicious! Spring was like an enormous breathe of fresh air!

He loved the land, he loved the people. All of the old memories came flooding back. There was his Mother. But where was his Father? Oh yes, his Father died in the War defending the Soviet Union from attack. War and more war. It was an endless game that accomplished nothing but death and devastation and heartache. He closed his eyes and drifted off.

CHAPTER 32

The days went by and Yuri did recover. He began to sit up and eating became easier. Leli also survived uninjured and had made it back to camp. She had stayed behind to help the wounded during those difficult hours after the battle.

One day when Christine was changing Yuri's bandages, he was watching her closely.

"Why do you look at me so?" She asked him.

"Because you are beautiful!"

Christine blushed. "Now I know you are better."

"Why?"

"Because you are starting to tease me again."

Yuri smiled. "No, you are very beautiful!"

"And are my fingers still cold and boney?" Christine wanted to know.

"No! I love your fingers" And he picked up each of her hands and kissed every one of her fingers tenderly. "I love each and every one of your fingers!" He assured her.

Christine laughed. Yuri always made her smile. "You are such a flirt!" She said and put her arms around him sweetly and kissed him on the cheek.

"I love you, Yuri." Yuri beamed his beautiful smile. "I know you are still very weak, but we must get you up and walking." Christine told him. "I will help you up."

Yuri's legs were strong, but his chest was still very tender, and his body needed to replenish itself. He was able to get up, but he leaned heavily on Christine. They walked down to the far end of the cave and back. That was all Yuri could manage.

"Yuri broken toy." He said.

"No! Yuri is healing and is making great progress!"

"Yuri needs jumper cables."

"No, Yuri is strong and is becoming stronger!" Christine assured him.

"You are my Saint! Saint Christina! I have the will and the power to move, but nothing happens."

"Your health will all come back in due time, Yuri. You must not expect too much."

Yuri did recover. It took him weeks to regain his strength. Each day Christine washed and re-bandaged his wounds. One day Yuri smiled at her and watched her intently as she worked.

"You must still be sick." She teased him.

"Why is that?" He asked.

"You are being so nice to me."

"I can be nice. I can be very nice, but you never give me a chance!" He placed his hand under her chin as if he was going to kiss her lips, but he did not. He just looked at her in a searching manner.

She moved away from him.

"Are my wounds better?" He asked.

"Yes, they are coming along very well."

"Thank you Christine for caring for me."

Christine looked at him intensely. Did he not realize the agony she had been through when he was so near death?

Every day Christine would make Yuri get up and walk, and she would make him sit in the sunlight with his bandages off so that the sun's rays would help heal his torn and shattered body. Slowly Yuri became stronger. As he became stronger, his breathing became better.

Perhaps his body had repaired whatever internal damage had been caused to his lung. The human body was an amazing feat! It had memory and damage control and emotions and thought and movement and the capacity to feel and to love and to reproduce itself.

One day after Christine had washed and bandaged Yuri's wounds, she was combing his hair with Leli's beautiful comb and caressing him.

"You are my favorite patient!" Christine confided to Yuri.

When you are in terrible pain, the soft touch of one's hand can feel so good and be so soothing.

"I dream of Nurse Blakely all the time." Yuri said.

"Do you?"

"I dream of lying with her on a bed of gardenias with the soft mountain breezes flowing sensuously over us and I am kissing her passionately."

"Really."

"Every night I dream she comes to me in the dark."

"What is she wearing?"

"She wears nothing! She just lies down beside me naked and beautiful. I love to touch her and feel her every breathe."

"Does she come to you every night?"

"Yes, she comes glowing to me in the dark. Then her glow becomes my glow."

"Really?"

"Yes, it is lovely." They smiled at each other. Yuri put his strong arm around Christine and he drew her to him. They exchanged a long kiss.

"Sometimes I feel so cold." Yuri told her.

"It is because you have lost so much blood and the cave is cold. But you are doing well!"

"Stay with me and keep me warm." Yuri said and he opened up his sleeping bag to Christine. Without a thought, she slipped in fully clothed and carefully lay down beside him. She knew any sudden movement on her part could send Yuri into a stream of unwanted pain.

"Kissing makes bodies heal faster." Yuri assured her. They were very close now. There was a shining light in their eyes.

"Does it? My medical school never taught me these secrets."

They exchanged an intimate smile in the soft light. In such uncertain times, it was wonderful to be safe and warm in Yuri's sleeping bag. Yuri was alive and mending! They lay quietly together and enjoyed each other's warmth and presence. Sometimes Yuri would nibble on Christine's ear and whisper 'I love you.'

Christine smiled with pleasure. She lay very still. She was careful not to cause Yuri any pain.

"Spend the night with me." Yuri whispered. "I am out of commission, but just having you near me makes all my mending cells work double time!"

"I love being with you, Yuri. Do you not want dinner?"

"Yes, let us eat and then go back to bed."

"You must not open up your wounds. Promise me no ardent splendor."

"I promise, but I can nibble, can I not?"

"Yes." Christine smiled.

The American made sleeping bags were engineered so that they could be made conveniently into a double sleeping bag. Yuri and Christine zipped together their two sleeping bags and enjoyed each other's nightly company. Christine vowed that if Yuri made any sudden movement, she would retreat to her own sleeping bag again. She was terrified of Yuri opening up his wounds. Yuri promised he would be good; and to be fair, he was still in some pain and still somewhat weak. But his passion was growing and he was regaining his strength.

One morning after a month had passed, Yuri woke up in the morning and placed his hand on Christine's long, beautiful body.

"Come to me naked tonight." He whispered into her ear. They looked at each other intently. Christine kissed Yuri lightly on his cheek and got out of the sleeping bag to start her day. Christine spent most of her days at the camp hospital helping the wounded who had been injured like Yuri. In the evening, she would stop by the Great Cooking Hall to pick up dinner and bring it back to Yuri.

Yuri had many candles blazing as Christine came into the cave that evening.

"Beautiful!" Christine said as she entered their cave. "Where did you ever find all of these candles?" Soft candlelight bathed the intricate stone walls that surrounded them.

Yuri just smiled.

"How is my sweet Yuri?" Christine asked him.

"He is in want."

"In want of what?"

"In want of his beautiful Christine."

"And what does he want?"

"He wants to kiss her and hold her always. What does Christine want?"

"She is wanting also. I have brought dinner. Let us eat."

They sat on the sleeping bag as they did so often and ate in the soft flickering light. When they were done, Christine took off Yuri bandages and inspected his wounds. She touched them lightly and covered them with disinfectant. She bandaged him up again.

"Your wounds look very good. Do they hurt much?" She asked.

"It is my wanting that is hurting."

Christine came to him and ran her fingers through his hair and kissed him. She got up and blew out all of the candles that Yuri had placed on the cave floor. She went over to the Coleman lantern and turned it off. Christine stripped down to nothing and carefully entered the sleeping bag next to Yuri.

Yuri was waiting for her. He could feel her long, lovely body slide down along side of him. He could feel her thighs and her legs and her breasts against him. He ran his hand along her smooth, magnificent body. He touched her erotic breasts and her buttock. He touched her in all the important places and he brought her to the edge of the cliff where she dove off into a deep blue glacier sea and the thick primeval sea kept flowing and flowing into every crack and crevice of her body like great ancestral swamp waters. The last thing that Christine remembered was Yuri kissing her as she fell into a deep erotic sleep.

In the morning when they woke, Christine asked: "You did not come with me?"

"No! This was just for my beautiful Christina. For her love, for her caring, for her being! Yuri very bad. He took all for himself; he left Christina with nothing! This was just for her!"

Christine kissed Yuri and they touched each other and became one all over again.

They spent the entire Summer together. Tung ordered that Yuri was on convalescence leave and that he must rest and recover. As Yuri got better, he and Christine spent many days down by their swimming hole enjoying the water. Yuri took Christine up the mountain to a gorgeous waterfall. They swam and sunned and had small picnics down near the stream. They touched and enjoyed each other in the hot Indochina sunshine.

There were only two people in the world—Christine and Yuri! They bathed in the long Summer days and in the intense erotic Summer nights. They were hot, steamy, and on fire. They lived full of sensuous and everlasting pleasure.

Yuri was gradually going back to work. One morning after breakfast, he got dressed and was about to leave.

"I am going to be spending the day with Tung." He said as he was leaving.

Christine looked up. Yuri was always with her. Now she must share him. She was not happy. "You forgot to kiss me goodbye." She said quickly rising to her feet.

"Oh, you American women are so demanding!" Yuri said smiling as he came towards Christine and held her tightly in his arms. He kissed her long and beautifully. All the blood rose to Christine's cheeks. She was blushing. She hugged Yuri tightly. How many times had Yuri left her without her knowing if he would ever return?

"Yuri loves Christina." He whispered into her ear.

"Christine so, so loves Yuri!" She whispered back.

"Goodbye, my sweet."

"Goodbye."

CHAPTER 33

"We have been invited to a party." Yuri said.

"A party?"

"Yes, Tung feels he needs to raise the morale of the camp. He is having a USA party."

"What is a USA party?" Christine asked.

"It is where everyone dresses up in their most prized War booty."

"You mean items taken from fallen US soldiers?"

"It happens on both sides." Yuri said in a low terse voice.

"I do not think I would be comfortable there."

"Please come. It is a celebration for those of us who have survived. There will be singing and dancing and music and much food. Everyone is looking forward to it! It is a celebration! You must not look on the dark side. This is a chance for people to come together and relax and enjoy each other. It is a festival and a celebration of life!"

"Celebration of life? So people can go back out and kill again?"

"You have been listening to Yuri too much! Please come Christine! If you are not comfortable, I will take you home."

Christine was not sure, but she did go. She wore her USA Army fatigues and her Army issued black combat boots. Yuri wore a US Army uniform with many medals on it and his USA made Colt 45 that clung to his thigh like a poisonous leech. What did Americans say? They had the right to bear arms with weaponry so lethal it could shatter a man's head into a thousand pieces and throw shrapnel everywhere with one bullet. It was the Americans who invented the cluster bomb and before that the nuclear bomb. They were a hearty people afraid of their own shadow. They had enormous resources, and they squandered them on war and destruction. Good for the profiteers, not so good for the innocent and the common man.

There had been many committees set up to organize the party! There was a Food Committee, a Decoration Committee, an Entertainment Committee, a Music Committee, an Acting Committee, and a Clean Up Committee. Everyone was involved in the event, and there was an excitement in the air!

The Decoration Committee had strung bright Chinese lanterns through the trees and had constructed a makeshift stage. The Food Committee had been busy cooking for days. The Music Committee had been rehearsing, and the Actors worked together to put on short comic sketches. Everyone talked about what they would be wearing. People were happy, and they were proud of their newly found possessions courtesy of the USA.

The camp would be separated into venues. There would be a War Story Venue, a Comic Venue, a Singing Venue, a Theatrical Venue, and the music would be playing from beginning to end. They had mandolins, gongs, and kettle drums. Everyone was practicing for the big event! It took their minds off of the War, the shared experience made them a tighter group, and it helped them to laugh and enjoy their lives during this very difficult time. The wounded would be moved to a special area within the celebration. The Venues would come to them, and they would be honored for their role in the liberation of their Country.

The special day finally arrived. Everyone came together. Christine was astounded by the celebration. She was overwhelmed with how pretty and festive the lanterns were. She loved the beautiful mandolin music that played nonstop with the bewitching gongs and kettle drums.

The music vibrated throughout the jungle. It had an eerie tone to it. It was soft and lovely and propelling!

The National Liberation Fighters and the Viet Cong in their light-weight black apparel moved from one venue to the next. They were in small groups and they greeted each other happily. They showed off their War booty to each other. They were proud of it. It was proof that they had outsmarted the enemy and had lived to tell about it! Some wore US flak jackets, some wore US made ponchos and rain gear, many wore US steel helmets or US canteens over each shoulder.

One man wore a peace medallion, another had a high-caliber binoculars around his neck. The best display Christine thought was the Viet Cong who wore four Rolex watches, two on each wrist. He greatly enjoyed showing his fellow warriors the watches with all the sophisticated gadgetry on them. But the most fitting display of the evening was the Vietnamese man who had a least four or five magazine clips draped over each shoulder. He was so bogged down, he could barely move. He reminded Christine of the United States of America's presence in Vietnam. It was a memory that would always stay with her.

The USA party started at 3:00 o'clock in the afternoon. The National Liberation Front could not risk burning torches at night so they started the party early. They knew the party would last well into the evening, but by then it would be moved into the Great Cooking Hall away from skyward detection.

Christine and Yuri walked around to all of the venues. They were certainly dressed for the event. At each venue, there were long tables filled with wonderful food. Near the Great Cooking Hall, they could smell chicken cooking, and word had spread that a large wild boar had been found, and it had been roasted and was waiting to be served.

The first venue they stopped at was billed as Tales from the French

War. It portrayed how the Vietnamese had with great innovation outwitted the French during the French War. An elderly Vietnamese man with a hard, weather-beaten face was an accomplished storyteller. People crowded about him to listen to their past. They sat on the ground, and listened to this ancient warrior unfold his stories and they did not want him to stop. However, each venue had a timetable and a new group of anxious and eager listeners who wanted to enter the venue. Christine and Yuri walked on.

A Vietnamese man who knew Yuri came up to them.

"Bonjour." He spoke French to Yuri. He had a US made mosquito netting draped around his neck like a long Montana scarf. He shared something with Yuri in French and both men laughed heartily. The Vietnamese man bowed to both of them and moved on.

"Where do we go next?" Yuri called out to him.

"The Comic Venue."

"We are off to the Comic Venue." Yuri told Christine.

The Comic Venue was a popular place. Everyone in the crowd was laughing. The Comic was a seasoned pro. He had great pauses and wonderful punch lines. Christine had no idea what he was saying, but the crowd was in tears of laughter.

"Do you speak Vietnamese?" Christine asked Yuri.

"No, but I think he is very good. He has great body language and the crowd loves him!"

Tung and Leli came up to Yuri and Christine. Christine embraced Leli. Tung was wearing a distinctive Yankees baseball cap, and Leli was carrying a small US made flashlight. She held it up for all to see.

"Very good for latrine." Leli said in English and she smiled showing her beautiful, ivory white teeth. She looked happier than Christine had ever seen her.

"I on Decoration Committee." Leli pointed to the Chinese lanterns proudly.

"I love them! It is so festive!" Christine said.

"Where have you been?" Tung asked.

"Just to the French War Tales and to the Comic Venue."

"Go to the Singing Venue and do not miss the Theatrical Venue. They are a group of Actors that were brought in especially for the party." Tung said.

Tung looked happy. He said hello to everyone, and he would call out slogans to people like 'fight, fight, sleep, sleep'. Tung would clap the Vietnamese soldiers on the shoulders and smile at them encouragingly. The Viet Cong loved seeing Tung and looked at him in awe. There were many white-haired Viet Cong who were still fighting the War for National justice. Tung paid special attention to them, and he treated them with the utmost respect. To see people strong and confident and committed was Tung's goal.

Tung and Leli said goodbye and moved on. Christine and Yuri watched the Vietnamese fighters. People were singing, dancing, and eating. They were standing in small groups laughing and exchanging stories. They were calling out to each other happily or they were making new friends. There was gaiety and good humor everywhere.

The day was pleasantly warm. The wonderful smell of food cooking and the sound of music and chatter floated upon the air. The Viet Cong were moving from one venue to the next and running into old friends and acquaintances. They shared their stories and showed off their War booty. Christine loved seeing the people so happy. They had suffered greatly. Now they joked and laughed with one another. The party was a great success! It brought the people together, it helped them keep their minds off of the War, and it helped them to relax and enjoy their lives. Victory Village had survived again! Inwardly, they were staying strong!

The golden glow of twilight set in. The light became soft and gentle. Quickly darkness fell. All the Venues had been visited and revisited. The insects were beginning to join the party in droves, and it was time for everyone to move into the Great Cooking Hall. The cave was cool, but with so many people laughing and chatting, it soon warmed up. More food was brought out, and the music continued to play well into the night. It had been a fun evening. Christine had blocked out what had gone before.

Christine and Yuri did not stay until the end. They walked back to their cave hand in hand. When they were in the cave, they unbuttoned each other's shirts and smiled and kissed each other. They both sat down half naked and took off their heavy boots and pants, and climbed into their much loved sleeping bag where they were always one. In the darkness they lay together and talked about the party as they softly touched each other.

"It was a lovely party. I am glad we went." Christine said.

"We had a good time."

"Tung seems to be highly respected among his people."

"Tung is a very popular leader. He does everything he can to build trust and confidence and to focus on the mission. He holds meetings with his people. He shares food with them, and lets them air their complaints or express their ideas. They discuss and make decisions as a group. They hold songfests and they share riddles and jokes and slogans. This builds unity." Yuri said as he kissed Christine's shoulder.

"It is odd that even if you cannot understand someone's language, you can learn so much just by watching and observing."

"Yes."

"Tonight, Tung seemed almost like a cheerleader. He would say something, and you could see in the body language how his people would instantly react positively to him." Christine observed.

"Old Tung has many slogans like 'Come unseen, go unnoticed' and 'Fight Today, Peace Tomorrow'. They are words that demand commitment and action."

"Those sound good!"

"Yuri has motto." He said in his velvety voice.

"Does he?"

"Make love not War!" He whispered softly into Christines's ear as he moved his warm hand over her smooth, lovely body and kissed her neck. He smiled inwardly to himself. Oh, to be a San Francisco hippie when the world was overflowing with enormous creativity, social justice, and the pursuit of pleasure!

Christine smiled and turned herself fully to him. They kissed each other passionately and enjoyed the immortal hours of love.

CHAPTER 34

One day in the late afternoon, Yuri took Christine up to their high mountain perch. They sat on the boulders and looked out over their valley. A large, dark bird crossed the sky. Yuri took Christine's hand.

"I am taking you back to the other side."

Christine just looked at Yuri in disbelief.

"I refuse to go!"

"Please, Christine. Be reasonable."

"I will not go."

"Do you think I want to send you away? Do you think this is easy for me? Do you not think that I want to come back to camp and just melt into your arms and kiss you and touch you and hold you?"

"I will never leave you! How could I?"

"This is not easy for me either, Christine. Do you think on these long marches when people are shooting at me and trying to kill me, and insects are eating me alive, and I am hungry, and I am tired, and I am hot, and I am exhausted; do you really think that you are not always on my mind? That I never stop thinking of you; that I never stop wanting you?"

"If you love me, you would not let me go."

"You are everything to me, Christine! Do you doubt that for one moment? You were once an enormous problem for me; a burden, a temptation. And then somehow we were able to transcend everything, and now I am your slave! I want only to please you, to make you happy, to sacrifice myself to you. I have become your captive! It is too dangerous for you to be here now. Why do you not understand this?"

"I don't care. I want only to be with you!"

"Christine, remember how you would beg me to let you go home. This is your chance. Take it!"

"I will not leave you. I cannot imagine living my life without you! Please, please Yuri! We have come so far. We have bridged mountains and oceans and have endured such a long desert. Please don't let us be torn apart! Not now!"

"There can never be a Yuri and a Christine. If we left and went to America, the KGB would hunt us down. My Government is absolutely ruthless. They will do anything unspeakable to remain in power. They throw their enemies out of high-rise windows, down stairs, or overboard on ships. They radiate people with terrible poisons or execute them in the middle of the night. That is how my Government deals with dissent. Believe me, they have no regard for human life! I know too much. They would kill us both! Is that what you want? And if you came with me to Moscow, the CIA would find you there, and they would wonder how you ever came from the depths of the Vietnamese jungle to the Capitol of the Soviet Union! Your CIA would question the extent of the Soviet involvement in Vietnam and that would have huge political repercussions.

We are in a world where there can never be a Yuri and a Christine. I have looked at this from every possible angle. These are two powerful forces that want only to control. It is not just the Government. It is all the special interests that want to keep control. It is the Military that wants more money. It is the leaders who find it in their best interests to terrify people and make believe there is danger everywhere! It is the Corporations that want to operate without any restraints in other Countries just to make money; just to make a buck. We are at their mercy!"

"I am so in love with you, Yuri. When you were wounded, I was wounded too! When I washed your wounds, I prayed to God—please, please let him live! Because without you, there is no me. I cannot leave you, Yuri! I won't."

Yuri looked down. His heart was breaking. He tried one more time.

"Christine, the Americans are dropping napalm bombs throughout the Ho Chi Minh Trail to destroy the jungle canopy so that they can find and destroy the enemy. We are on the Ho Chi Minh Trail! At any time the Americans could drop napalm bombs on this camp, and you would be burnt to a tiny little crisp. Is that what you want? Why can you not understand this? It is too dangerous for you to be here! Do you want to be burnt to death by your own Countrymen?"

"I will not go."

"The United States is dropping an unprecedented number of bombs on these mountain tops that could reduce this camp into one giant crater. Is that what you want, to be blown to bits? And the United States of America is dropping phosphorous on the land that if it touches your skin, it will burn right down to your bones. Is that what you want? To go through life being grotesquely disfigured? I am trying to save you, Christine. Do not be a fool!"

Night had fallen. Dark clouds swept across the moon. The sky appeared menacing and troubled.

"I won't go!" Christine said adamantly. "All of these things could happen to you as well. Why should I survive and you not? Please Yuri, we can only be together. That is the only way!"

Yuri just looked down. He knew she could not stay here now. That he could not let her stay. No more was said. They walked back to their cave hand in hand.

CHAPTER 35

A week later Yuri came into the cave. He approached Christine from behind and kissed her on the back of her neck.

"We have been invited to another party."

"My, but you are a social group!" Christine said as she turned around and kissed Yuri on his very sensuous lips.

He held her in his arms and rocked her gently. "How I love my beautiful Christina!"

"I love you too, Yuri. Please don't send me away!" Christine begged.

"We are going to have a dinner party and the men are in charge of arranging everything! The only thing the women must do is to come and look lovely." Yuri said holding her and kissing her.

"Who is coming?"

"Yuri, Christina, Leli, and Tung."

"Wonderful! I can't wait!"

The men had set the day and the hour. The dinner was to be in Yuri's cave. They decided upon the menu for the evening and there would be several courses! The men placed a warm American made wool blanket on the cave floor. This was to be a picnic dinner. Tung found some almost extinct candles, and he placed them strategically in the cave. Tung, always the technician! They had brought in a small hibachi to keep the food and the tea warm. Tung was very exact as to what they would eat that evening. It was to be a traditional Vietnamese dinner and celebration. The Coleman lantern would continue its yeoman duty of casting out light. Yuri touched his chin, and made sure he shaved extra well. Tonight, he would wear his high collared Russian tunic. He was looking forward to the evening!

The women were down by the river preening themselves. They were excited about the dinner party also. They were thrilled that the men had proposed the idea and had organized everything! The women both had on their beautiful raspberry pink Vietnamese ao dais dresses. Should we braid our hair? They wondered. No, this is such a special evening, let our hair be soft and flowing and free! Let it fall upon our shoulders like snow on the mountains!

The women combed each other's hair and adjusted each other's dresses, Leli had found a plant whose flowers produced an orange scent. They rubbed the blossoms of the plant onto their hands and necks. It was almost as if they were in a glorious orange grove at springtime when all of the small white flowers come forth and give out the most amazing scent of glory and ecstasy.

They both looked at each other and nodded. They were ready. These two women were like two flowers ready to be picked, savored, and enjoyed! They were full of life and beauty and joy. They walked up the well-used trail. A small, green lizard scrambled across their path. Both women screamed in fright and then giggled. The little lizard climbed up on a rock, cocked its head, and watched them go by. We must be something very special to look at if even this lizard can't take its eyes off of us they thought. They laughed and hurried on.

The women entered the cave slowly. The men had been chatting and as the women came in, they scrambled to their feet and hid something behind their backs. The young women smiled and came toward them. The men presented them each with a beautiful Lotus flower and placed it carefully behind the women's ears. The women were enchanting in their pink ao dais dresses, their beautiful pink Lotus flowers, and their long flowing hair! The soft light of the flickering candles made the cave warm and glowing. The men motioned to the women to sit down on the blanket they had spread out for them. The long-awaited evening had begun! Tung served up the first course. He had the hibachi working perfectly.

"Unfortunately, we have no Vodka." Tung shot Yuri a disapproving look. "But I managed to secure some very fine rice wine for our Victory Party!" Tung said smiling. He translated what he had said for Leli so she was a part of the gathering as well.

Everyone cheered. Tung poured out the wine and passed it around.

"I propose a toast." Yuri said as he lifted his glass. "Here is to these beautiful and very fetching ladies!"

Tung translated for Leli and everyone smiled and clapped. They started to eat their delicious food.

"We have a plan for when the War ends." Leli said.

Tung translated for her.

"We will have schools in every village, health care for the people, we will have more houses and better sanitation and plumbing, and we want a movie theatre in every village!"

Everyone cheered and said hooray!

"You must have a movie theatre." Yuri told them.

They were a happy group. They were young and full of ideas for the future.

"We are reconstructing our Country even while we are fighting this War of resistance. We have Bureaus of Agricultural Management, Irrigation, Schools, and Health Clinics. We have Bureaus of Forestry,

Mines, and Construction. When the War ends, we will rebuild our Country. The more we fight, the stronger we become!" Tung said proudly as he passed out more food and more rice wine.

"We want to conquer hunger, illiteracy, and disease, and we want the fighting to stop! We want our Country to be at Peace!" Leli said. She looked so beautiful in the soft candlelight glow. Tung gazed at her lovingly as he translated what she had said.

Both men were happy. Life was full and vibrant—soft candle light, flowers, beautiful women, rice wine, good food, friends! Both men drank the rice wine knowing full well that they were about to enter the battle of their lives. A paradox, isn't it, that one must fight for Peace?

How do four people from very different backgrounds come together and enjoy the gift of life, the gift of pleasure, the gift of love, the gift of sharing? The candlelight darted upon the cave walls, but the true glow was the happiness between these four. They came from North, South, East and West. They came together and enjoyed the gift of friendship and the gift of goodwill amongst mankind!

"Tung is a very good fisherman! He caught a fish this big!" Yuri said and he spread his hands out three feet wide.

"They have fish that big in the river?" Christine could not believe it!

"OK, Maybe this big!" Yuri said and he reduced the size of the fish in half."

Tung translated for Leli.

"No Yuri, the fish was only this big." Tung spread his fingers five inches apart and he bowed his head.

Everybody laughed. They ate and drank more. Tung and Yuri liked to tease each other and they bantered back and forth. They told stories of each other's exploits and the women loved to listen.

"Tung, take our picture!" Christine cried out.

"He does not have a camera." Yuri said and he looked perplexed.

"Tung always takes our picture."

The women moved together and Yuri put his great arms around both of these lovely ladies. They all smiled. Tung held up his hand and took their picture.

"Got it!" He said.

They all laughed like little children forever happy living in their own special world unencumbered by everything that flows around them. For now, they were totally suspended in time and space.

It was late. The dinner had ended. It had been a great success! Everyone was happy and full and content. Tung and Leli would take back the uneaten food to the Great Cooking Hall on their way back so that no vermin would be enticed into the cave looking for a snack; although it could be said that Yuri had enough charisma to charm a snake or anything else that came his way.

Tung hugged Christine tightly. Christine looked at him. She had never seen him so animated!

She hugged Leli also. They all said goodbye warmly.

"It was a great party. Thank you for coming!"

"It is our pleasure!" Tung bowed and they left carrying the bowls.

It had been a good evening with the flickering candle glow, the good company, and the happy smiles and laughter.

Yuri turned to Christine. "Does poor Yuri not deserve a hug also?"

"Oh yes! I love to hug my darling Yuri. How could I ever live without him?" Christine said as she held him in her arms.

"We will always have Paris." He whispered into her ear and he softly kissed her.

Christine smiled. This definitely was not Paris! Yuri was such a tease!

"I will always love you, Christina!" He whispered.

Christine held Yuri tightly in her arms. He seemed so needy tonight. They walked over to their bed hand in hand.

"Would the beautiful Christina like to sleep in her ao dais or could Yuri help her with it?" He asked.

"Christine would like the Count to slowly seduce her."

"Oh, my dear, he would be so pleased!"

When they were warm and naked in their beloved sleeping bag, they lay touching each other tenderly and giving each other soft tiny kisses.

"Think of all the months we could have so enjoyed ourselves. Instead we each clung stubbornly to our own side of the cave for some half-baked notion." Yuri said.

"I think you were very annoyed that I had entered your world."

"I was not pleased. Women do not belong in War!"

"Men do not belong in War!" Christine added.

They smiled at each other and kissed.

"This is true. Mankind is so foolish. They should just concentrate on the important things in life!"

"Like kissing Yuri." Christine suggested.

"Yes! Yuri needs many kisses!" He assured her.

They held each other tightly. They kissed and made love, and enjoyed the true sweetness of life. Christine did not have a clue what was coming. She had been in a cocoon full of love, and she was blinded by its immense power.

CHAPTER 36

When Christine was sound asleep, Yuri quietly got up and put on his US Army uniform from the party. He went outside of the cave and found the assigned Vietnamese medic. They came back into the cave, and Yuri pulled back the covers where Christine lay. The medic gave Christine a shot with a drug that would knock her out for seven to eight hours. Yuri thanked him and the medic left the cave.

Yuri picked up Christine's ao dais pink dress and her lovely comb. The silky dress felt as sensuous as Christine's beautiful body. He wrapped the dress around her comb. The silk dress was very lightweight, and it wrapped up into a tight bundle. He placed the bundle into the long thigh pocket of her Army fatigues. He hoped she would keep it always as a keepsake.

He dressed her in her Army uniform. Her arms and legs were totally limp. He put on her socks and tied her boots. He went outside of the cave and found the three Vietnamese men who were going to help him get Christine back to the other side. The men came into the cave and helped Yuri lift Christine onto a simple stretcher. Yuri turned off the Coleman lantern, and the three Vietnamese men and Yuri carried Christine down the mountainside.

The moon was full and all of the stars were out. The jungle was quiet. After an hour, the group rested for a bit, then they continued on their way. They walked along the river for another hour and came to a spot where the river flattened out. A sampan was waiting for them. This was a shallow bottomed boat that the Vietnamese used for travel on the Vietnam waterways. The Vietnamese men helped Yuri lift the limp

Christine onto the bottom of the sampan. Yuri got in and lay down beside her. It smelled like fish! The Vietnamese man who was in charge of the boat placed a fish netting over them so they could not be seen.

The Vietnamese man wore a conical bamboo hat. He pushed the sampan into the river, and he expertly steered it so that it quickly caught the current; and they moved swiftly downstream with the moon reflecting its presence in the shimmering water. The Vietnamese man did not have much to do except watch for rocks or logs because the River did all the work for them in its mighty flow to the Sea.

In about two hours-time, the Vietnamese fisherman pulled up to the riverbank where there was an ox cart waiting for them. The Vietnamese man helped Yuri lift Christine's lifeless body out of the boat and onto the ox cart. Yuri thanked the Vietnamese fisherman, and Yuri climbed into the back of the ox cart and lay down beside Christine. The driver of the cart covered them with a blanket and some stalks and brush. Yuri made sure Christine could breathe. He could feel her warm body beside him.

The ox driver had climbed back onto the cart, and the cart lurched forward. They were off again! There were many ruts in the road so the cart bumped along at a slow pace. Yuri looked up at the heavens above. The stars were magnificent and the nighttime sky was filled with them. Yuri hoped the stars would watch over them and keep them safe. And he hoped Christine would forgive him.

"I am so so sorry my dear, sweet. I had to get you back to the other side. It was the only way! As God and the great Heavens above are my witness, I have tried to do what is right." But was it right? He did not know. He knew he had just closed a door that could never be reopened. He could feel the tremendous ache in his heart.

They bumped along the road for an hour, and finally they came to a pretty seaside town with parks and beautiful flowered walks. It had been a French provincial center for many years, and you could see the French influence in the buildings, the tree-lined streets and the small outside restaurants. There was a large Catholic Church in the center of the town and a red Pagoda that stood on a cliff overlooking the Sea. The two cultures lived side by side.

The ox cart pulled up in front of the police station. It was four o'clock in the morning and the streets were deserted. There was no movement anywhere. There was a park bench in front of the police station. Yuri and the ox driver quickly moved Christine off of the cart and sat her upright on the park bench as if she was waiting for a bus. Yuri thanked the ox driver and the ox driver quickly moved on.

Yuri looked around. Still, he did not see anyone. Christine was sitting upright with her chin on her chest. She looked like she was sleeping peacefully.

Yuri had rented a room across the street to watch over Christine until she was found. He needed to move through the town first to make sure no one had seen him or was following him. After a short tour of the town, he doubled back to the police station. Christine was still resting with her eyes closed. Yuri unlocked the door of the rented space and went up the stairs. He unlocked a second door and went into the room that overlooked the police station. He took a chair and placed it in the shadows of the window as he watched over Christine.

He had on his US Army uniform with all the medals, and he carried forged US papers just in case he ran into trouble. But everything had worked out well so far. He looked down at his watch. Dawn should be breaking soon.

Just before sunrise was the hardest part of the night for Yuri. He looked down upon Christine and remembered how sweet it was to kiss her, and how much he loved her and wanted to be with her. He remembered how she had nursed him back to good health, and how she had saved his life when he was so badly wounded. He knew how much he loved to tease her and hold her in his arms and make love to her.

Like a long Russian night, in the beginning she had been so cold. She was mistrustful and angry and difficult. Just to get through that tough outer core of hers was hard work. She had been one feisty Montana Bobcat. How had he ever managed it? How were they ever able to put aside their differences and get along? He was not sure. But somehow they had done it, and each had gained so much!

Yuri looked up at the sky. The horizon was beginning to turn a golden hue. The sky was turning pink now and the earth began to lighten. Christine sat with her head down resting comfortably. Merchants began to come onto the streets and open up their shops. A single moped bike went slowly down the empty street. Yuri looked at his watch again. Christine should be waking up soon. He wished he could help her, but there was nothing more he could do. He had made his decision.

"I will always be with you, my sweet. Close your eyes and I will be there. I will be in your bed, I will be holding you, I will be kissing you. I will be thinking of you always. I will be there!" Those were his final thoughts as he watched over her.

Finally, Christine began to stir. She slowly raised her head and looked straight ahead as if she was in a trance. She looked to the right and to the left. Yuri could see that she was trying to figure out in her mind where she was. She tried to stand up, but the drug made her unbalanced and tipsy. She quickly sat down again on the edge of the bench and held onto it as if to steady herself. After a while, she tried to stand up again. She was able to stand. She moved slowly down the street.

Yuri watched her struggles and his fists were clinched.

"No, not that way, Christine! Turn! Turn!" He could not help saying.

Christine stopped suddenly as if she had heard Yuri. She looked about her. She turned and started walking in the opposite direction toward the bench she had been on. She saw the French colonial building with its pale, yellow stucco on the outside. She looked up. She saw the sign—Commissariat de Police. She stopped. She saw the steps.

"Go up the steps, Christine! Go up the steps!" Yuri was beside himself.

Christine went up the steps. The street was now empty. Yuri let out a huge sigh of relief. He had gotten her back safely, but he felt hollow inside. What had he done? Would he regret this decision for the rest of his life?

Nothing happened for 45 minutes. Then the town was crawling with Military personnel. Three Army jeeps pulled up smartly in front of the police station. Yuri could see Army snipers positioned on the tops of buildings. Did they think this was a trap?

Yuri watched as she was being escorted out of the police station. Christine looked heart stricken and lost. She kept looking, waiting, and searching. But the street was empty. There were only fierce men in full combat gear carrying M-16 rifles, grenades, and heavy magazine clips. The weaponry gave them power and power ruled the world. It was the death dance, the dance of death.

The soldiers helped Christine into the waiting jeep. Instantly all the soldiers dropped their cover and climbed into the waiting vehicles. The convoy took off in unison. Only the snipers were left behind. The street now was deserted again.

Yuri felt as if his heart would break in two. He would spend the night in this room for safekeeping and leave for the camp tomorrow night. He had his rice cakes to nibble on and his memories of Christine to keep him company. He was a miserable man. The worst thought was going back to his empty cave in the mountains and climbing into his cold sleeping bag where they had shared so much pleasure.

CHAPTER 37

I picked up my Embassy telephone. "Belmont Dexter, here." I said.

"Hello Colonel. How are you?"

"She's what?"

"Oh Jesus!"

"OK, thanks for the call!"

I stood up. Christine had simply reappeared unharmed from nowhere. I was on my way over to the base to see her, to help her, to do anything I could for her!

I had just left my Embassy office. The Saigon air was warm and sensuous. It was like a master and a keeper and a lover. It surrounded and caressed you. In a sense, it overpowered you. I will always remember the hot sun, the swamp smells, and the bustle of Saigon. These are the memories that are seared forever in my youth.

Christine had spent her tender youth here as well. She had seen the death, the broken souls, the maimed bodies, the tortured minds, more death and more destruction. Would she ever be the same? Why in God's name were we sent here? The decisions of old and powerful men? Raging egos? Political boundaries? Ideology? Arrogant will power? What was the reason again that so many young lives and dreams and futures had been placed on a game board and moved around like trifles? What was that reason that was so important that you must sacrifice a whole generation of young men and women for the good of the Nation?

But we were adamant about imposing our beliefs on others as if it was our divine right. Conquer the West or conquer the East. We knew no bounds. and with our long tentacles we would grasp and hold and finally diminish any opposing world views from our own. Yes, we pressed ourselves on the South Vietnamese. We maimed and destroyed in the name of freedom and sent a tough people into misery, sorrow, and pain. And in the end, they won!

You might say it was a misallocation of funds. So we simply declared Victory, and we left only to save the fight for another day because that was the American spirit. We had won the West and now we needed to broaden our horizons! We had the money and the know how, but we were crumbling from the inside out, and soon we would be paying a huge price for our arrogant and violent ways because the American Military Industrial complex was just aching for another War!

But we have always been led by our mercantile business interests that would supersede the individual, the community or our faith. We were a Christian Nation that had no Christian beliefs. We were willful and self-absorbed, and we had a short time on this earth to make our mark. Money ruled! We were American and proud of it! Did we care whose ox we gored? Not really, as long as it was in our own self-interest. And money was no object. Money was power and we had power! Power was our middle name. So sometimes people had to eat out of our hand and drink from our cup, and they were resentful! So what?

The Americans were brutal. Their honor was on the line. How could they lose this War? Under the Dominoes theory, everything would be lost! So we Americans were vicious. We dropped bombs, we coated the jungle with chemicals, and we killed, maimed and destroyed all in the name of freedom. And for what?

Americans think they live in a Democracy, but they do not. They are ruled solely by the special interests which will be their downfall! And mark my words--you poor Citizen, shall be left with nothing.

I hoped Christine was all right. She was a delicate, prickly little thing. I had always thought of her standing on the edge; and I felt it was my duty to save her, to protect her, and to make sure she did not take that final step. I was on my way over to the Officer's Club to find out if there was any more news about her. I stopped into the Canteen briefly to see if anyone was there.

The Canteen was a large makeshift area with naked light bulbs dangling from the ceiling. There were many empty tables and chairs. Food and coffee were always available at all hours of the day and night. I spotted Christine sitting alone in the Canteen. It was unusual that the Army would let her be all by herself after what she had been through. She looked like a lonely figure in the harsh light.

I slowly walked toward her.

"Christine! I can't believe you are here! Are you all right?"

She looked up at me. There was an unmistakable sadness in her eyes.

"Hello Belmont." She said softly.

"I heard about your ordeal! There is a huge battle going on in the Highlands right now. It's lucky you got out just in time!"

There was a flicker of emotion in her eyes. She had remembered Yuri and Tung exchanging a meaningful glance at the Victory party. Now she understood why. The Victory party was actually the Last Supper. She would never see her friends or Yuri again. She would never know if they were injured or if they had survived the attack. She was safe. They were still in the Highlands with the battles raging all around them. How many bullets can one person dodge in a lifetime?

"It is over." She said and her eyes went blank again.

"What are you going to do now?" I asked.

"I am going home."

Home! I didn't want her to go home. "Giving up?"

She looked at me and raised her chin slightly.

"No, I am not giving up."